P9-DCW-302

Angela's eyes dropped before Levi's steady gaze.

She forced a smile. "You're right."

Cradling her face, Levi stared deeply into her eyes. "I can't begin to presume to know what you've gone through, but I'm willing to help you get through this, Angela. I'm not your brothers or your father, so Robert Gaskin will be unprepared to deal with me running interference. Do you trust me?" he asked softly.

The word *trust* was like gall in Angela's mouth. She'd trusted Robert and had deceived her. She'd trusted Savannah, and she also had deceived her. [...] she trusted were family members an[...] was asking her to trust him. "Do I have a choice."

CHASE BRANCH LIBRARY
17731 W. SEVEN MILE RD.
DETROIT, MI 48235
302

He brushed a kiss over her parted lips. "No, you don't. What I'm not going to do is lie to you. I like you. You're pretty, intelligent, and you're not snobby or uptight even though—"

"I'm an SB."

"What's an SB?" he asked.

"Southern belle."

Smiling, Levi kissed her again, this one very different from the others they'd shared. His kiss was slow, surprisingly gentle and coaxing. It ended seconds later, leaving her mouth burning and wanting more.

Books by Rochelle Alers

Kimani Romance

Bittersweet Love
Sweet Deception
Sweet Dreams
Twice the Temptation
Sweet Persuasions
Sweet Destiny
Sweet Southern Nights

ROCHELLE ALERS

has been hailed by readers and booksellers alike as one of today's most prolific and popular African American authors of romance and women's fiction.

With more than sixty titles and nearly two million copies of her novels in print, Ms. Alers is a regular on the Waldenbooks, Borders and *Essence* bestseller lists, regularly chosen by Black Expressions Book Club, and has been the recipient of numerous awards, including the Emma Award, the Vivian Stephens Award for Excellence in Romance Writing, the *RT Book Reviews* Career Achievement Award and the Zora Neale Hurston Literary Award.

She is a member of the Iota Theta Zeta chapter of Zeta Phi Beta Sorority, Inc., and her interests include gourmet cooking and traveling. A full-time writer, Ms. Alers lives in a charming hamlet on Long Island.

Sweet
Southern
Nights

ROCHELLE
ALERS

CHASE BRANCH LIBRARY
17731 W. SEVEN MILE RD.
DETROIT, KIMANI 8235
ROMANCE
578-8002

If you purchased this book without a cover you should be aware
that this book is stolen property. It was reported as "unsold and
destroyed" to the publisher, and neither the author nor the
publisher has received any payment for this "stripped book."

He who finds a wife finds happiness;
it is a favor he receives from the Lord.
—*Proverbs* 18:22

KIMANI PRESS™

Recycling programs
for this product may
not exist in your area.

ISBN-13: 978-0-373-86248-1

SWEET SOUTHERN NIGHTS

Copyright © 2012 by Rochelle Alers

All rights reserved. The reproduction, transmission or utilization of this work
in whole or in part in any form by any electronic, mechanical or other means,
now known or hereafter invented, including xerography, photocopying and
recording, or in any information storage or retrieval system, is forbidden
without written permission. For permission please contact Kimani Press,
225 Duncan Mill Road, Toronto, Ontario M3B 3K9, Canada.

This is a work of fiction. Names, characters, places and incidents are
either the product of the author's imagination or are used fictitiously,
and any resemblance to actual persons, living or dead, business establishments,
events or locales is entirely coincidental.

® and TM are trademarks. Trademarks indicated with ® are registered in
the United States Patent and Trademark Office, the Canadian Trade Marks
Office and/or other countries.

www.kimanipress.com

Printed in U.S.A.

Dear Reader,

Riddle: What do you get when the heroine is secretly a romance novelist?

Answer: *Sweet Southern Nights.*

There is a very good reason why Angela Chase—aka Angelina Courtland—believes in happily ever after for everyone but herself; however, that's before she meets Dr. Levi Eaton. The question is, can the sexy pediatrician turn the serial dater into a real-life heroine worthy of her own happy ending?

Kentucky is the setting for *Sweet Southern Nights,* so put your feet up, grab a mint julep, rub shoulders with folks who think basketball is a religion and consider the first Saturday in May a holiday.

Also look out for my next Eaton book, when Crystal Eaton finds herself involved with Joseph Cole-Wilson. This title promises drama *and* passion as two prominent families plan to add another branch onto their family tree.

Read, live and love romance.

Rochelle Alers

THE EATONS

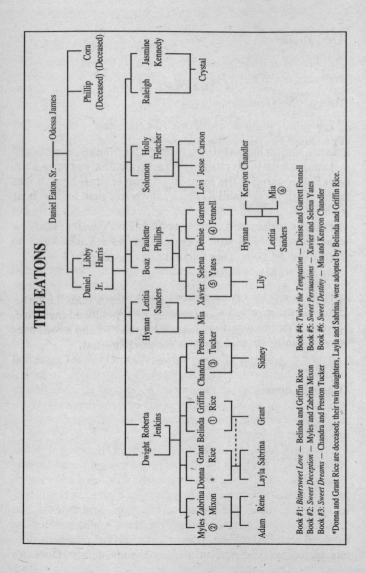

Book #1: *Bittersweet Love* — Belinda and Griffin Rice
Book #2: *Sweet Deception* — Myles and Zabrina Mixon
Book #3: *Sweet Dreams* — Chandra and Preston Tucker

Book #4: *Twice the Temptation* — Denise and Garrett Fennell
Book #5: *Sweet Persuasions* — Xavier and Selena Yates
Book #6: *Sweet Destiny* — Mia and Kenyon Chandler

*Donna and Grant Rice are deceased; their twin daughters, Layla and Sabrina, were adopted by Belinda and Griffin Rice.

Chapter 1

"Levi, do you have anything planned for Sunday afternoon?"

Leaning back in his chair in the bar of the dimly lit restaurant, Levi Eaton stared at the foam-filled mug of draft beer. It was Friday night in the small Kentucky town less than half an hour from Louisville, and there wasn't much else to do but hang out with the three men he'd come to regard as friends. He ordered a second round for everyone at the table even though he knew he should've gone home after the first.

He was scheduled to see patients the following day and needed to be alert, especially when dealing with infants and toddlers, many of whom needed booster shots and vaccinations. Unfortunately, in the rural community where Levi practiced medicine, insuring a child's health was secondary to keeping a roof over their heads and food on the table for most families.

It had taken almost four months, but Dr. Duncan Chase had helped Levi make the transition from big-city doctor to small-town practitioner. In fact, the town of Maywood Junction was so small the school was one building connected by breezeways separating the kindergarten from the grade school, and the middle school from the high school.

Duncan Chase, an oncologist, had been involved in a national research study on the effects of the workplace on cancer-related illnesses. The Centers for Disease Control data revealed industrial-related cancers were unusually high in several Kentucky communities like Maywood Junction. And Duncan had received a federal grant to open a clinic there. Additional funding from the state had allowed him to add a staff of part-time doctors, including a pediatrician, an ob-gyn and a dentist. Duncan's friend Levi had moved from New York to Kentucky to volunteer as the local pediatrician.

"What do you have in mind?" Levi asked.

Duncan Chase sipped the head of foam off his beer, and took a large gulp as he stared at Levi over the rim of his glass. "I'd like you to escort my sister to a family wedding." As soon as the words were out of his mouth, the two other men at their table pushed back their chairs and stood up to leave.

"This is where I bid you gentlemen good night," said Patrick Demorest, the dentist at the Maywood Medical Clinic. He dropped a twenty-dollar bill on the table. "That should cover the tip."

"Pat's driving, so I'm outta here, too," announced his twin brother, Andrew Demorest.

Levi sat up straight, staring as they quickly retreated. "Do they know something I should know?" There was a pause as Duncan stared into his mug. "What's wrong with your sister?" Levi asked, shouting in order to be heard over the applause once the house band returned to the stage for a second set.

Lines fanned out around Duncan Chase's large, dark brown eyes when he smiled. "There's nothing wrong with her."

Levi's eyes narrowed. "If that's the case, then why did Andy and Pat run out of here as if the hounds of hell were after them?"

Duncan glanced up, but didn't meet Levi Eaton's questioning gaze. "They have issues when it comes to Angela."

"What's wrong with her?" he asked again.

"Nothing, except…"

"Except what, Duncan?"

"Pat went out with Angela a couple of times and…"

"And what happened?" Levi asked when Duncan's voice trailed off.

Duncan stared directly at Levi. He didn't want to ruin his relationship with his colleague by asking him to escort his sister to a family wedding, but his mother had pressured him to find a date for Angela to avoid a possibly embarrassing situation. "Pat wanted more, and Angela didn't."

Levi gave Duncan a long stare. "Did more have anything to

do with commitment?" He didn't know why, but he felt like a police interrogator.

Duncan nodded. "Yes." He held up a hand. "And before you ask, she does like men. She's just not interested in becoming *that* involved."

Levi took another swallow of his ice-cold beer. He was four months into his six-month commitment, providing care in the underserved community. His cousin, Dr. Mia Eaton-Chandler, had decided to practice medicine in West Virginia, but he'd decided his skills as a physician were better suited to a mining town in northwest Kentucky.

Duncan's request reminded Levi that since he'd arrived in Kentucky, he'd only been on one date. Levi had been honest with the woman, telling her upfront that he couldn't commit to a relationship since he planned to return to New York in a few months. Since she wanted marriage and children, they decided to part amicably.

He was scheduled to work from nine until two the next day, and his Saturday afternoons were usually spent picking up dry cleaning and shopping for groceries for the week. He saw patients on Tuesdays, Thursdays, Fridays and Saturdays, and spent Sundays watching sports. He'd always been a fan of baseball and basketball. But since moving to Kentucky, he'd added football, tennis, golf and NASCAR. As much as he didn't want to admit it, he'd become a sports junkie.

"Where's the wedding?"

Duncan carefully concealed a smile as he brought the mug to his lips. "Louisville," he drawled, taking another swallow.

"I'll think about it," Levi replied.

Lowering the sudsy mug, Duncan set it on the scarred oak table. "How long do you intend to think about it, Levi? The wedding is in two days."

Levi gave him a pointed look. He and Duncan Chase were the same age—thirty-six—but Duncan's hair was prematurely gray. Despite that, Duncan was still one of Louisville's most eligible bachelors. Tall, slender with masculine features in a tawny-brown face, his large, deep-set, gold-flecked brown eyes were his most arresting feature.

"I'll let you know after I talk to your sister."

"What's there to talk about, Levi?"

He leaned across the small table. "Is she aware that you're trying to set her up with a date?"

Duncan averted his gaze. "Not really."

Levi smiled for the first time, angular lines creasing his lean jaw. "That's what I thought." He reached into the breast pocket of his jacket, took out his cell phone and handed it to Duncan. "Give me her phone number. I'll call her and then I'll let you know tomorrow if I'll be her escort." Although he hadn't had an active social life since leaving New York, he also didn't want to waste his day off spending time with a woman who was totally incompatible.

Duncan took the BlackBerry and added his sister's name and number to Levi's contacts. "When are you going to call her?"

"Tonight," he said. Levi glanced at his watch. "Sorry, but it's about time I leave so I can call her before it gets too late." He retrieved his phone, reached into the pocket of his slacks and dropped a few more bills on the table. "Enjoy the music." He stood and walked out of the restaurant.

The parking lot was quickly filling up with couples who'd come to The Rook for dinner, music and line dancing. He signaled to a driver in a late-model pickup that he was pulling out and could have his parking space. It was only nine-thirty—early enough for Friday date nights, but a little late for Levi. Even though his first appointment was at nine, he always arrived at least an hour early to go over patient charts.

Heading straight for his off-white BMW four-door sedan with NYMD vanity plates, he opened the door and slid in behind the wheel. He'd purchased the car a year ago and it still had that new-car smell. It had been years since he'd bought a new car, and Levi had taken a long time deciding whether he wanted another racy sports model or something different. For years he'd driven a two-seater Mercedes-Benz, but now that he was older he felt it was time to change his image. He was still a bachelor, but a bit more serious. Now, dating had taken a backseat to practicing medicine.

For whatever reason, Levi always felt more like a Philadelphian because of his family's roots. Whenever he returned home for family reunions, or to celebrate a wedding, christening or a milestone birthday, it felt more like a homecoming, even though he now lived in a two-bedroom condominium in Mamaroneck, New York.

His younger brothers, who were married with children, constantly teased him about being marriage shy. But what they didn't understand was that when it came to women, he'd always been very discriminating. He had a mental checklist, and intelligence and patience were his top priorities. Levi wanted someone who he could talk to, a relationship that went beyond sexual attraction. And patience was a necessity since doctor's hours were never nine to five.

He wanted to get married and start a family, yet Levi knew he couldn't begin that chapter of his life until he completed his obligations in Kentucky.

Angela Chase clicked on the print icon and watched the pages slide out into the paper tray. A slow smile tilted the corners of her mouth. She'd managed to complete ten pages of her latest novel in three hours. It was one of her better writing days. All she needed was another five thousand more words to finish the manuscript.

Lately the scenes and dialogue had been slow in coming. It wasn't that she had writer's block, but her characters seemed to have stopped talking to her. Before starting any new manuscript, Angela went through a carefully planned routine of setting up the plot, then reworking it until she could visualize every scene as if viewing a sequence of film frames. Next, she began the task of developing detailed sketches of her characters. Once she developed her characters, she began a chapter-by-chapter outline that resembled a storyboard.

No one, other than her aunt and her cousin Traci, who was also her business partner in their downtown Louisville gift shop, knew she moonlighted as a romance writer. Always a voracious reader, Angela began reading romance novels her first year of college. Her novels sometimes took priority over her class work. She'd lost count of the number of times she'd had to cram for an exam or stay up all night catching up on required reading because she hadn't been able to put down a romance novel. What she refused to admit was that she'd become addicted to them. So much so, that after graduating she'd tried her hand at writing one. Her first attempt was not fit to print, but the fact that she'd completed it gave her the confidence she needed to try again.

It had taken more than four years to achieve something readable. But by the time she'd celebrated her twenty-eighth birthday, she'd become a published author. Her first novel had received lukewarm reviews, but it was the second one that had garnered the acclaim she'd hoped for as a writer. Using the pseudonym Angelina Courtland, she guarded her true identity like a double agent.

She usually kept a low profile. Although she answered reader emails, she didn't have a website. She didn't make public appearances or do book signings since her publicist had explained that Angelina Courtland was agoraphobic. The pretense that she was afraid to leave her home or be photographed only added to her mystique. She'd even had her attorney set up a holding company for her work so that her name never appeared on the copyright page of her novels. It wasn't until after the publication of her second novel that she revealed her *nom de plume* to her cousin.

Traci thought Angela was delusional until she accidently read a draft of her novel on her computer. That was when Angela had sworn her cousin to secrecy. The two had always been confidantes, so Angela knew she could trust Traci not to tell anyone that she was a bestselling author.

What her readers didn't know was that she did leave her home and that she actually had an active social life. The exception was when she was facing a deadline. And, she didn't have to go very far for inspiration. She had five brothers, who were all single, as well as the men she dated to research her male characters. And for her heroines, she had her own experiences, as well as women friends and family to draw upon. But none of her characters had names of people she knew, and she only used snippets of their personalities in developing her characters.

Taking the pages she'd printed and a red pencil, Angela moved from behind her desk to a plush club chair with a matching ottoman. Light from a floor lamp provided enough illumination as she settled in to read what she'd typed:

His fingertips feathered down the length of her bare skin, his gossamer touch reminding Ericka of the gentle brush of a butterfly's wings.

Does that sound too cheesy? Angela mused.

Her red pencil was poised to make changes when her cell phone rang, shattering the quiet. She reached for her cell phone. "Hi. This is Angela," she answered, without glancing at the caller ID display.

"Is this Angela Chase?" came a deep voice on the other end of the line.

A slight frown etched on her forehead. "Who's asking?"

"Levi Eaton."

She went still. "Who are you and how did you get my number?"

There was a brief pause. "Your brother Duncan gave me your number, Miss Chase. I work with him at the clinic."

There was another pause. "Why would he give you my number?"

"He said you needed an escort for a wedding on Sunday."

It wasn't until she felt the sharp twinge in her jaw that Angela realized she'd been gritting her teeth. It was something she did whenever she was stressed or at a loss for words. Her brother had no right! Duncan had no right to interfere in her social life! Her mouth gaped open when realization dawned. She was willing to bet her first born that her mother had asked Duncan to find a date for her.

"Duncan's wrong. I don't need an escort."

"Look, Miss Chase, I don't need to get involved—"

"It's Angela," she interrupted.

"As I was saying, Angela, I don't need or want to get involved in any family fracas, but I did tell your brother I'd be willing to take you as a favor to him. I'm sorry if I bothered you."

"Don't hang up!" she practically shouted into the tiny mouthpiece. "Are you still there?" she asked after several seconds. A low chuckle caressed her ear.

"Yes, I'm still here. Have you changed your mind?"

Angela's mind was in tumult. There was something about Levi Eaton's voice she liked. And, if the rest of the man matched the voice, then he could at least be character development material for her novels.

"Yes, I have. I may have been a little too hasty. My brothers believe they know what's best for me when it comes to my social life."

"Are they usually right?"

Angela smiled. "Most times—no. Do you keep track of your sister's love life?" she asked.

"No, I don't. Because I don't have a sister. Now that we've established that I'll be your date for the wedding, I suggest we meet sometime tomorrow and talk so we'll be on the same page come Sunday."

I like his approach, she thought. The smile curving Angela's lips reached her eyes. It was obvious Levi Eaton was a take-charge guy. He'd mentioned he worked with Duncan at the clinic.

"How did you come to know Duncan?" she asked him.

"That's something we'll discuss tomorrow."

Her eyebrows lifted a fraction. *Mysterious,* she thought. "When and where do you want to meet?"

"I'm scheduled to see patients in the morning, so I won't be able to get to Louisville until late afternoon. We can talk over dinner. You're probably more familiar with the restaurants in Louisville than I am. Where would you like to eat?" Levi asked.

He'd answered one of Angela's questions. Levi Eaton was a doctor. "I'd rather not go out. If people spot us together, then it's going to generate a lot of questions. We can meet at my place."

"What if I bring dinner?"

Angela laughed for the first time. "That won't be necessary. I'll cook."

"I don't want to put you out, Angela. I don't mind bringing dinner."

"I have to cook for myself, so making a little more definitely won't put me out. Is there anything in particular you'd like?"

It was Levi's turn to laugh. "No. Surprise me."

Daring. "Maybe I should've asked if there is anything you're allergic to, or if you have any dietary restrictions."

"No and no."

Angela gave Levi her address, listening intently as he repeated it. "Is seven too late for you?"

"No. Seven is perfect."

She smiled. "I'll see you tomorrow at seven. Call me if you get lost trying to find my house."

"That's all right, Angela. My car has GPS navigation."

She wanted to tell Levi that even with GPS people still weren't able to find her house that easily since the area where she lived in the suburbs of Louisville was secluded with private roads and streets.

"If that's the case, then I'll see you tomorrow."

"Tomorrow," Levi repeated.

"Levi?"

"Yes, Angela."

"Thank you."

A full-throated laugh came through the earpiece. "You're quite welcome."

Depressing a button, Angela ended the call. She didn't know whether Levi was laughing at her. It wouldn't be the first time one of her brothers had dared a man to go out with her. It was as if they had taken a concerted interest in her love life since her former fiancé eloped with her maid of honor the day before her wedding.

They would've hunted him down and beat him to a bloody pulp if she hadn't convinced them it was better to find out that her fiancé was unfaithful before she'd married him. If she'd found out after they'd exchanged vows, then it might have been her who would have tried to pound the life out of him with a cast-iron frying pan.

It didn't matter if Duncan wagered or paid Levi Eaton to be her date because come Sunday, it would be the first time in five years she would come face-to-face with the duplicitous pair who'd turned her life upside down.

Soft meowing caught her attention. Shifting on the chair, Angela saw the tiny, white-coated cat with gleaming blue-gray eyes staring up at her. To say the cat was spoiled was an understatement. "What do you want, Miss Divine?" The cat meowed in response, arching her back and stretching out her front paws. Putting the manuscript pages and pencil on the table, she leaned over and picked up her pet.

Angela knew Miss Divine could jump up onto her lap without any help, but she was training her to stay off the furniture. The exception was when she sat at her desk working during the day. Miss Divine would find a spot on the corner of the L-shaped desk and settle down to sleep as sunlight poured in through the skylight and French doors.

She was one of those rare cats who had learned that the kitchen, dining and living rooms were off-limits. Angela had resisted having a cat or dog because of the pet hair and dander. And she refused to resort to covering her furniture if Miss Divine decided to sit wherever she pleased. But once she saw the tiny kitten, she knew she had to have her.

"Well, Miss Dee, it looks as if you're going to be on your own on Sunday," she said as the cat stared back at her owner as if she understood what Angela had said. "As much as I tried to fight it, yours truly has a date for Yvette's wedding."

Angela was more than willing to sit at the singles' table, but somehow Duncan—no doubt at their mother's urging—had recruited someone to be her date so Dianne Chase could save face. Her mother was the only one in her social circle whose daughter was unmarried. A society *grande dame,* she had been denied the chance to flaunt her status as mother of the bride when Angela's wedding was abruptly called off. Of course, the fact that the groom had run off with the maid of honor made it all the more embarrassing.

"What my mother doesn't realize is that I'm one of those women who happens to be quite content to be without a man in her life," as she continued her dialogue with the cat. Miss Divine blinked, meowing softly in response. "I'm sure you know what I'm talking about, Miss Dee, because you don't have a man in your life, either. Even if you did, I doubt whether anything would jump off because you can't have any kittens." She ran her fingertips over the smooth fur that felt like velvet. "If I hadn't had you spayed, you probably would've had an adorable litter."

No, she didn't need a man. Not when she was able to live out her fantasies vicariously through her characters.

Chapter 2

Levi had spent a restless night wondering why he'd allowed himself to be set up on a blind date. The last time he'd been on one was his second year in college when he'd taken his roommate's sister to her senior prom. Going to the prom with a college student as her date had appreciably elevated his roommate's sister's "geek" image. What her brother hadn't realized was that his sister wasn't a nerd, but really more of a *freak*. He was fortunate to have survived the night without being sexually assaulted. Of course, Levi didn't tell his roommate about his sister, but it was the last time he'd agreed to go on a date with a woman without first meeting and talking to her.

It was after two o'clock before he'd come to the conclusion that he hadn't been set up, but instead had willingly agreed to escort a woman to a wedding that was just a day away. Admittedly, his social life had been pretty much nonexistent over the past few months, and it was time he enjoyed a few hours of female companionship.

If Levi had been in New York, his free time would've been filled with dinners, parties, occasional trips to Philadelphia to see his relatives and having fun with his circle of friends in his off-hours. If he needed a date, all he had to do was call. He'd established a coterie of female friends who were willing to step in at a moment's notice, and he was always quick to reciprocate whenever they needed an escort. He made certain never to blur the lines between friendship and intimacy. Women he counted as friends he didn't sleep with. Those he'd slept with, he relegated to the past. When he ended a relationship, he never wanted to send mixed signals.

Levi planned to meet Angela Chase later that evening. He wanted to find out whether they both were on the same page in case someone asked how long they'd known each other or where they'd met. After all, the wedding guests were Angela's friends and family and he didn't want to do or say anything that would embarrass her.

His head popped up when he heard the knock on his office door. He stared at the receptionist-slash-secretary-slash-insurance claims manager as she peered through the slight opening. He turned off his tape recorder.

"Yes, Krista."

"I just got a call from a mother who would like you to examine her son."

Levi capped his pen, slipping it into the breast pocket of his lab coat. "What's wrong with him?"

"She claims he fell out of the back of her dad's old pickup and hurt his arm."

"Tell her to bring him in."

Office hours were over and he'd just finished updating notes for his last patients' medical records. If he hadn't been thinking about his dinner date with Angela Chase later that evening, he probably would have already left for the day. Ten minutes later Krista returned to tell him the patient was waiting in one of the examining rooms.

It took only a glance for Levi to know the boy was seriously injured, and would need X-rays. He gave the six-year-old a shot to minimize the pain, stabilized the limb with a splint and sling, and then called the local hospital to alert them that the boy's mother was bringing him in, and that he needed emergency medical attention. He promised to fax over the incident report.

He ended the call, and then turned to stare at the young mother sitting on a chair cradling her son to her chest. The boy's eyelids were fluttering. "Mrs. Godfrey, I want you to go and start up your car. I'll carry Jeremy for you."

Debra Godfrey stared up at the tall doctor with the friendly smile. Within minutes of bringing her son to the clinic, Dr. Eaton had managed to ease her son's fears by asking him what his favorite cartoon was. When Jeremy said *Sponge Bob Square*

Pants the pediatrician pretended to be one of the cartoon characters. It was enough to stop the flow of tears while Dr. Eaton deftly injected him with a painkiller so he could examine the child's arm to better determine the severity of the injury.

Debra nodded as she bit her lip to stop it from trembling. "I… I don't have enough gas in my car to make it to the hospital. "I'd hoped you would be able to take care of Jeremy's arm here at the clinic."

Levi gave the mother a reassuring look. Most of the patients who came to the clinic were hardship cases, living at or below the poverty level. Many were on Medicaid, and those who were uninsured were charged a nominal fee. He knew Debra Godfrey was the mother of three school-age children and had moved in with her parents after her husband was sentenced to an eight-year prison sentence for armed robbery. If she'd come into his New York office, Jeremy would've been x-rayed by a staff technician, an orthopedist would have set the child's arm and fitted it with a lightweight cast. The fully staffed medical group offered an array of services including minor surgery.

"I'll call Larry at the gas station and tell him to fill up your car."

Debra's eyes filled with tears. "I'll pay you back soon as I get paid next week."

Levi patted her hand. "Don't worry about paying me back, Mrs. Godfrey," he said, smiling in hopes of putting her at ease. "Just take care of your son."

Reaching into the pocket of his lab coat, he took out his cell phone, scrolled through his contacts, and tapped the button for the gas station. It took less than a minute to relay his instructions to the station owner. Scooping up the boy, he carried him out to the parking lot, placed him gently on the passenger seat of the old pickup truck, and fastened the seatbelt, adjusting it to prevent further injury to his arm.

Levi watched as the taillights disappeared when Debra Godfrey drove away. Treating the child had meant he'd have little time to prepare for his meeting with Angela Chase. He didn't want to read more into the blind date than just doing a favor for a colleague. He reasoned that this was only going to be a one-time thing.

Angela checked the table setting to make certain she hadn't forgotten anything. For reasons she couldn't fathom, she wanted dinner to be perfect. Maybe it had something to do with not having a man over for dinner in almost six months. It wasn't as if she'd soured on the opposite sex. It was just that she didn't trust men.

She'd decided to have dinner in the enclosed terrace. After making sure everything was perfect, she returned to the kitchen to check on the chicken that had marinated overnight. She opened the oven door and checked to see if the roast was fully cooked and perfectly browned. A smile tilted the corners of her mouth when tantalizing aromas wafted up to her nostrils. The stuffed bird was perfect for the cool late-spring evening.

Most nights when she returned home from work, she didn't go into her home office to turn on her computer, but retreated to the enclosed back porch where she spent countless hours catching up with her pile of reading material or watching a movie.

Glancing at the clock on the oven, Angela lowered the temperature, closed the door and walked out of the kitchen to the staircase that led to the second floor of bedrooms. She had an hour before Levi Eaton arrived.

Stripping off her tank top, sweatpants and underwear, Angela covered her hair with a shower cap and then stepped into the stall in the en-suite bathroom. She turned on the shower spray and adjusted the water temperature. She squeezed a generous glob of her favorite bath gel onto a sponge and went about soaping her body.

As his gaze shifted from the map on the dashboard to the road in front of him, Levi decelerated. Apparently Angela was right. The roads were confusing. It was the third time the automated voice had recalculated his programmed route. After his last patient, he packed an overnight bag and a garment bag with the suit he'd planned to wear to the wedding, and drove fifteen miles from Maywood Junction to Louisville. He planned to check into a downtown hotel where he'd take advantage of the hotel's full-service salon for a haircut and shave.

As he continued driving, a wooded area gave way to a paved road and a sign pointing the way to Magnolia Pines—a private residential community. The sun had set and the light from the nearly full moon reflected off the rails of the white fencing surrounding the property. The rails were a constant reminder that he was in horse country.

He'd come to Kentucky at the beginning of January and planned to leave at the end of June. And during his six-month stay, he'd made a promise to himself to attend a horse race. And his race of choice was the Kentucky Derby.

Reining in his thoughts, and remembering why he was driving along unlit roads in a Louisville suburb, Levi recalled the conversation he'd had with Duncan earlier that morning. He'd told him that he'd contacted his sister and would be meeting her for dinner tonight. Duncan seemed surprised that Angela had agreed to go out with him. But Levi didn't want answers from his colleague, but rather from his sister. The outline of the gatehouse came into view, and Levi maneuvered up to the security gate as the guard slid back the window.

"Good evening, sir. May I help you?"

He nodded, smiling. "Good evening. I'm here to see Miss Angela Chase."

"Your name, sir."

"Levi Eaton."

"I need to see your driver's license, Mr. Eaton."

Shifting in his seat, Levi removed a small billfold from his back pocket and handed his license to the guard. He drummed his fingers on the leather-wrapped wheel as he waited to be announced.

Angela stood in front of the full-length mirror, half an hour later, grimacing when she realized she looked like one of the heroines in her novels before her glamorous transformation. The white, man-tailored blouse, black cropped slacks and a pair of black patent high-heeled sandals were more appropriate for an afternoon luncheon than a dinner date.

A pair of pearl studs was the only jewelry she wore. Even her hairstyle was conservative. Instead of leaving it loose or in a ponytail, she'd pinned it into a chignon at the nape of her neck. She moved closer to the mirror and examined her bare face. She'd applied a moisturizer, lip gloss but nothing else. She went completely still when the distinctive buzzing from the intercom echoed through the house. She knew it was Levi Eaton—and he was early. Walking over to a wall panel, she punched a button on the intercom.

"This is Ms. Chase."

"Miss Chase. Mr. Levi Eaton is here to see you."

"You can let him in."

Well, her blind date was about to see Angela Maxine Chase without any artifice. It would be a test to see if Dr. Levi Eaton was as superficial as most of the men she'd dated over the past three years. She left the bedroom, walked the length of the carpeted hallway to the staircase leading to the living room. She unlocked the door, opened it and came face-to-face with a man whose masculinity literally took her breath away.

To say the man standing on her front steps was tall, dark and handsome was an understatement. Angela hadn't realized she was gaping until she saw his gaze shift from her eyes to her mouth. Opening the door wider, she gave him a bright smile.

"Please come in, Dr. Eaton."

Levi's expressive eyebrows lifted a fraction, and she wondered what was going through his mind. Now, she thought if his personality was as good as his looks, then Levi Eaton would definitely become the prototype for her next romance novel.

"Please, it's Levi."

Her smile grew wider as she extended her free hand. "And I'm Angela. Welcome." Her fingers disappeared in his large grasp.

He handed her a decorative bag filled with wine. "I didn't know what you were serving, so I bought a bottle of red, white and rosé."

She peered into the bag. "You really didn't have to bring anything."

Levi smiled for the first time, attractive lines appearing in his lean face. "I guess it has something to do with home training. My mother would be mortified if I showed up at someone's home empty-handed. At least the first time," he added, his smile becoming a full grin.

Angela angled her head, staring up at the man who made her heart beat a little too fast for comfort. It had been a long time—at least five years—since she'd found herself slightly off balance. It hadn't happened since she'd been introduced to Robert Gaskin. And if she could turn back the clock, Angela never would've given him a second glance. She opened her mouth to tell Levi that tonight would be the first and last time he would cross her threshold, but changed her mind when she remembered Levi was to be her date for her cousin's wedding.

"Please come with me. It'll be another twenty minutes before dinner is ready, so I thought we could take some time to become better acquainted," she said instead.

Levi glanced around the alcove off the living room where two facing club chairs, one with a matching footstool, a low mahogany table with rosewood inlay and two floor lamps with Tiffany-style shades created an inviting and comfortable seating area. A decoratively carved credenza doubled as a bar, its surface covered with lead-crystal decanters filled with clear and amber-colored spirits.

He hadn't known what to expect, but it wasn't the young woman who appeared to be no nonsense *and* all business. What he did like was her natural, flawless face. Beyond her beauty, he didn't know anything about her other than her name and that she lived in a sprawling, exquisitely decorated house in a gated community. Yet he was curious and wanted to know more about her.

A woman's looks were not as important to him as her intelligence and femininity. Levi had come to the conclusion that he was somewhat old-school when it came to women. He wasn't a chauvinist, but he liked women who were more traditional.

Angela suddenly turned and stared at him, her eyes large and her gaze unwavering in the flattering warm light. "Please sit down, Levi."

"After you, Angela," he said, smiling.

He waited for her to sit down, then followed suit, trying not to stare at her legs, which were stretched out and propped on a footstool. The soft light from the floor lamp spilled over Angela's delicate features, and her serene expression reminded him of the female images in Renaissance paintings. Her rich golden-brown complexion was reminiscent of autumn leaves and his gaze lingered on her temptingly curved lips.

Angela was slender but with enough curves to get a man's attention. If he had to describe her looks, Levi would have to admit that Angela Chase was easy on the eyes—very, very easy on the eyes.

He smiled. "I suppose you'd like to know a little something about me before our big date tomorrow." The question was more of a statement.

Angela's smile matched his, charming him with the gesture. "I'd like to know more than a little something about you."

Levi sobered. "Ask me whatever you like."

Settling back in the chair, she studied the man sitting only a few feet from her. His close-cropped hair, smooth jawline and dark suit, white shirt, striped navy and white silk tie and imported slip-ons bespoke exquisite taste and grooming.

"How old are you, and where were you born?"

"I'm thirty-six. Born in Philadelphia and grew up in Miami, Florida."

I know you're a doctor, but do you have a specialty?"

"Pediatrics."

Angela's expression did not change as she continued to stare at Levi, wondering why Duncan had neglected to tell her that he'd added a pediatrician to his staff. After he'd set her up with his part-time dentist, Patrick Demorest, she'd stopped visiting her brother in Maywood Junction to avoid Patrick. "Why did you decide to become a pediatrician?"

Levi stared at his hands. "I like children. Why do you ask?"

"If I had to take a guess as to your specialty, it wouldn't have been pediatrics."

"What did you think it would be?"

"I would've thought cardiology, or maybe obstetrics."

"One ob-gyn in the family is plenty."

"I take it you come from a family of doctors," Angela said.

Levi nodded. "There are quite a few doctors, lawyers and teachers. What else do you want to know about me?" he asked.

"How long have you lived in Kentucky?"

He paused before saying, "I'm only here for six months."

Angela sat up straight. "Why just six months?" she asked.

"When I was in med school I agreed to do community service and provide medical care to places like Maywood."

"So, when your commitment is up you plan to return to Florida?"

"No. I live and work in a suburb just north of New York City."

Angela digested this information. She usually spoke to Duncan several times a month, but he hadn't said anything about Levi. The fact that Levi worked with her brother provided the perfect reason for why they were attending the wedding together.

"Perhaps you should tell me about yourself, Angela, and why it's so important that your brother recruited me to be your date for tomorrow's wedding," Levi said, breaking into her thoughts.

"It's not that I couldn't get a date, but—"

"That's obvious," he interrupted, "because you're beautiful, and I assume you're quite intelligent."

Her cheeks grew warmer. "Should I take that as a compliment, Levi?"

He shook his head. "No, Angela. It's the truth."

Angela knew she had to be careful with Levi Eaton. Very, very careful or she would find herself succumbing to his charisma and obvious sex appeal.

A slow smile ruffled the corners of her mouth. "Thank you."

Levi shook his head. "There's no need to thank me."

"My cousin is marrying the cousin of my ex-fiancé."

Levi crossed his arms over his chest. "Is there bad blood between you and your ex?"

"No. The truth is I haven't seen him in five years."

"Is he married?"

Angela nodded. "Yes," she confirmed after a pregnant pause.

"You need a date because you don't want him to believe you've been pining away for him."

She wanted to tell Levi that she *hadn't* been pining away for Robert, since right after their canceled wedding she plunged back into the dating scene with a vengeance. It was only when she began writing in earnest that she'd slowed down so much that she hadn't been on a date in months.

"I need you to dispel any idea he might have that I'm pining away for him since I'm still single."

Levi's expression remained impassive. "Are you single by choice?" he asked. His voice was barely above a whisper.

Angela angled her head, offering him a smile that didn't quite reach her eyes. "Are you single by choice?" she asked, answering his question with one of her own.

"What makes you believe I'm single?" said Levi, asking her another question.

This time Angela's smile spread over her face like bright rays of morning sun. "If you weren't, or should I say if I were married to you, I doubt that I'd let you go away for six months without me. And I'd hope if you are married, you wouldn't accept an invitation to escort other women."

Levi leaned closer and gave her a prolonged stare. "Perhaps I'm more like your cheating ex than you think."

She went completely still, as if she'd been hit by a bolt of lightning. A slow, uneasy panic seized Angela, making it virtually impossible for her to speak. Had Duncan told Levi the circumstances of her breakup with Robert even though he, along with everyone else in her family had sworn never to talk about it?

"What makes you think he cheated on me?"

"Did he, Angela?"

"Yes!" she spat out, annoyed that she'd allowed herself to dredge up the past. "Do you cheat on women?"

"No. And even if I were seeing someone, I still wouldn't cheat. I didn't mean to put you on the spot, but I need to know what I'll be dealing with if we encounter your ex," Levi said apologetically.

"His name is Robert Gaskin."

He gave Angela a smile he usually reserved for his patients. "We'll be ready for Mr. Gaskin," he said confidently.

Angela noticed he'd said *we*. It was the first time a man, other than her father and brothers, had offered to protect her. It was too bad she wasn't looking for a man in her life, because Dr. Levi Eaton would've been the perfect candidate.

The grandfather clock in a corner of the living room chimed the hour. It was seven o'clock. She stood up as Levi rose to his feet with her. "Please excuse me, but I have to check on dinner."

"Do you need help?"

She glanced at him over her shoulder. "Do you cook?"

Levi winked at Angela. "I've been known to burn a few pots. Maybe next time we get together I'll return the favor and cook for you."

Angela stopped short, forcing Levi to bump into her. His hands went to her shoulders to steady her. He was close—close enough for her to feel his body heat, close enough to feel the whisper of his breath over her ear, and close enough to inhale the subtle masculine scent of his cologne.

"You want to go on another date?" Her query was a low husky whisper.

Levi's gaze moved slowly over her face. "Why wouldn't I? After all, you owe me one."

She tilted her chin. "When will I have to pay up?"

"At my family reunion. We always get together over the Memorial Day weekend. This year it will be in Philadelphia."

Angela shook her head. "You can't just spring something like that on me at the last minute. I have a business to run."

Levi dropped his hands. "What kind of business?"

"I operate a gift shop with my cousin in downtown Louisville."

"Do you ever take a vacation?" he asked.

"Of course I do."

"Do you have anything planned for that weekend?"

"My parents usually host a cookout that weekend."

"Maybe we can work something out so that we're able to attend both," Levi suggested.

Angela's smile reminded him of a high-wattage bulb. "Why

don't we wait until after the wedding to see if we can stand each other before we talk about a second date?"

"I'll agree, but under one condition," Levi said in a seductively deep voice.

Her smile faded. "What's that?"

"Tell me how I can get a ticket to the Kentucky Derby."

Angela waved her hand as if swatting away a fly. "That's easy. You can come with me."

Levi froze. "You're kidding, aren't you?"

"No, I'm not. Come, Levi. I have to take the chicken out of the oven before it's as dry as sandpaper."

A smile curved Levi's strong mouth as he stared at the swaying hips of the woman who was as charming as she was intriguing. Duncan was right. There was nothing wrong with his sister—at least not on the surface.

Chapter 3

Angela breathed an audible sigh when she opened the wall oven door to find the large roast chicken had cooked to a perfect golden-brown. "Is it okay?" Levi said, standing behind her.

Smiling and moving to her left, she winked at him. "Take a look."

"Hot damn! The girl *can* cook!"

"Bite your tongue! I don't know what kind of women you've been hanging out with, but one thing I'll readily admit is that yours truly can jam in the kitchen."

Levi took a step, his chest only inches from Angela's back. "The women I date usually don't cook."

"Don't or can't?" she asked.

He smiled. "Don't."

"How or where do you eat?"

"We make reservations, or I'll cook for her."

Shifting slightly, Angela stared up at Levi over her shoulder. The word keeper came to mind and she wondered why some woman hadn't become Mrs. Levi Eaton, except, of course, if he was afraid of marriage. And, if he was, then he would fit quite nicely into her plans since she had no intention of *ever* getting married. In that moment Angela decided she would try to keep Levi around until he went back to New York—unless he decided otherwise. After all, he appeared to be every woman's fantasy. He was gorgeous, intelligent and single. But, then she thought about Robert.

She saw Levi's mouth moving before she realized he was talking to her. "I'm sorry, but my mind was elsewhere," she apologized.

"I asked if you wanted me to help you bring anything to the table."

Angela blinked as if coming out of a trance. "Yes. After I take the chicken out of the roasting pan you can take it out to the terrace."

Taking off his suit jacket, Levi draped it over the back of one of the chairs in the breakfast nook. He then loosened his tie, unbuttoned and turned back the cuffs to his shirt. His gaze swept around the gourmet kitchen with stainless steel appliances. Double-wall ovens, two sinks, two dishwashers, a counter-depth refrigerator-freezer and a cook-top range and grill were a chef's dream kitchen.

The house had quintessential Southern architecture with a wraparound porch, second story veranda, window shutters and a trio of ceiling fans on the front porch.

"Is there someplace that I can wash my hands?" he asked.

Angela pointed to a door at the far end of the kitchen. "There's a half bath over there."

She watched as he walked toward the bathroom. Even his walk was sexy. He didn't walk or glide—he had a swagger. It was in that instant that she decided she was going to call on everything in her feminine arsenal to keep Levi Eaton around for as long as he remained in Kentucky. And if she and Levi became friends, then she would be more than willing to make the drive to Maywood Junction to see him. Having him around would assuage her mother's concern that she was ruining her reputation by seeing a different man every few months.

The women in Dianne Chase's social circle were quick to report that they'd seen Angela with a guy one week and another a month later, much to her mother's consternation. Not only did Dianne have an unmarried thirty-something daughter, but none of her sons were married and she still wasn't a grandmother. However, what her mother failed to realize, even after Angela informed her she wasn't sleeping with any of the guys she dated, was that she didn't really care about such salacious gossip.

Even though she told them on their first date that she had no intention of sleeping with them, that didn't stop her dates from trying to change her mind.

* * *

Levi returned to the kitchen just when Angela was taking the chicken from the pan and placing it on a platter. He smiled when he saw that she'd put on a black pin-striped bibbed apron.

"Let me do that," he offered, lengthening his stride until he was standing next to her. Lifting the rack from the roasting pan, he managed to slide the bird onto the platter with little or no effort. The tantalizing aromas titillated his nose. "What did you stuff it with?"

"Long-grain rice, raisins, finely diced apples and ground cinnamon."

"It smells amazing."

"It tastes amazing," Angela confirmed. "I can't take credit because it's my aunt's recipe. She threw a lot of dinner parties in this house, and her culinary style was to combine as many dishes into one that you can. She said if you're serving chicken, then stuff it so you don't have to prepare separate side dishes."

Levi gave Angela an incredulous look. "You live here with your aunt?"

Angela laughed, the sound resembling the tinkling of a wind chime. "No. She now lives in a chateau in France's wine country with her longtime lover. She gave me the house as a wedding gift." She compressed her lips. "It was the only gift that I didn't have to return."

He heard the throatiness in her voice when she'd mentioned *wedding gift*. "Your aunt sounds like a colorful character."

"Colorful wouldn't begin to describe her. Folks around her called her everything but a child of God. And those were the compliments. They'd failed to realize she was her own woman who lived by her own set of rules. If something made Nicola Chase happy then she made everyone around her happy. If not, then stay out of her way."

"It sounds as if you are quite fond of her."

Walking over to the refrigerator, Angela took out bottles of chilled white and rosé wines. Using her shoulder, she closed the door. "I grew up wanting to be just like her, much to my mother's horror."

Resting his hip against the cooking island, Levi crossed his arms over his chest. "Did you?"

"I wish."

"Don't you like how your life has turned out?"

"Please don't get me wrong, Levi. I'm quite satisfied with my life. It's other folks who don't believe I am."

She turned and walked out of the kitchen. Levi followed with the platter as she led the way to the glass-enclosed sunroom. Charcoal-gray solar blinds provided privacy from prying eyes. When he'd followed the private road leading to Angela's house, he noticed that it overlooked a lake surrounded by a copse of weeping willow trees.

His gaze swept over the room, the focus of which was a table covered in a white linen tablecloth with a black-and-white-striped runner, and set with china, crystal and sterling silver. White candles in varying heights flickered in crystal votives, hurricane lanterns and candelabras. Angela touched a wall switch and track lighting illuminated the space like starlight pinpoints, while soft music filled the room from concealed speakers.

He set the platter down on the table beside a vase of white and deep pink flowers. "This is very, very nice."

Angela met his eyes across the table. "Thank you."

Levi stared at Angela, whose face was illuminated by the soft light coming from the candles, his gaze moving slowly over her features as if committing everything to memory. He'd spent less than an hour with Angela and already he found her incredibly fascinating. She appeared conservative in her choice of attire, yet her home and furnishings were luxurious and exquisitely tasteful. She seemed reserved yet daring, somewhat of a contradiction.

"Who do you mean by others?"

"My mother in particular, and a few of my brothers would probably agree."

"They'd like to see you married with children."

She nodded. "What they don't understand is that I'm quite happy being single. Aunt Nikki never married and she enjoys being a free spirit."

"In other words she's content to live with her lover rather than marry him."

Angela gave Levi a mischievous smile. "She couldn't marry him even if she wanted to."

"He's married."

She nodded. "He and his wife have lived apart for more than two decades."

"Why doesn't he divorce her?" he asked.

"He would if his estranged wife wasn't a devout Catholic. They live apart, but he supports her financially."

Intrigued, Levi asked, "Did he and his wife have any children?"

"They had a son, but he drowned in a boating accident when he was a child."

"That's unfortunate."

Angela sighed audibly. "Yes, it is. He wanted my aunt to have a child, but she refused because she didn't want to have a child out of wedlock. Excuse me. I have to go back and get the salad."

Rounding the table, Levi pulled out a chair at one of the place settings. "Sit down. I'll get it."

"That's all right. You're my guest."

Leaning over her head, Levi took a deep breath, breathing in the subtle fragrance of the perfume clinging to Angela's body. The scent was like its wearer—subtle and sexy. "You cooked, so it's only fair that I help out."

"What if you open the wine and allow it to breathe while I get the salad and put the asparagus on the grill," she countered in a soft, but stern tone.

Levi resisted the urge to salute Angela. Her refusal to let him help told him more than he needed to know about her. She was stubborn and controlling.

"Yes, ma'am," he said, reaching for the corkscrew opener resting on a folded napkin. "Are you rolling your eyes at me?" he asked when she rested her hands at her waist.

"I'm not old enough to be a ma'am."

"How old are you?" he asked, removing the foil and inserting the corkscrew into the bottle of rosé.

"You should know better than to ask a woman her age."

Levi lifted broad shoulders under his crisp white shirt. "It doesn't matter. I can always ask Duncan."

Angela rolled her eyes again. "Thirty-two," she spat out, "and soon to be thirty-three."

He winked. "That wasn't so bad, now was it?"

"What else are you going to ask Duncan about me?"

The soft pop of the cork was the only sound in the room as Levi and Angela stared at each other. "If I wanted to I would've had Duncan tell me everything about you before we met. He asked me to do him a favor and I said I would. I'm willing to be your date tomorrow, and the only thing I'm going to ask is that you do the same for me at my family reunion, since my mother will undoubtedly have some woman there for me to meet. She thinks it's time I settled down and give her some grandchildren."

Angela compressed her lips. "As long as we understand each other I think we'll get along quite well. Excuse me, but I'm going to get the salad and grill the asparagus."

"Angela," Levi said as she walked away. She stopped but didn't turn around. "I'd like to sit down and enjoy the food you've prepared without talking about us."

"So what do you want to talk about?"

"Your aunt, sports, books, movies or TV for a start."

She half-turned and smiled at him over her shoulder. "Thank you, kind sir, for giving me a choice," she drawled in her best Southern accent.

Throwing back his head, Levi laughed, the rich sound echoing in the room. "You're quite welcome, ma'am."

Angela couldn't remember when she'd spent a more enjoyable evening with a man. Not only was Levi a great listener, but he was also a wonderful conversationalist. They'd discussed sports. He'd seemed surprised that she was so knowledgeable about the subject, but after she'd explained that she'd grown up with five brothers and a father who were sports nuts, he'd understood completely.

Between forkfuls of food, washed down with the chilled wine, dinner was a comfortable and leisurely affair.

Levi raised his water glass. "When you talk to your aunt

again, please let her know her roast chicken recipe is exceptional."

Angela inclined her head. "I'll definitely let her know."

"How often do you speak to her?"

After dabbing the corners of her mouth with her napkin, she placed it beside her plate. Resting her elbow on the table, Angela cupped her chin in the heel of her hand, and stared at Levi through lowered lids. "There are times when I hear from her a couple of times of month, and then it's like she disappears. Then out of the blue she'll call me and explain that she'd jetted off to some exotic destination. If it's not an African safari, then it's shopping in Hong Kong. The highlight of one of her trips was snorkeling in the Great Barrier Reef. She laughs whenever I say I want to be like her when I grow up."

Levi stared at her. "Are you?"

Angela smiled. "I'm halfway there."

"How are you halfway there?"

"I work for myself and make my own hours. Aunt Nikki was a set designer for film and stage, and she told me I would never be completely happy until I worked for myself. I was a teacher when my cousin Traci, who'd been through a contentious divorce, moved from Frankfort to Louisville and asked me to go into business with her."

Levi's expressive eyebrows lifted when he asked, "What about teaching?"

"I gave it up. Traci's paternal grandmother worked as a chef in a Frankfort country club and was a collector. Nowadays you'd call them hoarders. Whenever she catered private dinner parties, she'd ask her clients for their old china, stemware and silver in lieu of payment. The collection was so large and it took Traci three months to polish the silver and wash the china and stemware by hand. Then she hired an appraiser and after he gave her a figure, she decided to open a gift shop called the Garden Gate. We do quite well selling estate pieces, but most of the business comes from wedding registries. We carry Waterford, Lenox, Baccarat, Limoges plus a wide selection of wedding party gifts. Some of the items are what I consider luxuries." A mysterious smile softened her mouth. "I splurge and treat myself to two crystal pieces each year—one for Christmas and the other for my birthday."

Levi's gaze went from her mouth to the vase and candleholders. "They're beautiful."

"Thank you," she said softly. "If you ever need a gift for a wedding or a baby shower let me know and I'll give you the family discount."

"I'm going to take you up on your offer because there've been a few newborns in the family this year."

Angela traced the rim of her wineglass with a forefinger. The glow from the track lights and flickering candles flattered the planes of Levi's face. His gentle manner, deep voice and effortless conversation made her feel as if she'd known him for weeks instead of hours. "Let me know when you're free and I'll give you a private showing."

"I'm off on Sundays, Mondays and Wednesdays," Levi quickly offered.

"The Garden Gate is closed on Sundays and Mondays." Mondays were when she spent most of the day writing, and she rarely scheduled anything that day. Levi would be the exception. "When do you want to come in?"

"I'll call and let you know."

Angela was certain he'd heard her sigh of relief because she'd hoped to finish her manuscript by midweek. She normally would've indulged in a marathon writing session on Sunday and Monday. But her cousin Yvette's wedding had forced her to change her plans.

"I'd prefer you come on Sunday, since Traci and I usually meet with consignment customers and prospective brides on Mondays."

Leaning back in his chair, Levi studied the woman whose cooking skills were exceptional and who continued to amaze him. He found her guarded, much too guarded whenever she talked about herself.

"Where did you go to college?"

Angela picked up her wineglass and took a sip. "Spelman."

"Why did you decide to go there?"

"My mother and grandmother were both Spelman alums. And you, Levi?"

"Howard, and then the University of Pennsylvania med school."

Her brow furrowed. "If you were already at Howard why didn't you go to med school there?"

"I gave it a lot of thought, but realized I wanted to be close to my family in Philadelphia."

Angela sat up straight. "I thought you said you were from Miami."

"My dad's family is from Philadelphia. However, there are some Eatons who live in D.C., West Virginia, South Carolina and Texas now."

"Is your father a doctor, too?"

Smiling, Levi shook his head. "No. He's a judge."

"So he likes putting away the bad guys."

"He loves it."

Angela's eyes lit up in excitement when her mind churned with ideas. "Tell me about the Eatons, Levi."

Levi took a surreptitious glance at his watch. It was after ten—much later than he thought. Somehow he'd lost track of time talking with Angela, and for him that was a good sign. "Perhaps I'll tell you about them some other time. Besides, you know enough about me so that we won't seem to be total strangers tomorrow."

"What do I tell people when they ask how long we've been seeing each other?"

"We tell them the truth."

"And that is?"

"We've just started dating."

Angela nodded, wondering if that explanation would satisfy her mother. That was why she was always reluctant to introduce a man to her family—her mother in particular. She'd immediately launch into an interrogation. Her father was less concerned with her love life as long as word didn't get back to him that some guy had caused her grief.

Benton Chase had wanted to personally go after Robert when he ran off with her maid of honor. It had taken everything for

Angela to convince the men in her family not to inflict bodily harm on Robert Gaskin. She had always been a believer in "what goes around comes around." If he cheated on her, he would eventually cheat on his new bride or she would cheat on him.

When Angela's engagement had been announced, a collective sigh went up all over Louisville since she'd managed to snag one of the city's most eligible bachelors. They were the perfect couple—the children of two of Kentucky's most prominent African-American families. Uniting the Chase and Gaskin families was cause for celebration, and had Louisville buzzing.

However, what Angela didn't know at the time was that her fiancé had been sleeping with her best friend, Savannah, who was to be her maid of honor. They'd managed to keep their relationship a secret until the night before she and Robert were to be married. A few hours after the rehearsal dinner, Robert had called to tell her that he and Savannah were flying to Las Vegas to marry, because they were expecting.

What had surprised Angela most was that she didn't cry. Pain, humiliation and anger had rendered her emotionless. It was as if all of her feelings were suppressed, and as her life unfolded she seemed to be just going through the motions.

She shifted in her chair when she heard soft meowing. Miss Divine had emerged from her hiding place in the laundry room. Pushing back his chair, Levi stood up. "I didn't know you had a kitten." He stared at the tiny white feline with splotches of dark brown fur. Her eyes were blue-gray, and her nose was pink and black, with a long tail that was darker brown than the rest of her body.

"Miss Divine is not a kitten. She's almost four."

Levi approached the cat as she sat still, watching him come closer. "Is she the runt?"

"Miss Dee is not a *runt!*"

He gestured at Miss Divine. "What else can she be, Angela? She's no bigger than a six-month-old kitten."

Angela walked over to her cat. And when she leaned over to pick her up, Miss Divine scooted to sit between Levi's legs. "Come here, baby," she said, beckoning her closer. Miss Divine responded by rubbing her face against the leg of Levi's trousers.

"Why you little traitor," she gasped when Levi picked her up.

Levi rubbed a finger over the soft fur. "She knows I like cats."

Angela rolled her eyes. "Miss Dee is usually skittish around strangers. Whenever the doorbell rings she runs and hides."

"I've never seen a full-grown cat this small."

"She's what is called a Singapura. The breed originated from feral cats that lived in the drains of Singapore. Because they're quite scarce in the States, they are very expensive. I heard that an owner of a male Singapura was offered ten thousand dollars from a breeder."

"That's incredible." He smiled when the cat purred loudly. "You came to see who's taking up your mama's time, didn't you, Miss Divine?" He winked at Angela. "Do you think she's a little jealous?"

"Don't flatter yourself, Levi." He gave her a smile that made her heart stop, and then start up again much too quickly.

"You wouldn't say that if I took her home with me."

Angela let out a gasp. "You wouldn't!"

He winked at her. "I would if you let me."

"That's not happening. I would've thought you were a dog lover, not cats." Levi angled his head and stared at Angela as she stared up at him. It was the first time he noticed that her head only came to his shoulders, even though she was wearing heels. He was six-two, and if he had to guess, Angela was at least eight inches shorter than him in her bare feet.

"I like dogs, too. But cats are different. They're more independent and completely unpredictable. You have to walk dogs, play fetch, and they hog up the space on the sofa when you're trying to watch a game. I doubt whether this little darling weighs more than six pounds."

"She weighed four pounds during her last visit to the vet."

His gaze shifted to the cat purring contently in his arms. "She likes me."

"I like you, too. But that doesn't mean I'm going to let you live with me."

Without warning, Levi's expression became stoic. "Did I ask if I could live with you?"

Her face reddened, the color settling in her cheeks. "I didn't mean for it to come out like that."

Levi handed Miss Divine to Angela. "You can cradle your baby, while I clear the table."

Angela shook her head. "That won't be necessary. There's not much to clean up."

He smiled, but the expression did not reach his eyes. "You cook, I clean."

She wanted to tell him not to push his luck, but decided better of it. After all, there was more than one way to skin a cat. *Sorry, Miss Dee,* she thought. There was something about Levi Eaton that reminded her of the male characters in her romance novels— pushy, arrogant, and oozing with enough sex appeal to earn an R-rating. Smiling sweetly, she said, "Leave everything on the countertop and I'll take care of it."

"Okay," he agreed.

Twenty minutes later, she stood on the front porch with Levi. "I'll see you tomorrow."

Levi took a step closer, cradled her face, dipped his head and brushed his lips against hers.

She froze, and then relaxed as he deepened the kiss. "I'll see you tomorrow."

He was there and then he was gone. Angela stood watching the taillights of his car fade into the darkness. Steadying her shoulders, she closed the door and locked it. It wasn't until after she'd cleaned up the kitchen, put everything away and extinguished the candles that Angela finally admitted that Levi Eaton was exactly what she needed to put to rest any notion that she'd been pining for Robert Gaskin. She'd never been one to seek revenge, but this was one time she was looking forward to it.

Spending time with Levi had convinced Angela that she was more than ready to face her past and finally put it behind her.

Chapter 4

The telephone on the bedside table rang twice before Angela raced over to answer it. "Hello," she said, trying to catch her breath.

"Hey, you. Do you still need a date?" asked a familiar voice.

"What have you done now, Traci?"

"Nothing."

Cradling the cordless receiver between her chin and shoulder, Angela returned to the en suite bathroom. "I'm going to put you on speaker while I put on my makeup."

"Okay."

Sitting down at the vanity, she picked up a small sable brush and deftly applied shadow over her eyelid. "Talk to me, Traci."

There was a brief pause before Traci's voice came through the speaker. "Reggie's brother said that he's willing to be your date for the wedding if you can't find anyone else to go."

Angela groaned, still unable to understand why her cousin continued to date her ex-husband. Although she'd always liked Reggie, it was his brother that she could only take in small doses. His ego was as large as his waistline.

"Thanks for looking out, but I have a date."

"Who is he?"

"You'll see," she said cryptically as she carefully outlined her lids with a smoky-colored eye pencil.

"Come on, Ang, give me a hint."

Angela leaned closer, checking her handiwork in the lighted makeup mirror. She smiled. She hadn't lost her touch. There was a time when she wore makeup every day. But once she began working in the gift shop, her makeup routine was a light dusting of face powder, one coat of mascara and a tinted lip gloss. She still had a standing appointment every week to have her hair and nails done, but shadow and eyeliner were for special occasions.

"Don't think you're going to badger me until I tell you. You're going to have to wait like everyone else to see who I bring. Now, please hang up so I can finish putting on my makeup. I'll see you and Reggie in about an hour."

"Should I tell Reggie's brother that you don't want him to pick you up?"

Angela shook her head. There were times when she thought Traci played dumb because she didn't like making men feel insecure, when in fact her cousin was a genius. Two years her junior, Traci had married and divorced not once, but twice—Reggie was her first—and swore she'd never marry again. Nevertheless, her cousin liked being in a relationship.

"Tell him thanks, but no thanks. I have a date."

"Okay. What are you wearing?"

She smiled. "You'll have to wait and see that, too."

"I hope it's real sexy, Ang, because I want Robert to realize what he lost."

"Robert Gaskin made his bed, and now he'll just have to lie in it. Look, cuz, I have to go if I'm going to be ready when Levi gets here."

"Levi. Now that's a name you don't hear too often. Personally I like biblical names. They always sound so strong and masculine."

Angela exhaled a deep breath. She knew if she didn't get off the phone with Traci she wouldn't be ready when Levi arrived. She still had to get dressed. "Bye, Traci. We'll talk later."

"Do you know if Yvette put us at the same table?" Traci asked, prolonging the conversation.

"Yes. I told her I wanted us seated together."

"Okay, then I'll see you later."

"Later, Traci." Angela ended the call, and concentrated on finishing her makeup.

Adjusting the light surrounding the vanity mirror, she surveyed her face under the flattering glow. Her makeup was subtle, and her eyes were dramatic with a smoky look. She turned off the lights, washed her hands and dried them. She walked out of the bathroom and into the bedroom to the dressing area where her dress and matching day coat hung from a padded hanger.

Taking off her robe, she slipped into a pair of midnight-blue bikinis, a halter-top bra and sheer pantyhose. She had just put on her dress and slipped her foot into one of the blue-suede, peep-toe pumps when the intercom rang at the same time as the clock on the fireplace mantel chimed on the half hour.

"Levi."

His name unconsciously slipped past her parted lips. A smile spread across her face as she tried to recall everything about him—the deep, soothing timbre of his voice, the sexy-looking lines that creased his sharp jawline whenever he smiled, and the way he angled his head whenever he'd listened to something she said. He was perfect—perfect enough that she could easily see him as Mr. Right Now.

Pushing the speaker button on the intercom, she said, "This is Ms. Chase."

"Are you expecting Mr. Eaton?"

"Yes, I am."

"Thank you, Ms. Chase."

Angela put on her other shoe and then picked up her light-weight coat and evening purse. She made her way down the stair-case, carefully navigating the steps in her four-inch heels. She walked across the living room floor, opened the entry door and stared out the storm door, watching for Levi's car. The weather had cooperated for her cousin's wedding. Afternoon temperatures were expected to reach the high sixties without a chance of rain. The sky was bright blue with a few puffy clouds.

She felt something soft brush against her leg and looked down to find Miss Divine sniffing the black silk bow on her shoe. "Not the shoes, Miss Dee. I left you food and water, so I know you're not hungry."

Her head popped up when she saw the sunlight reflected off the car as it approached the driveway to her house. She shooed Miss Divine away from the door, activated the alarm system and locked the door. Angela approached Levi's car as he came to a stop, and got out to meet her. There was no mistaking his surprise when he greeted her.

Angela's eyelids fluttered. Levi looked strikingly handsome in a dark blue tailored suit that looked as if it had been custom-made for his tall, slender physique. A white shirt with French cuffs, a royal blue Windsor-knotted silk tie, and black wingtip shoes made him look as if he'd stepped off the pages of a men's fashion magazine. She felt her heartbeat kick into overdrive as he closed the distance between them. Her high heels put the top of her head level with his nose.

She tiptoed and pressed her cheek to his. "How are you?"

Turning his head slightly, Levi pressed his mouth to the column of her scented neck. "Wonderful." Reaching up, he cradled her face in his hands, his eyes moving slowly over her features. "You look incredible." He couldn't disguise the approval in his voice.

Angela Chase was a chameleon. Gone was her natural look and casual attire, and in its place was a stunning femme fatale. The curly hairstyle framed her delicate features, falling a few inches beyond her shoulders. Large, wide-set eyes highlighted in subdued hues of dark-colored eye shadow met his direct gaze. He managed to curb a smile when he noticed mascara had added length and volume to her lashes. False eyelashes had always been his pet peeve with women. He disliked women who were fake-looking, but instead used makeup to enhance their natural beauty. His gaze traveled from her face to the diamond studs in her ears and lower to her legs in sheer stockings that displayed the perfection of shapely calves and slender ankles. His eyebrows lifted when he saw the dark blue, peep-toe heels with a black bow that adorned her delicate feet.

"Thank you," she said, demurely lowering her gaze. She didn't know why, but she wanted him to find her attractive. It'd been so long since she'd found herself attracted to a man.

"Are you going to be able to dance in those?"

Angela smiled, bringing his gaze to her parted lips. "Do you dance?" she asked, answering his question with a question.

"Of course I dance."

She winked at him. "If that's the case, then we'll see how well I can dance in my heels."

Levi leaned closer. "Is that a challenge, Angela?"

"Do you want it to be, Levi?"

Pressing his mouth to her left ear, he breathed a kiss. "I've never backed down from a challenge," he whispered.

Angela laughed softly. "Neither have I."

Standing back, Levi stared at the woman who unwittingly had captured him in a spell of desire. The few hours they'd spent together the night before had only served to whet his appetite and his curiosity.

He knew her old fiancé would be at the wedding, and that he'd cheated on her, but to Levi there was cheating and then there was *cheating*. There was having an affair with another woman, and then there was cheating with your partner's friends and family. The former he could rationalize somewhat, but he drew the line when it came to friends and family.

He knew what it was like to be cheated on. During his junior year at Howard, he learned that the girl he'd been sleeping with was also seeing four or five other guys on campus. Of course, it made him wary of the opposite sex, but it didn't ruin his social life. The truth was he liked women and they liked him. Yet, he was never one to take advantage of a woman. He readily admitted he wasn't ready for marriage or to become a father. And most of the women he'd dated appreciated his honesty.

Angela had asked him if he liked a challenge, and he'd said yes because she was a challenge—a very beautiful and complicated challenge. He took her hand in his, and led her around to the passenger side of the car.

"Are you ready for this?" he whispered.

"Only if you have my back, Levi," Angela answered.

"That's something you don't have to worry your beautiful head about, because I have your back and your front."

"That's a lot, Levi," she deadpanned.

"Haven't you realized yet that you're a handful, Angela?"

"No." Angela ducked her head and slid into the black leather seat.

Levi rounded the sedan, slipped in beside her and secured his seat belt. He opened his mouth to say something, but changed his mind. They were going to a wedding—a celebration—and he planned to spend the time enjoying her company, not arguing with her.

He'd driven past the gatehouse, heading back to the local road when he took a quick glance at Angela staring out the side window. "You're going to have to tell me how to get there."

She turned, staring at the gold monogrammed cufflinks. She met his eyes for a second before he turned his gaze back to the road. "Stay on this road for two miles, then you'll see marker pointing the way to Manor Oaks. When you come to the stop sign, make a left. The property is about a quarter mile from there."

Levi glanced at Angela again, this time at her long legs that stretched from the mid-thigh hemline of her dress and ended at her heels. "Are you a guest of the bride or the groom?" he asked, pressing a button on the steering wheel to turn on the radio. He had to say something to avert his attention from the woman sitting inches from him. Levi still couldn't believe her startling transformation. For a moment he hoped she'd dressed that way for him and not to make her ex jealous. Regardless, he was happy to be her date.

"The bride is my first cousin. She and her fiancé, Craig, are high school sweethearts who've broken up and reconciled so many times that when they finally sent out wedding invitations no one believed them."

"Don't you think starting out in such a shaky relationship doesn't bode well for marriage?"

Angela let out an audible sigh. "I hope not. Yvette is such a drama queen. If something doesn't go her way she resorts to histrionics. Originally I was supposed to be a bridesmaid. Eventually I gave her an ultimatum: either she cooperated or I was out."

Levi smiled. "Did she change?"

"She was okay for about a week, then she threw a mother of a tantrum and I bowed out. Yvette begged and pleaded, but I refused to give in. There is just so much verbal abuse I'll take, even if it's from family. She'd asked my cousin Traci, but she also declined. And knowing Traci she would've punched Yvette out. In the end she decided to have her twin sister as her only attendant."

"What's Robert's connection to the groom?"

Angela groaned inwardly. She didn't want to talk about Robert. Not today. It was enough that she would see him again after five years.

"He's his cousin."

Levi took another quick glance at his passenger. Her expression was as neutral as her tone. "What's up with the women in your family marrying these guys?"

"You don't understand," Angela said.

"If it didn't work out with you and Robert, why would your cousin believe it would work for her and Craig?"

"Craig isn't a cheater."

"Cheating isn't the only thing that can…" Levi's words trailed off when he spied the stately gleaming white mansion in the distance. Red-jacketed valets were parking cars as wedding guests arrived at the antebellum Greek revival mansion with its massive columns that supported the upper floor.

Slowly, he maneuvered behind a black, late-model Lexus and within seconds a parking attendant raced over to his door as Levi lowered the driver's side window. Levi got out of the car and gave the valet, who didn't look old enough to have a driver's license, his keys. The attendant handed Levi a red ticket, then put another one on the dashboard. "I'll take it from here, sir."

Levi opened the back door, reached for his jacket in the backseat, slipped it on, and walked around the BMW to help Angela out of the car. One blue-suede pump touched the ground, then the other, as he gently eased her up.

Curving an arm around her waist, he pulled her close to his side. Lowering his head, he brushed a light kiss over her lips, aware that she'd be shocked by the public display of affection. Her breath caught.

"Are you ready?"

Angela quickly recovered. "I was born ready," she answered, her voice filled with confidence.

They followed several couples up the stairs and into the expansive entryway of the landmark mansion. The house and surrounding three-hundred-acre estate had once belonged to one of the wealthiest tobacco-growing families in the county. Light from a massive chandelier reflected off the highly polished marble floor. Baskets and vases of white flowers in every variety lined the walls, which were covered in oyster-white silk fabric.

The cocktail hour was scheduled for two, the wedding ceremony for three, immediately followed by a reception that was to take place in another part of the mansion.

An elderly woman dressed in black approached them. "May I please take your coat?" she asked Angela.

She smiled. "Yes." The word was barely off her tongue when Levi helped her out of her coat, and handed it to the woman who gave him a yellow ticket. With her back to him, Angela felt Levi go completely still when he stared at her dress. "What's the matter, sweetie?" she whispered, glancing over her shoulder.

Leaning in close, Levi pressed his mouth to her ear. "Sweetie's wondering where the rest of your dress is."

Extending her arms, Angela pirouetted on her toes, allowing him to view the front and the back of her dress. The halter dress clung to her body like a second skin, the soft swell of breasts visible above the décolletage whenever she took a breath.

She smiled a sexy mouc. "Halters always have a bare back."

Levi's fingers splayed at the small of her back as they stood in the foyer. "I couldn't imagine what you were hiding under your coat, but I wasn't expecting to see so much of you."

Angela noticed his strained expression. "It's not that low cut." Looping her arm over his, she said, "Didn't you tell me that you had my back and my front?"

"No comment," he said under his breath. "Let's go inside."

She had got not only his attention, but also that of the men milling around the entryway as they stared, slack jawed at her lithe figure.

Levi escorted her through the throng waiting to enter one of the three ballrooms in the historic mansion. A string quartet played softly, as white-jacketed waiters circulated with trays of hot and cold hors d'oeuvres. Bartenders at portable bars set up at opposite ends of the ballroom were busy mixing and pouring drinks.

The light from half a dozen chandeliers reflected off the precious gems that adorned the ears, necks, wrists and the manicured fingers of the women in attendance. It was as if Louisville's most prominent African-Americans had come out to see and be seen. Levi saw Duncan standing off to the side next to a pretty, petite, dark-skinned woman with short, curly hair clinging to his arm. He recognized her as one of Maywood Junction's schoolteachers.

"Come with me, Levi. I want to introduce you to my mom and dad."

He followed Angela as she led him across the ballroom to where a tall, attractive fashionably dressed couple stood talking quietly to another couple. When the woman turned slightly he smiled, knowing what Angela would look like in three decades. Her mother was stunning!

Levi stood beside her as Angela hugged her mother and kissed her father before she acknowledged the other couple. He forced back a grin when her father raised his eyebrows after looking at the back of Angela's dress. She whispered something in her father's ear, and his gaze shifted to Levi.

Angela reached for Levi's hand. "Mom, Dad, I'd like you to meet Levi Eaton. Levi, these are my parents, Benton and Dianne Chase."

"I'm honored to meet you," Levi said, shaking Dianne's hand before repeating the gesture with Benton.

Tall and slender with coppery skin and snow-white thinning hair, Benton narrowed his deep-set dark eyes and stared at Levi. "You're an Eaton?"

Levi nodded. "Yes, I am," he said proudly.

The older man squinted slightly behind the lenses of his glasses. "You look a lot like Solomon Eaton."

He smiled. "He's my father. Do you know him?"

Resting a hand on Levi's shoulder, Benton led him away from his wife and daughter. "I met your father a couple of years ago when we got together for a fundraising golf tournament in Palm Springs. I'd heard through the grapevine that the president wanted to appoint him to the federal circuit court. I was sorry to hear Solomon declined. It's not often someone of your father's stature turns down a position like that. Forty years ago black judges were as scarce as hen's teeth—especially in the South."

"Are you a judge?" he asked Benton.

"Yes."

Levi managed to mask his surprise behind an impassive expression. "I expected you to talk to me about dating your daughter, not talk about my father."

Benton waved in a dismissive gesture. "I promised myself I would stop commenting on the men Angela dates. It's a lost cause. She claims she doesn't want to be involved with any of them." He shook his head. "The only thing I can do is hope for the best for my baby girl."

"Hey, Dad, Levi," said a familiar voice. Levi turned to find Duncan standing behind them. "I see you've met the best pediatrician I've ever had the honor of working with."

Benton's smile was dazzling. "So, you're a doctor?" He patted Levi's shoulder. "How do you like working in Maywood Junction?"

"It's a lot different from my New York practice."

"You should see him with the kids, Dad. He's incredible. I don't know what we're going to do when he leaves in a few months."

Levi felt slightly uncomfortable. "We'll cross that bridge when we come to it," Levi said.

"You're thinking about…" Duncan was interrupted when Dianne and Angela joined them. His eyes swept over Angela's revealing dress. "Who are you trying to hurt in that getup?"

Dianne shot her oldest son a stern look. "Duncan, please."

Levi shifted his position, wrapping an arm around Angela's waist. "I happen to like what she's wearing," he said defensively.

Angela flashed a Cheshire cat grin. Tilting her head, she smiled into Levi's laughing eyes. "Why thank you, sweetie."

Duncan wasn't amused. "I just hope sweetie doesn't have to bust a few jaws tonight."

Shaking her head, Dianne managed a brittle smile. "Levi, you're going to have to excuse my son. There are times when he can be a little overprotective of his sister." She looped her arm through Duncan's. "By the way, where's your pretty little girlfriend?" Her voice changed, becoming syrupy sweet.

Duncan's dark mood vanished when he smiled. "Myla went to the ladies' room."

Resplendent in black silk and brilliant diamonds, Dianne Hitchcock Chase patted her coiffed hair. "Now that the weather is warmer I'd like to have a little something at the house next Sunday. Duncan, I'd like you to bring Myla." She smiled at Angela. "Of course I'd love for you and Levi to join us."

Angela met Levi's gaze. "Levi and I will have to talk about it."

He shook his head. "I promised Angela I would cook for her next Sunday, but there's always the following Sunday. We'll be there, won't we, darling?"

At that moment Angela wanted to drive the heel of her shoe into his foot, but thought better of it. She was accustomed to making decisions in her relationships, but apparently she'd underestimated her date. He was as good at playing the game as she was.

She gave her mother a plastic smile. "You can count on us being there." She dug her nails into the palm of Levi's hand. "Do you mind getting me something to drink?"

A slight frown furrowed his smooth forehead. "What would you like?"

"Surprise me," she drawled facetiously.

Her eyes narrowed when she glared at his departing figure. Angela felt as if she was losing control, that it was as if Levi could read her mind and had flipped the script. She'd promised to take him to the Derby, but still hadn't agreed to go to Philadelphia for his family reunion. Now he'd invited himself to Sunday dinner with her family.

Duncan carefully observed the exchange between his sister and Levi, and winked at Angela. "Play with fire and you'll get burned, Sis," he whispered in her ear.

"Go find Myla," she countered.

Grabbing her hand, Duncan led her away from earshot of their parents. "I'm going to ask you a question, and I need you to tell me the truth." Angela nodded. "Do you like Levi?"

"What's there not to like. He's perfect but…"

"But what, Ang?"

She averted her gaze. "You know I don't want to get involved."

"Neither does Levi."

"How do you know that?"

Duncan leaned closer. "Levi was seeing someone, but he broke it off when she wanted more than friendship."

Angela stared at her brother. "Are you saying he's only interested in a platonic relationship?"

"Look, Sis. Levi and I don't have detailed conversations about who we do or don't sleep with. But he's told me that he doesn't want a permanent relationship. What I do know is that he's a good guy and the kids love him, and you're both looking for the same thing."

She gave him a skeptical look. "Why are you playing matchmaker?"

"Because I hear that you're still going out with losers. The best way to get over Robert is to date a decent guy. Excuse me, but I have to look for *my* woman."

Angela stared as her brother walked away, her eyes landing on the one person she loathed seeing again standing only a few feet away.

Chapter 5

Angela felt a shiver run up her spine. Recovering quickly, she tilted her chin defiantly as the man with whom she'd once planned to spend her life came face-to-face with her. To say that time had *not* been kind to Robert Gaskin was an understatement. He was only thirty-eight, but appeared much older. There was a sallow undertone to his light brown face. His shoulders were rounded, and what had been a thick head of hair was now thinning. She noticed a slight puffiness under his eyes and a gauntness that belied fatigue. His suit hung from his body as if his six-foot frame had shrunken.

Karma is a bitch, she thought, as she suppressed a smile. But her sense of triumph turned to shame when the possibility that maybe Robert was sick suddenly occurred to her. That was something she wouldn't wish on her worst enemy. The anger she thought she would've felt dissipated in an instant as Angela stared impassively at the man she believed she'd been in love with.

"I was hoping you'd be here," Robert said, smiling.

Angela's cool expression did not change. "How have you been, Robert?"

His light brown eyes moved slowly over her face. "Let's just say, I could be better. You look absolutely beautiful."

"I agree."

Angela turned when she heard the familiar baritone. Levi had come up behind her. "Thank you, sweetie," she crooned when he handed her a Bellini. She winked at him. "Love, I'd like for you to meet Robert Gaskin. Robert and I were what you would call an item back in the day. Robert, Levi Eaton."

Levi offered his right hand. "It's nice meeting you," he drawled facetiously.

Robert was slower in extending his hand. "How long have you and Angela been…been together?"

"Not long," Angela and Levi chorused. They shared a grin.

Massaging his forehead with his fingertips, Robert glanced down at the toes of his shoes. "Levi, can you please excuse us? I'd like to speak to Angela *alone*."

A look of annoyance shadowed Levi's face. "If you want to talk to Angela, then I suggest you ask her directly."

Robert stood up straight and pulled back his stooped shoulders. "Angela?" His expression was hopeful.

"I'm sorry, but there's nothing to talk about," she said.

"Angela, please."

"She said no," Levi intoned. A harsh edge had crept into his voice, as he and Robert engaged in what had become a stare down.

Robert was the first to look away. "It doesn't matter. Savannah and I are moving back to Louisville, so I'm sure I'll see you around—especially at family functions."

"I doubt that," she countered. "We have nothing to say to each other. You said it all five years ago. The only thing I'll say is that I wish you and Savannah the best."

She turned her back, struggling not to lose her temper, and unable to believe she'd felt even an iota of pity for that selfish cretin. For Robert it'd always been about him. That is what had drawn her to Robert. Despite being considered an egghead by his friends, there was another side of the man few got to see. She'd been the exception. Whenever they went away on vacation together, Robert was always the life of the party. He was the first and the last one on the dance floor. And after one or two drinks he was completely uninhibited—especially in the bedroom. And with her limited experience with the opposite sex there were occasions when Angela felt overwhelmed and uncomfortable. If or whenever they argued it was usually about sex. He'd called her a prude, and said she didn't know what it took to please and, therefore, keep her man. Well, in the end she didn't please or keep her man and he'd strayed. If it had been any other woman but her best friend, Angela wouldn't have taken it so hard. Savannah Jenkins was the sister Angela never had. She trusted Savannah, confided her deepest secrets and her unconditional love for Robert.

Resting her hand on Levi's jacket sleeve, she leaned into him for physical as well as emotional support. "Get me out of here before I take off my shoe and clock his ass."

Smiling, Levi led her across the ballroom and outside through a set of French doors to the patio. Wedding guests strolled along the paths leading to English, boxwood and Japanese gardens. They stopped next to a planter with a large palm.

What she hadn't known at the time was that her fiancé had been sleeping with her best friend, who was also her maid of honor. They'd managed to keep their affair a secret until the night before she and Robert were to be married. At the time, she hadn't cried, because she wasn't able to. Pain, humiliation and rage had shut down her emotions. It was as if she was on autopilot.

"Were you really going to hit him?"

Angela took a long sip of her cocktail. "I don't know." She stared at a flowering azalea bush. "I've never hit anyone in my life."

Levi pressed his chest against Angela's back. "You never had a fight when you were a kid?"

She shook her head. "No. Not when I had four older brothers and one younger. We're only two years apart."

He kissed her hair. "Are your other brothers coming to the wedding?"

"No. Ryder, he's the youngest, owns a cattle ranch in North Dakota. When he's not herding cattle, he's riding them in rodeos. Zane, Langdon and Jared decided to stay away, because they didn't trust themselves not to, as they put it, 'stomp the hell out of Robert.'"

Angela took another sip of her cocktail. The blend of peach nectar infused with dry champagne lingered on her palate. She rested the back of her head against Levi's shoulder, closing her eyes and moaning silently when he wrapped his arm around her waist. It had been so long since she'd felt the peace she felt now that Angela thought she was dreaming.

"What happened between you and Robert?" Levi whispered in her ear, shattering the spell.

She opened her eyes. "He cheated on me with my best friend who was my maid of honor. I have no idea how long they'd been sleeping together. Most of the time Savannah claimed she didn't even like Robert and thought he was all wrong for me."

"He was wrong for you but right for her."

Angela smiled. "I didn't realize they were involved until Robert called me a couple of hours after the rehearsal dinner to inform me that he and Savannah were at the airport. They were flying to Vegas to get married because she was pregnant."

"Why did he wait until the last minute to tell you?"

"Because he's a coward. He was afraid to face my father and brothers," she said. "We'd decided beforehand to keep his condo because it was larger than my place, but I didn't know that Robert had sold his condo months before, and had paid the new owner not to move in until after the wedding date. I also didn't know he'd bought a house in Frankfort and had gotten a position teaching engineering at Kentucky State University. I was blindsided from all directions."

Levi noticed some of the guests were watching him and Angela. Had they thought of him as another of the guys she dated who was here today, gone tomorrow?

"Now he's back," Levi spat out. The three words were filled with anger.

Turning to face Levi, Angela stared up at him. "I'm over him, Levi."

"You may be over him, but it's apparent he isn't over you."

"It doesn't matter."

"Robert wants you."

She shook her head. "He can't have me."

Eyes narrowing, Levi leaned in closer. "Do you hate him?"

"No. Though there was a time when I believed I couldn't live without him. But hate had a way of eating you up inside, and I'd found myself going to bed angry and waking up even angrier. Then, one day I stopped and I told myself it was best that it happened before we were married and had children. I wouldn't want my children to ask me where Daddy is or why he isn't coming home because as sure as the sun rises each morning, I would've thrown him out without batting an eyelash."

"What about Savannah?"

A wry smile crossed her lips. "The only thing I can say is if Robert cheated on me, he'll cheat on his wife."

"So it's over?"

The smile on Angela's face made her look angelic. "It's beyond over."

"What if I make certain it stays over?"

"What do you mean?"

"I can help you out, but I don't want to be mister one-oh-one."

"What are you talking about?"

"Your father told me you weren't serious, that you're seeing a lot of guys."

A wave of heat suffused Angela's face. "I haven't dated that many guys."

"How many is not many?" Levi asked.

"I don't know."

"Give me a figure, *sweetie.*"

Angela compressed her lips. "It could be around a dozen."

"It has to be more than a dozen, Ang," Levi drawled, using her nickname.

"Okay, less than twenty."

There was a hint of amusement in Levi's dark eyes. "Do you realize some women don't have twenty dates in a lifetime?"

"I didn't sleep with any of them. And there were times when months would go by and I wouldn't have a date." Angela knew she sounded defensive but she didn't want Levi to believe she was a *loose woman,* as her grandmother used to say.

"Then let's be exclusive."

Her gaze caught and held Levi's. She thought about his proposition and decided that Levi Eaton was not only a good candidate to be Mr. Right Now, but he could also provide great material for the hero of her novel. For Angela it was a win-win.

"Okay," she said softly, "I'll go out with you."

Levi set his glass on a nearby table and took Angela's, placing it next to his. Cradling her face in his hands, his eyes softened into a smile. He'd never had to work so hard to get a woman to agree to out with him but there was something about Angela Chase that made it worth it. Lowering his head, Levi kissed her forehead. "Do you know what this means?"

Angela blinked, feeling slightly lightheaded. She anchored her arms under his shoulders to keep her balance. "No. What does it mean?"

"We are officially a couple." She lowered her thick, black lashes in a demure gesture, charming Levi completely.

"Does that also make you *my man?*"

Levi kissed her forehead again. "Do you need a demonstration?"

"No…no," she said much too quickly. "I believe you."

"Then, I guess it's all good." They shared a smile, a smile usually reserved for lovers. "Are you ready to go back inside?"

Angela nodded. Levi was perfect. He was someone her mother would approve of and someone her father seemed to like. She liked him and so did Miss Divine. Yes, she mused, dating Dr. Levi Eaton was the best of all possible solutions, if only to prove to Robert that she hadn't been pining over him.

"Yes, I'm ready." What Levi didn't know was how ready she really was.

Hand in hand Levi and Angela returned to the ballroom, which was a lot more crowded now. She spied Traci craning her neck, no doubt looking for her.

"There's my cousin waving to us. Come, Levi. I want to introduce you to her."

Traci Freeman wove her way through the crowd toward Angela and the most delicious-looking man she'd seen in a long time. Now, if Angela wanted to trade him in for the next one, then Traci was more than willing to take him off her hands.

"Hey, you," she said, crooning her usual greeting. Bending slightly at the knees, she pressed her cheek to Angela's. "Nice surprise," she whispered in Angela's ear. "You look fabulous," she continued in a normal tone.

Angela smiled and nodded. "So do you." Looping her arm through Levi's, she pressed closer to his length. "Levi, this is Traci Freeman. Traci, Levi Eaton."

Jackpot! Traci mused as she exchanged a handshake with Levi. She couldn't wait to get the details from Angela as to how she happened to hook up with a man who seemed to be the total package.

"Charmed," she drawled, while fluttering her eyelashes.

Levi went still, trying to remember where he'd seen her before. Realization dawned when he remembered seeing her in fashion magazine ads. A smile touched the corners of Levi's mouth. Traci Freeman was a flirt. She was pretty, but much too thin for his tastes. Her short curly hair, makeup, body-hugging little black dress and designer shoes screamed supermodel.

"The pleasure is all mine," he said politely.

Traci turned, craning her neck. "I sent Reggie to get me something to drink, and he appears to have gotten lost. That's one of the reasons I divorced the man. He would take off and then forget to come back like I was an afterthought." As soon as the words rolled off her tongue he appeared by Traci's side carrying a martini glass and a cold beer.

Levi stared at the man standing six-six and weighing close to two hundred sixty pounds. He was an imposing figure in a dark suit designed to conceal his massive size. He could hardly believe that Traci's date *and* ex-husband was the same man whose football career he'd followed since becoming a number one draft pick until he'd been forced to retire because of injuries. Their wedding had been a lavish spectacle, and their breakup had become fodder for the tabloids. Neither had divulged details of their split, citing irreconcilable differences, but they continued to see one another after their divorce.

Angela made the introductions, Levi pumping the hand of the former Philadelphia Eagles' defensive end. "I tried to make every home game during football season just to see you play," he said.

Reggie's round face softened when he smiled, his dimples creasing his smooth cheeks. Large dark eyes twinkled. "Where you from, brother? You don't sound like someone from Philly."

"I lived in Philly for six years before my folks moved to Miami."

"Do you…" Whatever Reggie was going to say was preempted

when they were directed to another ballroom for the wedding ceremony. "We'll talk later," Reggie promised Levi, as Angela and Traci engaged a knowing look.

Angela sat next to Levi on the bride's side of the room, in chairs covered with white organza secured with black satin ribbon tiebacks. The ballroom was exquisitely decorated in flowing white fabric with black accents. Levi's shoulder touched Angela's bare one when he leaned to his left.

"Why didn't you tell me your cousin was once married to pro-football-player Reggie Goddard?"

"Traci and I promised each other that we wouldn't discuss the men in our lives. Traci is as close to me as a sister, and we're very careful to maintain separate personal *and* professional relationships."

Levi glimpsed at Angela's well-toned thighs when she crossed her legs. He still found it hard to believe any man had cheated on her. Even though she had five brothers and a father who wouldn't hesitate to step in and protect her, Levi felt responsible for her. He'd agreed to be her escort and that meant he would make certain Robert Gaskin kept his distance.

Resting his arm over her shoulders, he pulled her close. "Will you forgive me?"

She turned her head, their mouths inches apart. "For what?"

He stared at the outline of her sexy mouth. "For telling your mother that we're coming to her house next Sunday."

"There's nothing to forgive. You'll learn that once Dianne Hitchcock Chase sets her mind to something, only a natural disaster can make her change it."

"So we go to your mother's next week, and the following Sunday you'll hang out with me."

"Are you asking or telling me, Levi?"

He smiled. "I'm asking."

"Well?"

"Well what?"

"Ask me, Levi?"

His smile faded. "Will you please share Sunday dinner with me?" he said, his tone contrite.

Angela leaned closer, her mouth pressed to his ear. She closed her eyes, unable to believe he smelled so incredibly good. "Humility doesn't suit you," she whispered.

"What does?" he asked.

"Arrogance."

He pulled back, giving her an incredulous stare. "You think I'm arrogant?"

"You're a doctor, aren't you?"

He nodded.

"Then you're probably arrogant with a God complex. I've never a met a doctor who wasn't, and that includes Duncan."

"More than judges?" Levi countered.

Her eyes narrowed. "I know you're not talking about Daddy."

"Could be yes, could be no."

Angela went completely still. "What did my father say to you?"

Levi trailed fingertips down the length of her bared back. "We didn't talk about you." He felt her shiver under his light touch.

"Then who did you talk about?"

Levi gazed longingly at her, as a strange feeling made it virtually impossible for him to formulate a reply. He suddenly realized just how sexy Angela was. Her sexiness wasn't obvious as with some women, but her femininity was.

As he sat through the ceremony, he recalled some of the Eaton weddings he'd attended over the past three years. He had lost count of the number of Eaton babies that had been born. Whenever he opened an envelope it was either a wedding invitation or a birth announcement. The last wedding he'd attended was a year ago in Dallas, when Mia Eaton had exchanged vows with Kenyon Chandler. Mia made it known then that she and Kenyon planned to wait a year before starting a family.

"Levi?"

Angela's voice shattered his reverie. "Yes?"

"You didn't answer my question."

He blinked. "We discussed my father."

"My dad knows your father?"

The melodious sound of an electronic keyboard filled the ballroom.

"I'll tell you later," he whispered when Benton Chase, clad in a black robe walked in and stood in front of the altar.

Angela watched, unable to move, as she witnessed the procession of the best man and Yvette's twin sister arm-in-arm down the length of the white-carpeted aisle.

She closed her eyes when the familiar notes of the "Wedding March" echoed in the room as Levi reached for her hand, threading their fingers together and giving hers a reassuring squeeze. His touch communicated silently that he was there for her, that everything would be all right.

Angela knew she couldn't sit through the entire ceremony with her eyes closed, so she opened them and stood up when Yvette's father escorted her down the carpet to where Craig stood with his best man. A wry smile twisted her mouth. Her cousin was an absolutely stunning bride. She'd waited, endured several breakups, but in the end she'd managed to get her prince and her happily ever after.

She hadn't based her plot on Yvette and Craig's off-and-on romance, but rather she lived vicariously through her protagonists experiencing her own happily ever after.

However, her life was very different from those of her heroines. She didn't have an ex-husband or children. What she had was a supportive family, a twenty-five percent interest in a small business, and instead of a therapist she had a hobby in which she could vent her frustrations.

Somehow she managed to remain calm, staring at her cousin's hand-beaded gown. But when Yvette extended her hand to her groom, and Craig kissed her fingers the floodgates opened for Angela. One tear found its way down her cheek, followed by another and before she knew it, they flowed unceasingly.

Levi glanced over at Angela, his heart turning when he saw her tears. Letting go of her hand, he reached into his breast pocket and took out a handkerchief. Cradling her chin, he carefully blotted her face, taking care not to smudge her makeup.

"Are you all right, baby?" he whispered in her ear.

Angela sniffled softly, resisting the urge to blow her nose. "Yes. I always cry at weddings."

Giving her a skeptical look, Levi forced a smile, aware that Angela hadn't been completely honest. Not only was she crying, but she was also trembling. Was she, he mused, thinking about the time when she should've walked down the aisle?

He stared deeply into the brown eyes that reminded him of rich dark coffee, and it was in that instant he promised himself that he would make certain that during their time together, if she cried again, it would be because she was happy.

He pressed his mouth to her forehead. "I want you to remember something," he said.

Angela's eyebrows lifted inquiringly. "What's that?"

"As long as I'm in Kentucky I'll take care of you."

Chapter 6

As long as I'm in Kentucky I'll take care of you. Levi's words settled in Angela's mind like a mantra. She sat through Yvette's wedding and the reception that followed as if she was in a trance. She laughed at the appropriate times, engaged in conversation, barely touched the food on her plate and sipped water instead of the wine, champagne and cocktails at the open bar.

Robert was seated at a table close to where she was, and every time she glanced around he was staring at her. She was surprised that Savannah hadn't come with him, which made Angela wonder if they were still together. But she recalled him saying that he and Savannah were moving to Louisville. Had he convinced her to stay home because he knew it would be socially awkward?

Dianne Chase didn't want to believe her sons, who were raised to behave like perfect gentlemen, could become thugs when it came to their sister. Thugs or not, it kept guys with ulterior motives at a distance.

"Come, Ang, get up!" Traci said, pulling her onto the floor when the all single women were encouraged to gather in the center of the ballroom to catch Yvette's bouquet as Beyoncé's "Single Ladies" blared from the speakers. "Get up, Angela!" she shouted, when Angela didn't move.

Clutching Levi's hand, Angela whispered, "Get me out of here."

Levi heard the panic in her voice before seeing the look of fear seize her. "What's wrong?"

"You promised to take care of me. If you don't want me to

have a meltdown and ruin my cousin's reception you will get me out of here now."

Levi needed no further prompting. Cupping her elbow, he helped her to her feet and placed his hand at the small of her back. "She's not feeling well," he said to those who turned to stare at them. Angela leaned against limply his body as he escorted her out of the ballroom.

"Shall I call for a doctor, sir?" asked the maître d'.

Levi shook his head. "I'm a doctor."

"You can use the business office if she needs to lie down."

"Please just take me home, Levi," Angela said under her breath.

Levi nodded. "Thank you for the offer, but I'll take her to my office."

Ten minutes later she sat in the BMW, eyes closed, the back of her head pressed against the leather headrest. It was as if she couldn't draw a normal breath.

She reached over and pressed a button to lower the passenger-side window, letting the cool night air wash over her face. Angela thought she could've been able to attend the wedding and be unaffected, but she had failed miserably.

Levi gave Angela a sidelong glance. "Are you all right?"

Her eyelids fluttered. "I will be in a few minutes."

Slowing, he maneuvered over to the shoulder, coming to a complete stop. Lines of concern appeared between his eyes. "Are you sure you don't want me to check your heart?"

Her head came around. "Why would you want to do that?"

"Your pulse is racing."

"How can you tell? " she said quickly. "Of course, you're a doctor, so you would notice something like that."

Levi leaned in closer. "Don't forget an arrogant doctor," he teased.

"That, too."

Removing his seatbelt, he turned toward her in his seat, staring intently at her. "If you're all right, then I'd like to know why you wanted to leave."

Angela averted her eyes so he wouldn't see the tears welling up. "I thought I could do it, Levi."

"Do what, Ang?"

"Attend the wedding and pretend everything was okay. It felt as if I was reliving what should've been my wedding day. It was as if nothing had changed. And when Traci wanted me to get up and stand with all the single women in the hope that one of us would catch the bouquet and be the next one to marry, that was the last straw."

Levi massaged the nape of her neck, kneading the tight muscles. "I don't know why you thought you had to put up a brave front. You could've declined the invitation and sent her a gift like your brothers."

"My brothers had a different reason for not attending."

"Yes and no, Angela. They didn't want to lose control when they saw your ex. What he did to you was humiliating and traumatic. And his moving back to Louisville is certain to complicate your life. I know you wanted to support your cousin, and also show Robert that you'd moved on. But the best way to show that you've moved on is to be yourself."

"Keep dating a different guy every two or three months?"

"No, Angela. That's the only thing that's going to change."

Shifting slightly, she turned to stare directly at him. The light from the dashboard cast shadows across Levi's face. There was hardness in his lean face that hadn't been there before. "It's only going to be us?" she whispered.

He nodded. "Just us. And if he comes anywhere near you I'll tell your brothers to kick his ass, because I've taken an oath 'to do no harm.' What I might do is to postpone giving him medical attention until the last possible moment."

Angela managed a smile when she felt like crying. "My brother Zane was in the military and runs a security company. He employs professional bodyguards who protect wealthy people around the world. All he has to do is send one of them to Robert's house and it's lights out. So, I'm not that worried about him harassing me."

"By the way, where was Mrs. Robert Gaskin tonight?"

"I heard someone say she was home with the flu."

How convenient, Levi thought. "You should've told Duncan

to make a house call." Angela laughed. The sound was so infectious that Levi couldn't stop his own laughter.

"I don't know how well you know my brother," she said, sobering, "but Duncan isn't as passive as he seems. He's also taken an oath 'to do no harm,' but when provoked he can be one nasty *hombre*."

"Enough talk about your loser ex," he said, deftly changing the topic of conversation. "Where do you want to eat?"

Angela stared numbly. "You want to eat?"

"I'll settle for coffee and dessert, but you need to eat something. You barely touched your food."

She knew Levi was right. She'd had a cup of tea and two slices of toast earlier that morning and nothing else since she'd planned to eat at the wedding reception. However, anxiety had her stomach in knots and she'd only managed to eat the salad.

"I'll eat something once I get home."

Levi buckled his seatbelt, then shifted into gear and maneuvered off the shoulder onto the roadway. "You need more than leftovers. Is there someplace nearby where we can get a quick bite?"

"I know a truck stop that serves incredible food but…"

"But what?"

"It's not fancy and it's on the other side of the interstate."

"My hotel is closer," he said, accelerating into the flow of traffic. "Besides, what you're wearing is a tad bit fancy for a truck stop."

"Hotel?" Angela asked, giving him an incredulous stare.

"I checked into a hotel downtown last night rather than make the drive between here and Maywood."

She settled back in her seat. "Don't bother to reserve a hotel room during Derby week, because my parents will put you up at their place."

Levi gave Angela a quick glance. "Why can't I stay with you? After all, you have more than one bedroom."

"I don't believe you."

"What don't you believe, sweetie?"

"You're inviting yourself for a sleepover at my house?"

"What's the big deal, Angela? When you come to Maywood

for dinner you can stay with me. I'm renting a place with two bedrooms. The only thing I'll say is that room service at the Eaton Inn is exceptional. We offer clean linens, turndown service, fluffy towels and a breakfast menu that's guaranteed to please the palate. It will be so sumptuous that it may be impossible for you to move for an hour or two."

Angela laughed. "I like the sound of that."

"It sounds like we're going to have a lot of fun, Ang."

Angela gave him a dazzling smile. "That's something I'm looking forward to."

He winked at her. "When do you want to start?"

"How about now?" she asked. Levi slowed the car, pulled over, and then without warning executed a U-turn. "Where are you going? Downtown is the other way."

"We're going back to your place so you can change into something less revealing."

"What's wrong with what I'm wearing?"

Levi rolled his eyes. "You'll see once we get there."

"Where, Levi?"

"You'll see," he said cryptically.

Folding her arms under her breasts, Angela stared at the lights on the dashboard. "What about you? Aren't you a tad bit overdressed?"

"All I have to do is take off my jacket and tie, roll up my cuffs and I'm good. By the way, what time is your curfew?"

She smiled. "I haven't had a curfew since I moved out of my parents' house. Why are you asking?"

"I'm going to take you to a place where the guys at the clinic usually hang out on Friday nights. It's something of a honkytonk, juke joint, sports bar and local watering hole all rolled into one. They serve wonderful food and have better than average live music. They also have line dancing and karaoke."

Angela was hard-pressed to contain her excitement. Levi had promised her they were going to have fun, and apparently he was a man of his word. It had been a long time since she'd been able to let her hair down, throw caution to the wind and just enjoy herself.

"In other words, the joint is jumpin'," she said, smiling.

"That it is. I asked how late you can stay out because even though I don't have office hours on Mondays, you might have made plans for tomorrow."

"I'm not going into the shop tomorrow." What she didn't say was that she'd planned to spend the entire day writing.

Angela stared at his distinctive profile. She'd noticed a lot of the women at the reception staring at Levi when they thought she wasn't looking. It was as much curiosity on their part as it was taking note of his handsomeness.

Angela had never been attracted to a man because he was good looking, but if she'd had to choose the man of her dreams, then Levi Eaton would've definitely be on top. His classically masculine looks were a throwback to the days when men dressed conservatively, had close-cropped hair, were clean-shaven, and never had piercings or tattoos. He reminded her of the distinguished-looking men in her grandfather's photos. Not only was Levi easy on the eyes, but he was also intelligent, articulate and had impeccable manners.

Levi gave her another quick glance. "If that's the case, then are you willing to stay overnight? We'll stop by the hotel and I'll check out. I'll bring you back to Louisville tomorrow after brunch."

"First it was breakfast and now it's brunch?"

He smiled. "It's whatever you want it to be. If you're an early riser then it's breakfast. If not, then it's brunch. It's your call, Angela."

"What if I ask for a rain check?"

Levi nodded. "When do you want to take your rain check?"

Angela met his eyes when he slowed and stopped for a red light. "Let's wait until Derby weekend. We usually start partying Thursday night and don't end until late Saturday into Sunday morning."

"Do you really wear those big fancy hats?"

"Yes."

He shook his head. "So you wear a salad bowl on your head because it's customary."

Angela softly punched his shoulder, her hand hitting solid muscle. Her eyebrows lifted a fraction. Levi's tailored attire concealed a rock-hard body. "You'll eat those words when you see my chapeau."

"We'll see about that." The light changed and he stepped on the gas pedal. "When was your first Derby?"

"I went to my first Derby at thirteen. I wasn't as excited about seeing the race as I was about my outfit. I had to have the perfect dress, hat and shoes. It was also my first time wearing makeup, so I had to make certain not to overdo it or my mother would've made me scrub my face until it was raw. She has a thing about women looking like hookers."

Angela told Levi about Kentucky Derbys she'd attended once she was old enough to go to the pre- and post-race parties, and her first mint julep.

"I've never had a mint julep," Levi admitted. "Is it that special?"

"Yes. I may sound biased, but I'm going to recommend that you don't have one until you've tasted a mint julep made with aged bourbon from Chase Brothers distillery."

"Your brothers are distillers?"

Angela laughed softly. "Jared and Langdon took over a failing distillery more than ten years ago, and have a reputation of making some of the finest bourbon in the state. They've concocted a blended bourbon and a Kentucky whiskey that are ninety and ninety-seven proof."

"Is it true the best bourbon comes from Kentucky?"

"We Kentuckians know it's the best. One of these days I'll take you on a road trip along the Bourbon Trail. You'll be able to sample the different brands from most of the distilleries. And if you want I'll take you on a tour of some of the horse farms."

Levi maneuvered onto the local road leading to Angela's house. Initially, she seemed to have reservations about seeing him beyond the wedding, and now she was planning road trips with him. He didn't know what had prompted her to change her mind. What he had to remind himself was that he'd come to Kentucky to practice medicine and not become involved with a woman, especially if that woman was his colleague's sister.

He also had to remind himself that he'd never used a woman

to satisfy his sexual needs, but Angela's aversion to committed relationships wasn't reason enough for him not to see her.

Once they reached the gatehouse, the guard waved them through when he noticed Angela in the car. "Where's Miss Divine?" Levi asked when Angela opened the door. "I thought she would be here to greet you."

She glanced up at him over her shoulder. "Miss Dee isn't allowed in the kitchen, living and dining rooms."

"Why not?"

"Because I don't want cat hair everywhere."

"It's nothing that can't be vacuumed up."

Angela turned, narrowing her eyes at Levi. "Not when I have to clean a house with a dozen rooms."

He took off his jacket and slung it over his shoulder. "Don't you have a cleaning service?"

"No."

"Well, you should. They can send someone in once or twice a week to clean everything."

"That's all right, Levi. Miss Dee is fine just the way things are."

"There's no reason why she shouldn't have the run of the house, Angela."

"What!" The word was barely out of her mouth when a blur of ivory and chocolate fur streaked past her, heading directly for Levi. "Miss Dee!"

Bending down, Levi gathered the cat who nuzzled him under his chin. "Hey, beautiful!" Rubbing the feline's back, he winked at Angela. "Your mama is a meanie. She has you under house arrest." He pressed a kiss to her head. "Daddy's going to report her to the authorities for animal abuse."

Angela glared at Levi. "For your information, I've never abused my cat. And if you want Miss Dee to roam the house, then you pay a cleaning service to come in and vacuum up pet hair."

He buried his face in the soft fur. "That's not a problem. I'll call a cleaning service Monday and arrange for them to contact you. I'll also have them bill my credit card."

"What happens after you leave Kentucky, Mr. Big Shot?

There's no way I'm going to retrain Miss Dee to stay out of those rooms after she's run amuck throughout the house."

"Don't worry, Ang. I'll still pay for it. After all, it's only money."

It's only money, she mouthed, still glaring at him. "Go on and put her down so she can shed everywhere. I'm going upstairs to change."

Levi smothered a chuckle. "Mama's mad, baby girl. But she'll get over it," he said to the blue-gray eyed cat staring up at him.

"Whenever you have children they're going to be spoiled," Angela shouted, as she walked up the staircase to the second floor.

"They are going to be wonderful and you know it. We Eatons make beautiful, intelligent babies."

Angela paused midway up the staircase. "Don't sleep on the Chases," she countered.

"I'll let you know when I see a few Chases running underfoot."

This time she didn't have a quick comeback.

"One of these days you'll eat those words," she challenged. "Let's hope you don't choke on them."

Levi pretended to cough and choke as Angela continued up the staircase. "Your mama's okay, Miss Dee. But she has to let you be a cat and explore." The cat blinked. "Yes, I know. You and I are going to become best buds."

There was a time when Levi had considered becoming a veterinarian. He'd had a habit of bringing home injured birds, cats and dogs until his mother laid down the law and said that she wasn't running an animal hospital, and suggested he become a vet. He'd considered it until he realized he would have to deal with exotic animals like snakes, and quickly changed his focus from treating animals to treating humans.

He loved medicine, and caring for children in particular. And he was beginning to like Angela Chase more than he wanted to. Levi knew he had to be careful not to cross the line with her where his emotions were concerned.

However, there was something about the sassy Southern belle

that had him thinking about her when he least wanted or expected. In a few months he would be returning to New York, and Levi didn't want to bring back any extra emotional baggage.

Chapter 7

Angela walked into the living room and stared at Levi sitting in the alcove with Miss Divine lying in his lap. The cat was purring, enjoying the long fingers stroking her fur. She tried imagining those same fingers stroking her bare skin, and wondered if she would moan in ecstasy and beg Levi to make love to her.

Reel it in, the voice in her head warned. She knew it had been a long time, much too long, since she'd slept with a man. But Angela couldn't forget that Levi wanted an uncomplicated relationship—one that was probably free of sexual entanglement. She didn't know whether it was because he was involved with a woman in New York and hadn't wanted to cheat, or that he didn't want to become involved with her because she was Duncan's sister. Angela found it hard to believe that she'd just met Levi the day before and twenty-four hours later she'd attended a wedding with him. Now she was getting ready to go out for dinner, live music and dancing, and even agreeing to sleep over at his place in less than two weeks.

Had she lost her mind, or was she just that comfortable with him because he worked with Duncan? Maybe it was because he'd said he wanted what she wanted—a no-strings-attached relationship. That had become her dating philosophy—friends without benefits. Angela knew if she slept with any of the men she dated, it would've complicated things when it came time to break up. It would be different with Levi. He would leave Kentucky and return to his home and medical practice in New York. She couldn't have scripted a better storyline.

Angela didn't want to think or fantasize about making love to Levi Eaton. She'd been able to survive her self-imposed celibacy only because she went out with guys she knew she would never sleep with.

The subject of her fantasy had removed his tie and rolled up the French cuffs of his shirt.

"I'm ready, but I can wait until you finish spoiling Miss Dee."

Levi turned to find Angela standing several feet away. Setting the cat down on the floor, he stood. A sensual glow illuminated his eyes as he stared at her. She'd changed her diamond studs for a pair of large gold hoops and wore a pair of fitted black jeans that hugged her hips, a black knit pullover and matching high-heeled booties. Her presence shifted his libido into overdrive. His gaze moved from her curvy hips to the sweep of hair cascading over her shoulder. Angela was a chameleon. Every time he saw her she looked different.

"You look very nice." He wanted to tell her she looked sexy, but didn't want to send mixed signals.

"I hope I'm not too casual."

Levi shook his head trying to will his erection to go down, and praying that Angela wouldn't notice the growing bulge in the front of his pants. "No, no," he said, much too quickly. "You're good."

"Are you all right?"

Folding his hands in front of him, Levi shifted slightly in an attempt to conceal his hard-on. Much to his chagrin, he became more aroused. "Perhaps I should use your bathroom before we leave."

Angela's expression brightened. "Of course. Meanwhile, I'll put Miss Dee in the laundry room. Despite your accusation that I'm abusing her, I still don't trust her to have the run of the house while I'm away."

She picked up the tiny cat, cradling her under her arm, and carried her into the laundry room. Miss Dee crawled into her bed, tucked her head against her side and closed her eyes. Angela left the door slightly ajar. By the time she'd retrieved her favorite shoulder bag and lightweight wool jacket, making certain she had her driver's license, keys, credit cards and cash, Levi had returned. She punched in the code for the security system, and then closed the front door.

"Do you always leave so many lights on when you go out?" Levi asked, tucking her arm into the bend of his elbow as he led her to the car.

"I don't like coming home to a dark house."

"Are you afraid of the dark?"

"No."

Levi opened the passenger door, and waited until Angela was seated and had buckled her seatbelt before closing the car door. He came around, took his seat behind the wheel and started the engine. With no traffic, he could make it to The Rook within half an hour.

Angela stared up at the chimney atop a large barnlike building constructed in the shape of a chess piece, which gave the establishment its name. Bright lights and the sound of music spilled out into the darkness whenever the door opened.

She shared a smile with Levi as he pulled into one of the few empty parking spaces. "There's no doubt the joint is jumping."

"That's every night."

She unbuckled her seat belt. "How often do you come here?"

"A few times a month. The staff at the clinic comes here to hang out sometimes. Duncan only joins us when he doesn't have a date."

"What about you, Levi?" Angela asked.

"What about me?"

"Have you dated anyone since coming here?"

He cut the engine and only the sound of their breathing punctuated the silence. "Before you, I dated a woman a few times," Levi admitted.

"What happened?"

He managed a wry smile. "She wanted more than I was willing to offer her at this time in my life. And, before you ask, I'll tell you. She wanted marriage and babies, but I don't see that in my immediate future. Maybe if I was going to relocate to Kentucky I might've possibly entertained the idea."

"Would you ever consider living here permanently?"

"I don't know." Levi traced the outline of Angela's ear with his forefinger. "Would you ever consider moving somewhere else?"

She blinked, swallowed a breath then slowly blew it out. "I suppose I would if the right opportunity presented itself."

"What about the Garden Gate?"

Angela dropped her gaze. "The gift shop is Traci's brainchild. We're not equal partners. She has a seventy-five percent interest and I have the remaining twenty-five."

An expression of concern crossed Levi's face. "Is that enough for you to live on?"

She nodded. "We pay ourselves salaries, so it's not as if we have to wait until the end of the year to take money out."

"Levi, I'm not destitute," she continued when he stared at her, wondering if that was what he meant when he said as long as he lived in Kentucky he would take care of her. Well, she didn't need his financial support. She needed friendship, an uncomplicated relationship where she could learn to trust again.

"I'm not implying—" The ringing of Angela's cell stopped his words. "Aren't you going to answer that?"

Angela tilted her head at an angle, while peering at Levi through a fringe of lashes. "No." It was Traci's ringtone. There was no doubt her cousin wanted to know where she was. She would call her back tomorrow. "You promise to feed me, Levi, and right now I'm so hungry I could eat a plate of French fries."

Levi's deep laughter echoed in the car. "You're kidding, aren't you?"

"No, I'm not. Some people are addicted to drugs. For me, it's fries. One fry and I blow up like a blimp. One minute they're on my lips, but forever on my hips."

"There's nothing wrong with your hips," Levi said, pushing open his door and coming around to help her out of the car.

In fact, there was nothing wrong with Angela, *at all*. Wrapping an arm around her waist, he escorted her to the door of The Rook. Music and singing and waiters carrying large trays of food greeted them at the door. A man in a Stetson stood on stage singing karaoke to a Trace Adkins song.

"Welcome back, Doc," the hostess greeted Levi, shouting to

be heard over the din. Her face appeared almost geisha-like in contrast to the raven straight hair falling around her shoulders.

"Thanks, Becky." He'd met the young woman for the first time when she brought her daughters to the clinic to get their booster shots. He glanced around the crowded restaurant, "How long is the wait?"

Becky's blue eyes shifted to the seating floor plan at the hostess lecturn. "Do you want to sit close to the stage?"

"What else do you have?" Levi asked.

"I have a table for two in a corner not far from the emergency exit."

He pressed his mouth to Angela's ear. "There's a table near the stage. Are you all right with that?" Her eyes met his as she nodded. "We'll sit up front," Levi told the hostess.

Becky signaled a waiter, and handed him two menus. "Table nine."

Holding Angela's hand, Levi followed the waiter through the maze of tables until they were seated less than twenty feet from the stage. "Are you sure you're all right sitting so close?" he asked Angela.

"It's okay, Levi."

The Rook was nothing like the upscale restaurants she was used to, but there was something about the down-home crowd, the noise, and the delicious aroma from the kitchen that was appealing. It was a place where music, animated conversation and the unrestrained roar from sports fans watching a game on the flat screen above the bar that made her relax. There were pinball machines, a jukebox, an area set aside for dancing, and tables where patrons were playing checkers, chess and dominos.

As she scanned the menu another waiter set a pitcher of water, cola and beer on the table. The entrées ranged from roast turkey, southern fried chicken, braised lamb shanks, beef stew, catfish fritters, chicken fried steak with white gravy, grilled shrimp and trout along to an array of side dishes that included mac and cheese, dirty rice, mashed potatoes with giblet gravy, collard greens, string beans, potato salad, coleslaw and fried okra. There was an entire page dedicated to barbecue—spareribs, pork baby back ribs, beef back and short ribs, lamb ribs, chicken, steak, brisket and sausage—all prepared on the premises.

"What do you recommend?" she asked Levi.

"Everything's good, but the first time I came here I ordered the sampler. You get three choices of meat, two sides and one dessert."

A slight frown furrowed her brow. "That's a lot of food."

"The portions are smaller than if you ordered the entrée."

Angela continued perusing the menu. Her stomach rumbled, reminding her that she needed to eat something. "I'll order beef, chicken and fish and a side of potato salad and collards."

Smiling, Levi gave her a sidelong glance. "What about dessert?"

The corners of her mouth tilted when she returned his smile. "You can eat the dessert."

"Going once, going twice. The pretty lady has decided she doesn't want cake, so that means I'm not sharing."

Angela gave him a sexy moue, drawing his gaze to her mouth. "And I'm not going to ask."

"We'll see about that." Levi signaled their waiter. "We're ready to order now." Angela selected a sampling of smoked brisket, grilled shrimp and a fried chicken wing, along with her sides. Levi ordered coffee with a slice of red velvet coconut cake.

"I've never had red velvet cake with coconut."

Resting a hand on her back, Levi leaned closer. "It's to die for, sweetie."

Angela stared at the strong mouth so close to her own. And in a moment of madness she wanted to kiss Levi. Not the brush of lips, but a deep open-mouthed kiss so that she could taste him. Her gaze moved to his eyes. There was a silent message in them that made her breath catch, a signal she recognized—desire.

It was apparent he wasn't as unaffected as he'd led her to believe. There was no doubt Levi Eaton was a normal man with a healthy sexual appetite that made him want to make love to a woman. The very thought of making love to Levi made Angela acknowledge what she'd ignored for far too long. She'd denied her own physical needs.

She'd told herself there was no time in her life for romance.

Her romance novels were a poor substitute for the man sitting next to her. He was more real than any fictional character, and if she wasn't careful she might blur the lines between fantasy and reality by getting involved with Levi. That would be nothing short of disaster—at least for her.

"Sorry to disappoint you, love. But sweetie's not biting tonight," she said softly. Levi froze. Nothing moved. Not even his chest. "You can breathe now, Dr. Eaton," she whispered.

Levi exhaled an audible breath. His left eyebrow lifted a fraction. "Didn't you say that you never walk away from a challenge?"

She blinked slowly. "I did. But this is not a challenge, Levi. The next time we come I'll…"

"So you want a next time?" Levi interrupted.

"Of course I want a next time. I like this place."

Levi wanted Angela to like The Rook, but he also wanted her to like him. And it wasn't ego that drove him to want Angela to be attracted to him. "We can come back anytime you want. But somehow I thought…"

"Thought what, Levi?" Angela asked when he didn't finish his statement.

Levi stared over her left shoulder. "I thought you would look down your nose at a place like this."

"Why would you think that?"

"You're the pretty, pampered Southern belle."

"No, I'm not!" she protested.

"You have an impeccable pedigree, Angela. You're third generation Spelman, your father is a state supreme-court judge, and I'm certain you and your mother are probably members of the Junior League. And I'm also willing to bet you were a debutante and were presented to black society at a cotillion."

"And you think that makes me a snob, Levi?"

He smiled. "I didn't say snob, Ang. I said Southern belle."

Angela leaned back, wanting to put some distance between her and the man who'd affected her in a way no other man had. She didn't want to spend her time trying to figure out what had made him so very different from other men she'd known. And despite Levi's assertion, she wasn't a snob. That was more like Dianne Hitchcock Chase.

Dianne had been quite vocal when she announced that her sister-in-law had been a bad influence on her daughter whenever Angela expressed her desire to be a free spirit. Nicola Chase never defended her lifestyle and Angela was no different.

Angela smiled. She was a free spirit, and she was going to show Levi a different side. "As soon as I finish eating, I'm getting up on stage to sing."

It was Levi's turn to lean back in his chair. "*You* are going to sing?"

"Pick your jaw up off the table, sweetie. I promise not to embarrass you."

Angela winked and gave Levi a smug grin. She'd wondered whether he'd suggested bringing her to The Rook as a test—to see if she could "hang." Well, what he didn't know about her was that she could hang with just about anybody.

Levi and Angela turned their attention to the stage when a petite, plump woman with lots of piercings and flyaway ink-black hair took the stage and the microphone. She looked as if she'd been stuffed into a black tank dress. There were a few titters of laughter and whispering until she opened her mouth and sang the first note to "Lady Marmalade." Then complete silence, as the audience listened raptly to the sound of her voice belting out the raunchy song. Everyone was on their feet whistling and cheering when she took her bow.

"Are you certain you want to follow that?" Levi said in her ear.

Angela rolled her eyes at him. "What happened to you having my back?"

"I do have your back, baby."

She winked at Levi. "I guess only time will tell if you do."

The waiter returned with their order, and over the forty-five minutes Angela ate slowly, savoring every bite she put into her mouth. What The Rook lacked in decor the chefs more than made up for with their food.

Feeling full, she touched the napkin to her mouth. "I'm ready."

Levi stood up and pulled back Angela's chair, and watched

as she made her way to the line of would-be Karaoke performers. Leaning back in his chair he crossed his arms over his chest. An expression of pride and admiration shimmered in his eyes as he observed Angela, with a cascade of curly hair around her shoulders and the curve of her hips in the body-hugging jeans.

There were a few whistles and catcalls when Angela stepped up to take the microphone. He hadn't realized how nervous he was, reminding himself to breathe. The hubbub of conversations stopped, creating an eerie silence in the cavernous space when she opened her mouth to sing, "Looking out on the morning rain. I used to feel so uninspired." It was the Aretha Franklin classic, "A Natural Woman."

Levi couldn't ignore the shivers inching up his spine when he realized Angela had an amazing singing voice. It was almost impossible to distinguish her voice from the Queen of Soul. Putting two fingers in his mouth, he whistled loudly when she took her final bow. Several guys raced up to the stage, tossing bills at her. Angela ducked her head, and quickly walked back to their table where Levi waited with outstretched arms.

He pressed a kissed to her head and pulled her close. "You missed your calling. You were beyond extraordinary."

Angela filled her glass with water and took a big gulp. "That felt good," she gasped, as she sat down. She felt free, freer than she had in years and she had Levi to thank for it.

"Where did you learn to sing like that?"

Angela smiled at Levi. "I took lessons—voice, dance, piano and etiquette."

"I told you that you were a Southern belle," Levi reminded her.

He kissed her cheek. "What really matters is that you're *my* Southern belle."

Angela wanted to be his Southern belle and more. But she wasn't exactly certain what she wanted that more to be. Before she decided to go up on stage to sing, her first choice had been an upbeat Tina Turner song. But waiting and staring at Levi looking back at her changed her mind. There was something in his eyes that made her feel that she could be herself with him. That she could be a natural woman—free and uninhibited—and with a man who was willing to accept her.

"Isn't it too soon for me to be your anything?" she asked Levi.

"I don't think so. Now that your ex and his wife are moving to Louisville, we're going to have to convince them that we're a couple. And if we're going to be convincing then we're going to have to act and think as one. Only we know how it's going to end."

Angela didn't want to believe Levi could sound so cavalier about it. Well—if that's what he wanted, then she was more than willing to play the game. After all, she'd become quite adept in hiding her feelings, especially with men she had no interest in. She forced a smile. "You're right."

Caressing her face, Levi stared deeply into her eyes. "I can't begin to presume to know what you've gone through, but I'm willing to help you get through this, Angela. I'm not your brothers or your father, so Robert Gaskin won't be prepared to deal with me. Do you trust me?" he asked softly.

The word trust was like a rock caught in her throat. She'd trusted Robert and he'd deceived her. She'd trusted Savannah, and she also had deceived her. The only people she trusted were family and now Levi was asking her to trust him. "Do I have a choice?"

He brushed a kiss over her parted lips. "No, you don't. What I'm not going to do is lie to you. I like you. You're pretty, intelligent and you're not a snob or uptight even though—"

"I'm an SB."

"What's an SB?" he asked.

"Southern belle."

Smiling, Levi kissed her again, this time it was very different from the other kisses they'd shared. His kiss was slow, surprisingly gentle and coaxing. It ended seconds later, leaving her mouth burning and wanting more.

Angela pressed her mouth to his ear, inhaling his clean masculine scent. "Thank you for looking out for me."

"That's what friends are for. We look out for each other."

Chapter 8

Angela rose early Monday morning, showered, slipped into sweats, cleaned Miss Divine's litter box, and gave her food and fresh water. By the time the sunlight poured in through the skylight and French doors she was deeply engrossed in her manuscript. Miss Divine had curled up on the corner of the desk, her favorite spot.

She saved what she'd typed, then walked out of the office and into the kitchen.

Filling the kettle with water, Angela placed it on the heating plate and plugged it in. As she opened the refrigerator to get a container of sliced melon, the intercom from the gatehouse buzzed. Minutes later she opened the door for Traci.

"Oh, good," Traci said, her sultry drawl almost raspy as she followed Angela into the kitchen. She cleared her throat. "I'm just in time for breakfast."

Angela gave her a cousin a pointed look. "I know you didn't leave Reggie's bed this early in the morning to come here for breakfast."

She blushed. "How did you know I slept with Reggie?"

Angela pointed to the side of Traci's neck. "He left his brand."

"Oh damn!" Traci hissed, turning up the collar of her man-tailored blouse to hide the strawberry-red hickey. "I don't know why he does that."

"Like a dog he probably feels the need to mark his territory."

Taking off her jacket, Traci hung it over a high-back stool at the island and plopped down. "He's not a dog, Ang," she said, defending her ex-husband.

Angela turned around and looked at Traci. Even without makeup, Traci was stunning. Her slender figure, flawless sable-brown skin, delicate features and curly hair turned heads—especially those of the opposite sex.

Traci had been seventeen when she was approached by a modeling agency. Her parents balked since they'd planned for their daughter to attend college. But Traci was able to convince them that she would go to college once her modeling career ended. She became a supermodel overnight with her signature walk and curly hair flowing down her back. She'd modeled for eight years, and in that time she had married and divorced twice, opened the Garden Gate and recently had enrolled in college as a part-time student.

"I didn't say he was a dog, Traci, just that he's marking his territory to keep other men away."

"There are no other men."

"Do you want toast?" Angela asked, taking a loaf of multi-grain bread from the refrigerator.

"Sure."

"Now, back to Reggie," she continued. "Are you or aren't you going to become Mrs. Reginald Goddard again?"

Traci waved her hand dismissively. "I didn't come here to talk about me and Reggie, but about you and Levi Eaton."

The soft click of the kettle signaled the water had boiled. Angela dropped several bags of green tea into the clear pot to steep. "There's not much to talk about. He's a pediatrician who works with Duncan. End of story."

Resting her elbows on the granite countertop, Traci cradled her chin on the heel of one hand. "Are you going to see him again?"

Angela dropped two slices of bread into the slots of the toaster. "Yep."

"Do you like him?"

"Yep," she repeated.

Traci clapped a hand over her forehead. "Please don't tell me you're starting up with the serial dating thing again."

Leaning her hip against the countertop, Angela gave her cousin a determined look. "No. I've decided Levi is a keeper."

"A real, real keeper or someone you'll get bored with in a couple of weeks?"

"It's not like that with me and Levi."

Traci's eyebrows shot up in surprise. "What's so different about you and Levi?"

The seconds ticked off as the two cousins stared at each other. Angela knew she had to tell Traci about what she and Levi had agreed to. She watched an expression of shock cross Traci's features as she told her everything, including going to The Rook after they'd left the wedding reception.

"He heard you sing?" Angela nodded. "Did you tell him that you'd been offered a recording contract after a record producer came to see you in a high school musical?"

"No. I told him I'd taken music and voice lessons, which is the truth."

"Do you ever think of how your life would've turned out if you'd become a singer?" Traci asked.

Angela inhaled a breath and focused her gaze on the tiny buds on a potted miniature rosebush. "I never look back, Traci, because then it would be I woulda, coulda shoulda. That's no way to live life. I get up every day looking to do or experience something different than the day before."

"Like singing karaoke?"

"Yes. Like singing karaoke." A hint of a smile softened Angela's mouth. "I must admit getting up on stage and singing was a rush—something I'd like to do again."

"You know they have karaoke competition every Saturday night at Tubbs. The top prize is five hundred dollars. Don't look at me like that, Ang. I know it's not the nicest neighborhood, but I think we'd be all right if Reggie and Levi go with us as backup."

"You know Tubbs is nothing more than a bucket of blood. Someone is always getting stabbed or shot," Angela argued softly.

"Not anymore."

"What changed, Traci?"

"The owner hired some of Zane's people. I'd heard that they're armed and ready for anything."

Angela hesitated. She knew Traci wanted to double-date

because it'd been years since they had gone out together. And she knew if they went with Levi and Reggie they wouldn't look as if they were out patrolling the club looking to be picked up. It would be like old times when she and Robert would team up with Traci and Reggie. This time there would be no Robert Gaskin.

"I think bringing Reggie along will be all the protection we need."

Traci laughed. "No lie. Levi may not have Reggie's size, but I doubt if he's a punk. Come on, Ang. Please…."

"I'll think about it."

"Don't think too long, because Reggie was hinting that he wanted to do something this coming weekend."

"Don't forget my mom is having a little something at the house on Sunday."

"I won't. Now back to Levi. So, you've decided to have a relationship that excludes sex?"

"It's called friendship, Traci."

"Friendship my behind, Angela. I saw the two of you together, and if you think you're going to have a platonic relationship with Dr. Levi Eaton, then you need to be committed like yesterday."

"That's because you think with your hormones and your heart and not your head. Don't forget, I've dated more than a dozen guys and never slept with any of them. What makes Levi any different?"

Traci rolled her eyes upward. "You may have dated more men than me, but I have a lot more experience with men. After all, I was married to two of them. I've seen the way Levi looks at you, and it's the same way Reggie and I look at each other."

"I'd believe that if you weren't divorced."

"You know very well why we divorced. I was working in Europe eight months of the year, and when I returned Reggie was playing ball. We were like two ships passing in the night. But, it's different now."

"You're really reconciling?" Angela asked, as she emptied the tea into a hand-painted porcelain teapot.

Biting on her lip, Traci nodded. "We've been talking about it." She got quiet. "I know this can't be easy for you, Ang—me talking about getting married again."

Angela patted Traci's arm. "Don't worry. It doesn't bother me."

"Like me asking you to get up to catch the bouquet didn't upset you?"

"Your dragging me on the ballroom floor was like waving a red flag in front of me. Especially since Robert told everyone I was frigid." Reaching into an overhead cabinet, Angela removed two cups with matching saucers. "Do you want butter or preserves on your toast?"

"Preserves? You didn't answer my question, Ang. Who told you Robert said you were frigid?"

"No one told me. I was in a stall in the ladies' room when I overheard two women whispering about it." Angela pushed down the handle on the toaster. "My nerdy ex-fiancé just happens to have a kinky side. He was into threesomes. He wanted me to make out with another woman and make a video to replay later."

"I don't believe it. That's not kinky. That's perverted! He probably couldn't get it up unless he fantasized about two women. Do you think Savannah does that?"

"I really don't care if they do or not. Enough about Robert, Levi and Reggie. Who's coming into the shop today?"

"Olivia Knowles."

"Better you than me," Angela said, wincing. "Do you mind eating on the back porch?"

"Of course not," Traci replied. "Let me help you carry something."

Balancing the tea on a tray, Angela made her way out of the kitchen to the enclosed back porch. A white wicker sofa and love seat with olive-green paisley cushions, a glass-covered coffee table, four rocking chairs, beautiful plants and a hammock suspended between two massive columns provided an inviting space year round.

Over green tea, toast and sliced fruit the two cousins talked about the prospective bride who wanted to add antique Baccarat crystal to her wedding registry.

"I've tried to talk Olivia out of only having Baccarat, but she claims she doesn't like Lenox or Waterford."

Angela took a sip of tea, while staring at Traci over the rim of her cup. "There's nothing wrong with Waterford."

"You're preaching to the choir, cuz," Traci countered. Setting down her teacup, she patted the seat cushion when she spied Angela's cat. "Come here, Miss Divine." The cat sprang from the floor, landing on Traci's lap. "I'd get a cat if Reggie wasn't allergic to them."

"You could always get a dog that's hypoallergenic."

Traci ran her fingers over the cat's back. "Don't even go there, Ang. Reggie's idea of a dog is something that resembles a pony. He's partial to Rottweilers and Dobermans."

"I don't think…" Her words trailed off when the phone rang. Angela excused herself as she reached over and picked up the cordless phone on a side table. "Hello."

She listened as a woman from a cleaning service introduced herself. "Miss Chase, your fiancé called and made arrangements to have someone come and see your house before we set up a cleaning schedule with you. All of our employees are bonded," she explained, "and when we assign someone to clean your house we ask for your feedback. If you like her, then she'll become your permanent housekeeper. I'd like to send someone over to look at your place."

Angela closed her eyes. Levi had followed through with his promise to provide her with a cleaning service so Miss Divine could have the run of the house. But why, she wondered had he referred to her as his fiancé? "I'm usually home on Mondays, so if you're going to send someone it would have to be today."

"Will you be available in an hour?"

"Yes." Angela gave the woman her address, directions and then hung up. Cleaning her own house had never been a chore because she dusted and vacuumed the entire house on Wednesdays and cleaned the half bath, kitchen and en-suite bathrooms early Saturday mornings before going into the Garden Gate. That would change once she had a cleaning service.

Traci set Miss Divine on the floor, touched a cloth napkin to her mouth and then stood up. "Thanks for breakfast. It sounds as if you're going to have company and I need to psych myself up for Olivia. Call me later and let me know if you're down for Tubbs."

Angela knew Traci would haunt her day and night until she

gave her an answer. "I have to talk to Levi first, and then I'll let you know."

Traci combed her fingers through her short hair, fluffing up the damp curls. "You know we can't tell our mothers we're going because they'd both have a stroke."

The Hitchcock sisters were notorious snobs. Traci's mother had taken to her bed, refusing to leave when Traci had announced she was marrying a pro-football player, referring to them as "dumb jocks." Reginald Goddard may have been a jock but dumb he wasn't. He'd earned an undergraduate degree in biology, and gone on to earn a graduate degree in physiotherapy. He was now a licensed physiotherapist.

Angela pantomimed zipping her lips. "They definitely won't hear it from me."

Levi reclined on the back porch, legs crossed at the ankles, a baseball cap pulled low over his forehead and arms crossed over his chest. He'd gotten up at dawn to jog two miles, returned home to the two-bedroom guesthouse he rented from an eccentric widow, and settled down to enjoy his day off. He'd promised Angela he would pay for cleaning her house, and had followed through with a telephone call that put everything into motion.

When the woman who'd taken the information asked him what his relationship to the client was, he'd told her that Angela was his fiancée. Once the lie was out, he couldn't retract it, knowing it was easier to call her his fiancée rather than a friend. And because they also cleaned his house, Levi knew they would take special care with Angela's because of their relationship.

With his pager and cell on vibrate, attached to the waistband of his jeans, Levi reached for his iPod's earbuds. He inserted them in his ears, and listened to the eclectic playlist he'd downloaded from his extensive music collection. One day he would be in the mood for jazz and on another it could be hip-hop, R&B, pop or occasionally country. His musical tastes were as varied as his moods.

He closed his eyes and lost track of time as the sun rose higher in the sky. It was the perfect spring day in the Bluegrass State. The morning temperature had reached the mid-sixties with an expected high of seventy-two. After living in the Northeast for more than a decade he'd come to appreciate the milder temperatures. If he'd been in New York Levi knew he still would've been wearing a jacket.

His cell phone vibrated, and he sat up and looked at the caller ID. It was Duncan. Pulling the earbuds out of his ears, Levi answered the call, hoping there wasn't an emergency.

"What's up, Duncan?"

"I just got a call from the chief of staff down at Clarke County General and they need a doctor to head their pediatric unit."

A slight frown furrowed Levi's smooth forehead as he thought about Duncan's statement. "How did they get my name? Have you forgotten that I work for you *and* I still have a practice in New York?"

Duncan's laugh came through the earpiece. "There's no way I can forget. First of all, the patients who come here have been singing your praises whenever they go to Clarke General. Secondly it's a temporary position. The doctor who heads the department went hiking at Mammoth Cave, fell and broke his leg. The prognosis is that he'll be out for at least three months."

Levi had been caught off guard. It had been a while since he'd worked in a hospital, and he wondered if he'd be able to adjust to the frenetic energy. "What about the clinic, Duncan?"

"Not to worry. I'll look for a physician's assistant to fill in for you, or a retired pediatrician willing to put in a few hours. Look man, this is an opportunity of a lifetime for you. How many thirty-six-year-old doctors do you know become head of a hospital department, even if it is only temporary? Not many," Duncan said.

Levi knew Duncan was right. Even before he'd joined the medical group in New York, it had taken him a while before he resigned his position with the large New York City hospital. There was something about the challenges, the nonstop pace of the hospital emergency room that had always energized him and reminded him why he became a doctor. Treating patients in a hospital wasn't as personal as in private practice, but for Levi all of his young patients were special.

"When do they need to know?" he asked Duncan.

"It has to be today. McGill is the chief of staff, and he'll be available to see you any time after two this afternoon. I hate to lose you, Levi. But if you don't accept the position then I'm going to fire you."

It was Levi's turn to laugh. "What if I quit first?"

"You can't. Don't forget your commitment is for six months. You will also be paid for the position which is slightly higher than the stipend you're getting now. Another perk is there's free staff housing."

Clarke General, or CG, as most of the locals referred to it, was halfway between Maywood Junction and Louisville, and that meant he could drive to downtown Louisville in less than ten minutes. Levi knew Duncan could hire a physician assistant to fill in for him, but even before accepting the hospital position he was already experiencing anxiety about leaving.

"Give me McGill's number and I'll call him." Picking up a pen off the table, he wrote down the number on a pad.

"I hope when you call him you're going to tell him you'll accept the position," Duncan said.

"Don't worry, Chase. I'm not a fool."

Duncan laughed again. "I was beginning to think you were when you agreed to take my sister to the wedding."

"Don't worry about me and your sister. We're doing just fine."

"Are you telling me you guys are getting together?"

"That's none of your business, Dr. Chase. What goes on between Angela and me stays between us."

"Point taken, Dr. Eaton. I wouldn't have asked you to go out with her if I didn't have the utmost respect for you—as a man and a colleague."

"Enough with the sucking up, Duncan," he teased. "I'll call you after I talk to McGill."

Levi met with Dr. Neil McGill and afterward took a tour of the renovated facility. The renovation project had increased the capacity from sixty to a hundred twenty-five beds. His responsibility would be to supervise three med school interns and two residents. As a department head he was provided with free housing—a furnished two-bedroom apartment with amenities like twenty-four-hour security on the premises, concierge service and private parking. He'd been assigned a second-floor apartment with a living room, dining area, kitchen, two baths and a balcony that spanned the entire apartment and overlooked the parking lot. Dr. McGill had given him one week to see his clinic patients before joining the hospital staff.

Reaching for his BlackBerry, he punched the speed-dial feature. "Hey, sweetie," he crooned upon hearing Angela's voice.

"Hey, yourself," she said, laughing softly. "Or should I call you fiancé?"

Levi sobered. "Sorry about that, but it was the first thing that came to mind when the woman asked me my relationship to you."

"No harm, Levi, as long as we know where we stand with each other. Someone came out to see the house and because I live alone they don't see a need to come in more than once a week."

"One person is going to clean the entire house?"

"No. They say it'll be quicker with a two-man team."

"I'm calling because I need your help."

"What do you need?"

Levi told her about Duncan's call and his new position at the hospital. "I'm moving in this weekend."

"Congratulations. I know Duncan isn't happy about losing you, but it's an opportunity you can't afford to turn down."

He smiled. "That's what your brother said. I won't know what my schedule will be, but as soon as I find out I'll let you know."

"We're going to have to go out and celebrate."

Unlocking the sliding glass door in the master bedroom, Levi stepped out onto the balcony. "Okay, but I want to wait until after your mother's get-together and the Derby."

"Are you doing anything Saturday night?" Angela asked, catching him by surprise.

"No. Why?"

"Traci and Reggie Goddard and me are going to a club and I'd like you to join us."

"What time do you want me to pick you up?"

"Let me check with Traci, and I'll call you back."

"Levi."

"Yes, Angela."

"Congratulations again on your new position."

This time it was Levi's turn to pause. He hadn't wanted to leave the clinic. He'd grown close to his patients, something he wouldn't be able to do at a hospital—even one as small as CG. He preferred the one-on-one contact with his patients to that of a hospital.

"Thank you, Ang."

"You're welcome. By the way, plan to sleep over Saturday. It'll save you the hassle of driving back to Maywood, just to come back on Sunday for my mother's get-together."

Levi's smile was dazzling. "So, I rate a sleepover?"

"Don't get too excited, sport. Traci and Reggie are also staying over."

"Good. It's been a long time since I've been to a coed sleepover. How's my girl?"

"Who are you talking about?"

"Miss Divine."

"She's good."

"Tell her I said hello."

Angela laughed. "You're sick."

"Tell her, Angela."

"Okay. I'll tell her. Please hang up, Levi. I have to finish some paperwork."

Levi smiled. "Later." He ended the call, left the balcony, closing and locking the door behind him.

Standing in the middle of the empty bedroom he stared down at the wood floor. He had to tell his landlady he was moving out, contact the concierge and have them make arrangements to clean the apartment, and he had to remind himself that Angela Chase was looking for a friend and fun, even though his thoughts were not so friendly. He'd dreamt about Angela and woke up with a painful hard-on that refused to go down until he took a cold shower.

He knew he had to be careful—very, very careful or he'd want more from her than friendship.

Chapter 9

"Your total is eighteen hundred, thirty-one dollars and fifty-seven cents." Angela smiled at the middle-aged woman who'd become one of the Garden Gate's best customers. It also helped that she was the mayor's wife.

Priscilla Turner put her credit card on the counter. "I don't want you to send it out until the middle of next week. That way it'll arrive exactly on her birthday."

"I'll ship it Wednesday for a Thursday delivery." Mrs. Turner had ordered a Waterford heritage collection claret decanter for her daughter's thirtieth birthday. The exquisite piece was made with intricate detailing and craftsmanship, making it a crystal piece to be treasured for generations.

"Your daughter will love it," Angela continued, processing the credit card. She smiled as Priscilla patted her short, coiffed silver hair. The woman came from old money. Her family had made a fortune in tobacco, coal and oil. As a leading philanthropist, Priscilla sat on at least half a dozen boards of Louisville's charitable organizations.

Priscilla smiled, her eyes shimmering like polished topaz. "I'm certain she will. You carry the most exquisite pieces in the city."

Angela returned her smile. "Why, thank you."

"Well, it's true, Angela. If you speak to your mother before the Derby, please let her know that my secretary will be sending her an invitation for our post-race party."

Angela glanced up when she heard the distinctive chime signaling someone had walked into the Garden Gate. A slight gasp escaped her lips when she saw Levi. It'd been almost a week since their last encounter, and as he approached she felt slightly lightheaded.

She tried unsuccessfully to stop her hands from shaking as she handed Mrs. Turner her credit card. Angela had to get the woman out of the shop before she started up a conversation with Levi. Louisvillians had said for years that Priscilla should have run for mayor instead of her husband, because there wasn't anyone she couldn't engage in conversation. The running joke was she could get a rock to talk.

"Thank you so much, Mrs. Turner. I'll make certain your gift will be shipped as instructed."

Priscilla tucked her card into a compartment in her handbag. "Thank you again, Angela. Don't forget to tell your folks to look for the invitation."

"I will."

Priscilla turned to leave, then hesitated when she spied Levi standing off to the side. "Good evening, sweetie."

He nodded, smiling. "Good evening, ma'am."

She squinted at him behind the lenses of her rimless glasses. "Are you new in Louisville, because I don't remember seeing you around?"

Levi met Angela's amused gaze. "I don't live in Louisville."

"Where do you live?"

"Right now I'm in Clarkesville."

Angela decided to step in because she knew before long that the word would get out that Dianne Chase's daughter was dating Levi Eaton. "Levi, this is Mrs. Turner. Her husband is the mayor of Louisville. Mrs. Turner, Dr. Levi Eaton."

Priscilla rested a manicured hand on the strand of pearls resting on her ample bosom. "My, my, my. A doctor."

Levi's left eyebrow lifted a fraction. "Yes, ma'am."

"Do you know that Angela's brother is also a doctor?"

"Yes, ma'am," he repeated. "Angela and I are keeping company."

At that very moment Angela wanted the floor to open up and she fall through. She couldn't believe Levi had said *keeping company.* It was a term her grandmother had used. And to tell Priscilla Turner they were a couple was like taking out a full page ad in *The Courier-Journal.*

Priscilla beamed like a two-hundred watt bulb. "Aren't you just darling." She winked at Levi. "There aren't too many young men like you out there nowadays who'd say they were keeping company. Most of the time, it's we're seeing one another or hooking up. Oh, I hate that term. You hook up a horse to a plow or a wagon, but not one human being to another. And I'm so glad to see Angela with a fine young man such as yourself."

Levi leaned in closer. "My mother would agree with you. She also hates that word."

She patted his arm and pursed her rose-colored lips. "You're so much better than some of those other men she wasted her time with," Priscilla said as if Angela wasn't standing a foot away. She glanced at her watch. "I'd love to stay and talk, but I have to get back home for a ladies auxiliary meeting. Angela, you and your young man are also invited to come to the post-Derby party with your folks." She wagged a finger at Levi. "Promise me you'll be there, Dr. Eaton."

He gave her a warm smile. "I promise, Mrs. Turner."

Angela forced a brittle smile. The woman was at it again. Her sugary-sweet-buttery-melt-in-your-mouth manner had roped Levi into attending a social gathering where women brought their unmarried daughters, granddaughters and nieces in hopes that they'd meet an eligible man.

"Enjoy your evening, Mrs. Turner." Angela followed her to the door and then locked it. Waning sunlight was refracted by the stained glass insets in the decorative door. Angela closed the wrought-iron gate that gave the shop its distinctive name and slid the bolt in place.

Turning around slowly Angela stared at Levi. He was so incredibly sexy in a pair of jeans, a black pullover and a well-worn black leather jacket that she found herself holding her breath. The stubble along his jawline only added to his rugged masculinity. She approached him with her arms outstretched and kissed his chin. He leaned in so that his mouth covered hers in a slow kiss that weakened her knees. Angela felt wet in the area between her legs as her breathing quickened. Somehow she mustered the strength to pull away, ending the kiss. She was certain Levi had felt her runaway heartbeat.

"I can't believe you told her we were keeping company," she said softly. "That's what my grandma used to say when she asked me about a boy."

Levi gave her a wide smile filled with straight white teeth. "That should tell you that I'm old school."

"So old school that you're saving yourself for marriage?"

"Oh, hell no! That's not old school. That's downright crazy."

Angela laughed and shook her head. "You are so silly."

"No I'm not, sweetie. I'm a realist. Celibacy only works for some people."

"But not you," she countered.

"Not for an extended period of time."

"What do you consider an extended period of time, Levi?"

"Definitely not five years."

Turning away from him, Angela wound her arms around her body in a protective gesture. "That's cold. Maybe I shouldn't have told you how long it's been since I've slept with a man."

Levi gently pulled her arms down, wrapping his around her waist. He kissed the top of her head. "That's where you're wrong. I'm not judging you, Ang. You asked me a question and I gave you my answer. Since I became sexually active, I've never gone that long without making love to a woman. If you don't want to sleep with me, then you don't have to. No matter what happens between us, I want you to remember that you're the one controlling this relationship."

Angela turned around in his embrace, burying her face against his shoulder. The scent of his cologne and the smell of his leather jacket were heady and hypnotic. Thoughts raced through her mind, bringing with them a familiar throbbing between her legs that reminded Angela of how long it'd been since she'd had sex. She'd had nearly a week to recover from her meltdown at the wedding reception, and it had been enough time for her to think about what she really wanted from the man who'd promised to take care of her.

She wanted a friend, someone she could talk to about her problems and concerns. She wanted someone to accompany her to social functions. And she also wanted to realize what being a woman felt like in every way, to explore the full range of desire, passion and fulfillment that comes from making love.

"Right now I don't know what it is I want from you." Her voice was barely a whisper.

"It doesn't matter, baby. I'm not certain what I want from you, either. But we have time to figure it out. Let's just enjoy being together. We're adults, capable of making decisions without anyone's approval. Neither of us is naive, so if we *do* sleep together there's no guilt or regret. I like you, enjoy your company, and you certainly know that I think you're sexy as hell. And if you don't know then let me be the first to tell you that you are." Anchoring his hand under her chin, he raised her face and kissed the end of her nose. "I'm going to be around for a while, so let's enjoy our time together."

She wanted to say to him that they didn't have much time. "You're right," she said, smiling.

"Don't you know the doctor is always right?"

Angela rolled her eyes. "Sure, and I have a crystal ball that predicts whose going to win the Derby."

"Do you really?"

"Please, Levi. Don't New Yorkers have a saying about selling a bridge in Brooklyn?"

"Don't go there, Angela. There are certain subjects that are off-limits and New York landmarks are one of them."

"Have you ever been to Yankee Stadium?"

Levi nodded. "I have season tickets."

"If I come to New York, will you take me to a game?"

"If the Yankees make it to the World Series, I'll arrange for you to come with me."

"What if they don't make it to the Series?"

"Surely you jest, Miss Chase. Regardless of who the Yankees play or, heaven forbid, they don't make the World Series, I'll still take you to a game."

"If you renege, Levi, I'll raise holy hell."

"Damn, woman! There's no need for violence."

"There are plenty of ways to raise holy hell without inflicting pain," she said.

Levi angled his head. "If it involves handcuffs, chocolate syrup and whipped cream then I'm game."

Her eyes nearly popped out of her head.

He shook his head. "You're something else, you know."

"Why would you say that?"

"I never thought you'd be so gullible."

"I'm not gullible," she said defensively.

"Then why do you believe everything I say?"

She looked away, staring at the bouquet of white roses in a round crystal bowl. "I believe you because I trust you, Levi." Her gaze swung back to him. "You're the first man I've been able to trust in five years. Please don't make me regret it."

Lowering his head, Levi kissed her again. It was more to reassure Angela and let her know she could trust him. "Never," he whispered against her soft, moist lips.

Angela breathed in Levi's scent, and enjoyed feeling the hardness of his chest against her breasts. She wanted and needed him so much it hurt. All she had to do was ask Levi to make love to her and she was certain the pain would go away.

"Didn't you work today?" she asked, changing the subject.

He pulled her closer, staring down at her under lowered lids. "I went into the clinic, but didn't see patients. Why did you ask?"

"You didn't shave."

"Yeah, I know. I'd decided to give my face a rest. Don't worry. I'll shave for tomorrow."

Angela smiled. "You don't have to. I don't mind a little stubble."

"I'll shave anyway," Levi insisted. "Are you closing for the day?"

"Yes." Angela gently pushed against his chest, wanting and needing to put some distance between them. The longer she remained in his arms the more her body betrayed her. "Mrs. Turner was my last customer."

Levi dropped his arms, crossing them over his chest. "I guess I got here just in time."

She blinked. "I wasn't expecting you until tomorrow."

"I thought I'd surprise you. I did want to stop by and pick up some gifts for my cousins, and then take you out to dinner."

"I thought we'd do that when the shop is closed."

"That was before I knew I'd be working at the hospital. Once my staff is onboard I'll be responsible for putting together a schedule. I'll probably work four days on and three off."

Angela met his direct stare. "Will you be off for the Derby?"

He smiled. "Most definitely." Levi was willing to work double shifts so he could be off that weekend.

"In Louisville we start partying Thursday night and we usually don't end until late Sunday night, especially if you've bet on the right horse."

"I can get by on little to no sleep."

"We'll see about that, Mr. Big Time."

"I guess you will. By the way, where's Traci?"

"She went home. Traci works from nine-thirty to two, then I come in from two to six. Thursdays we stay open until eight." Traci had gone home early because her stomach was upset, so they'd decided to postpone going to Tubbs.

Levi glanced around the Garden Gate rather than stare at Angela. It was as if he'd actually entered a garden. China, crystal and collectibles were displayed on glass-topped tables, in showcases and armoires, amid potted plants as prerecorded music played softly in the background. A trio of bistro tables covered with blue-and-white-check tablecloths and chairs with matching seat cushions were set up in the far corner. Decorating magazines occupied a wrought-iron stand beside a daybed.

He turned back to Angela and stared at her. He'd realized her vulnerability, and it touched him in a way that would make it difficult for him to walk away from her.

Angela Chase was different from the other women he'd been involved with. She was outspoken, fiercely independent, stubborn, beautiful and unpredictable. Whenever he saw her, he didn't know what to expect. And that kept him slightly off-balance.

If Angela only worked four hours a day, Levi wondered what she did in her spare time. He just couldn't imagine her staying at home cooking, cleaning or watching television.

"If it's more convenient for you I can wait until next week to buy the gifts."

"How many gifts do you need and what are their ages?" Levi reached into the pocket of his jeans, took out a folded piece of paper and handed it to her. Angela smiled. "There're quite a few baby girls."

"The girls are definitely outnumbering the boys."

"Do the girls have pierced ears?"

Levi closed his eyes, trying to remember if they did. "I think so."

"Find out if they do because I have tiny diamond studs that are simply adorable for little girls. Also find out if the boys are into sports, and if they are then what teams they like. Come with me and I'll show you what I have."

Angela led Levi around the corner of the shop, past an antique armoire to a display case that held an array of gold jewelry—many with precious and semiprecious gems.

She removed the elastic band from her wrist, inserted the key in the lock and took out a tray with diamond studs in varying sizes. Angela pointed to several small carat diamond studs. "These are perfect for young girls. The smallest would be appropriate for a baby. They all have slender posts with screw backs. Once on, they'll stay on."

Levi peered at the earrings. The overhead track lighting reflected off the stones casting blue and white prisms of light. "I have a few cousins who are teenage girls now that would probably like the larger pair."

"A local jeweler was going out of business, so Traci bought a lot of his inventory. We've had the stones appraised and the diamonds are of the highest quality. We sell a lot of jewelry to brides and grooms as gifts for their wedding party. The brides like earrings and the grooms usually prefer engraved ID bracelets for their groomsmen. Everything in this case is gold and in the other one is silver."

"What do you suggest?" Levi asked Angela.

"I like the earrings for the girls, but I'm not sure about what to get for young boys. Whatever you decide, I think you should ask their parents."

"I'll definitely go for the earrings, because all of the women in my family have pierced ears. But, didn't you mention something about sports teams?"

"When you come to my house tomorrow you can go online and search the Waterford site for sport-themed gifts."

Levi groaned audibly. "This is becoming more complicated than I thought. I usually give the kids a check, but somehow that seems so impersonal."

"You're making this a lot more difficult than it needs to be. Why don't you think about buying a digital camera for the older kids and have them take pictures of family gatherings. Then, you can always go with gift cards for their favorite stores. Savings bonds for the little ones are always a good gift. Don't forget about e-book readers and tablets for the school-age kids, and gift cards so they can download books without asking their parents for money."

A slow smile spread across Levi's face. "Damn, girl! You really know your stuff."

It was Angela's turn to wink at Levi. "I only do what I know, which is running a gift shop. And I know how to shop."

"I'm completely clueless when it comes to shopping."

"Who buys your clothes?"

"I have a personal shopper at a men's store. He picks out everything from shirts and pants to underwear and socks."

Angela smiled. "He has impeccable taste."

Levi glanced down at his jeans and shoes. "He's really good." He gave her a long, penetrating stare. "Are you ready to lock up and go to dinner with me?"

"Where are we going?" Angela asked.

"You're from Louisville, so you pick the spot."

She removed the trays of jewelry from the showcase and stored them in a wall safe. "Do you like Middle Eastern food?"

"Yes."

"Then we'll go to Saffron's."

Levi sat across from Angela at a table in Saffron's, which specialized in authentic Persian cuisine. The establishment's cozy atmosphere, the mouthwatering aromas of the food and his dinner partner made the night close to perfect.

They'd been served a complimentary order of sabzi—a green salad with fresh herbs, feta cheese, and thinly sliced cucumber and radishes. He'd watched Angela spread the cheese on warm pita bread, add the sabzi herbs and then roll it together before taking a bite. She'd ordered grilled salmon topped with caramelized barberries served over dill-infused basmati rice. Levi ordered shisk-leek—a kebab of grilled New Zealand lamb with fresh vegetables and saffron rice. Their waiter had recommended Chateau Muscar Hocher, a Lebanese wine that was the perfect complement to their meal.

Levi admired the delicate angles of Angela's face in the flickering glow of candlelight. "Excellent choice," he said. "The food is delicious, the service exceptional and my dinner partner just perfect."

A wave of heat stung Angela's cheeks as she demurely lowered her eyes. "Thank you." Seconds ticked by before she met his eyes. "This is one of my favorite restaurants."

Levi wondered if she had come here with her ex. "I can see why. I'd like you to answer one question for me."

"Only one?" she teased with a smile.

"Okay, maybe two."

"What is it?"

"If you work part-time at the Garden Gate what do you do with the rest of your time?"

She slowly lowered her arm. "I read, walk, watch movies and I write," she admitted.

He gave her an incredulous stare. "You write?" Angela nodded. "What do you write?"

"I write reviews of the movies I've seen."

His eyebrows lifted. "Are you a movie reviewer?"

"No, Levi." There was a trace of laughter in her voice. "I have an extensive movie collection and every three days I watch a new one then write a review."

Angela hadn't lied. She'd always been a movie buff, and once she'd decided to become a novelist she began writing movie reviews to analyze plots and characters. The exercise had become useful in writing her own novels.

"How many movies do you have?"

She lifted a shoulder. "Thousands. They include every genre from action, adventure, to musicals, to comedies, drama and horror. I've set up a database for each title that includes the cast, director, studio and gross receipts along with my review."

"Do you ever see a movie more than once?"

"Hardly ever, but I do have my favorites. What's your second question?"

"Why do you wear your hair like that?" He gestured in a circular motion.

Angela patted the coil of hair at the nape of her neck. "It's easier this way."

"I like your hair when you don't pin it up in that schoolmarm bun."

"No, you didn't! We're not schoolmarms but educators."

"My bad," he said. "Do you think you'll ever go back to teaching?"

Angela turned her head to hide a smile. "I haven't ruled it out," she said. Although she didn't want to think about it, there was a possibility that her writing career could end, or that Traci would decide she didn't want to continue running the gift shop. She'd enjoyed teaching but writing romance novels had taken precedence.

"What do you do in New York when you're not treating patients?" she asked Levi.

"During the baseball season I try and make every Yankee home game. I also go to Knick games whenever possible. I'm more of a TV spectator when it comes to football. A group of us usually gets together on Sundays to watch the games."

"It sounds as if you're a frustrated jock."

Levi laughed. "That's where you're wrong. I'm not into pain."

"Did you ever play football?"

"Unlike Reggie Goddard, my idea of fun isn't having three hundred pounds of muscle tackling me. You can't imagine how many teenagers I've treated who get injured playing contact sports."

"Are you saying you wouldn't let your son play football?"

Levi gave her a withering look. "That's exactly what I'm saying."

"What if he wants to?"

"It's not what he wants as long as I'm responsible for him. Once he's old enough, he can do whatever he pleases."

"My brothers played football and they came out all right."

"Your brothers are not my sons."

Angela knew she was treading into dangerous territory with Levi and decided to drop the topic. Maybe because he was a pediatrician and had treated sport-related injuries, he was so adamant that his children not be involved in contact sports.

Levi signaled for the check, settled the bill and helped Angela to her feet. He drove her back to where she'd parked her car in a parking lot not far from the Garden Gate. Waiting until she was settled into her car, he leaned over into the driver's side window and kissed her.

"I'll follow you home."

"That's all right," Angela said, staring at him. "I'll make it home okay."

"I'll still follow you to make certain."

"Levi—"

"Shh," he interrupted. "Whenever I take a lady out, I always make certain she gets home safely. Please don't fight with me, darling, because I'm a lot bigger than you."

"You're a bully, Levi."

"That's where you're wrong, Angela. I like you a little too much to think of something happening to you."

"He likes me! He likes me!" she repeated.

Shaking his head, Levi couldn't help but laugh. "All right, Sally Field. Start your car and I'll be right behind you."

He got into his car, started it up and sped out of the lot just in time to see the taillights of Angela's two-seater Audi turn a corner. He followed her as far as the marker for Magnolia Pines, then reversed direction. *I like you a little too much to think of something happening to you.* The admission had just slipped out, but Levi wasn't certain if Angela's humorous response was because she didn't believe him or because she wasn't ready to acknowledge the depths of his feelings.

Chapter 10

Levi woke later than he'd planned Sunday morning. Rolling over, he gazed at the travel clock on the bedside table. It was after nine and he'd promised Angela he would pick her up at one. He stifled a groan, closed his eyes and flopped on his back. After seeing her home, he'd driven to an all-night supermarket to pick up groceries to stock his refrigerator and pantry.

It had taken three trips before he'd moved all of his belongings from the cottage into the new apartment. It was after midnight when he'd finally put away his clothes, made up the bed and stored bedding and towels in the linen closet and stocked the pantry. The only thing that remained was unpacking the boxes with pots, pans, cutlery and dishes and hooking up the television.

He sat up and swung his legs over the side of the bed. He walked into the adjoining bathroom. He went through the motions of brushing his teeth and shaving, then stepped into the shower stall. The warm water managed to revive him, and when he returned to the bedroom his step was lighter.

He walked into the kitchen and searched for the single-cup coffeemaker in one of the three boxes labeled "Kitchen." Levi plugged in the small appliance, and within minutes, the smell of brewing coffee filled the room.

He sat in one of the chairs, propped his feet up in another chair, and sipped the strong mug of Sumatra. He stared at the furniture and decided it reminded him of the functional, big-box-store style pieces sold in Ikea.

He'd finished brewing a second cup of coffee when his cell phone rang. A smile crossed his lips when he saw the name on the caller ID display.

"Hello, stranger."

"Bite your tongue, Levi Eaton. You're the stranger. You know you owe me a call."

"That's where you're wrong, Crystal. I called you just before I left New York, and the call went directly to voice mail." There was silence on the other end. "Cryss, are you still there?" Levi asked after a lengthy pause.

"I'm here." A sigh came through the earpiece. "I need a favor of you."

Levi sat up straight, giving his cousin his full and undivided attention when he heard something in her voice. It was fear. He'd always been particularly close to Crystal Eaton, and felt more like a brother than a cousin. Her father, Raleigh Eaton, was now on his fourth marriage and Crystal had spent her childhood competing with her father's wives for his attention. Her mother never recovered from losing the man she'd considered the love of her life. When she did talk to her only child, it was as if she were a total stranger. There were times when Crystal spent more time at Levi's house than she did at her own.

"What is it, Cryss?"

"Can I hang out at your place for a while?"

"You want to come to Kentucky?"

"No, Levi. I'm talking about your condo in Mamaroneck. I'd like to stay there—at least until you get back."

"What happened to your apartment in Fort Lauderdale?"

"I sold it."

"Why?" Levi asked.

There came another pause. "I...I couldn't stay in Florida."

He listened and was stunned when she told him she was pregnant, and hadn't told the man she'd been involved with that she was carrying his child. "How far along are you?"

"I just began the second trimester. You're the only one who knows."

Levi ran a hand over his face. "Are you going to tell your mother or father?"

"No!"

He was taken aback by the tone in her voice. "Have you at least been to see a doctor?"

"Yes. He says everything looks good."

"I want you to call my practice and ask for Dr. Webster. Tell him you're my cousin. He's one of the best obstetricians in the New York City area. I'm going to check in with him periodically to see how you're doing."

"What happened to doctor-patient confidentiality, Levi?"

"I'm not going to violate your privacy. He's going to be your ob-gyn and I'm going to be your baby's pediatrician, so it stands to reason that we will consult with each other. By the way, where are you now?"

"I've checked into a hotel in Manhattan. I'd like to stay at your place until you get back, then I'll look for something suitable for me and the baby."

"Don't worry about moving. You can stay as long as you want, Crystal," he told her. "I'll call the building manager and tell him to give you a set of keys. The only thing I'm going to ask you to do is call me regularly to let me know how you're doing."

"I promise, Levi. And thank you."

He smiled for the first time. "There's no need to thank me. Just take care of yourself and that baby."

"I will. And don't worry about your apartment, Levi. I'll make certain it'll pass the white-glove test."

"You will not be doing any housework or heavy lifting that might jeopardize your baby. The building has a contract with a cleaning service. Tell the concierge you want them to come in twice a week. You don't have to be there to let them in. And don't worry about paying them, because it's charged directly to my monthly maintenance. I'll call you back to let you know when you can pick up the keys."

Levi ended the call. He scrolled through his contacts on his cell for the name and number of the building manager. It only took a few minutes to tell the manager what he wanted before he called Crystal to tell her she could move into his condo the next day. He couldn't imagine what had happened between Crystal and the man who had fathered her child to make her not tell him she was pregnant.

Crystal was by most measures a late bloomer. She didn't begin dating until after she'd graduated from college. Levi knew her reluctance to become involved with a man stemmed from her father's many failed marriages and her mother's inattentiveness. Both had contributed to her trust issues.

Her father Raleigh Eaton's striking good looks made him a magnet for the opposite sex. The running family joke was that Raleigh could afford a harem since he'd made a sizable fortune in the stock market. It was as if the self-made millionaire had a sixth sense when it came to buying and selling stocks and bonds, but not when it came to women.

His uncle was going to be a grandfather for the first time. But unfortunately, his daughter didn't plan to include him in her life and that of her unborn child.

Angela sat on the back porch, watching the Weather Channel. The wind was gusting more than twenty miles an hour and there was a forecast of rain. But so far the skies had remained cloudy. Bad weather was never a factor when it came to Dianne Chase's social events. An outdoor party was simply moved indoors.

She had waited until eight to call Traci to find out if she was going to the cookout, but the call went directly to voice mail. She hoped Traci was feeling better than she had the day before.

It had been a week since she'd first met Levi Eaton. But for some reason it seemed like they had known each other so much longer. She felt an emotional calm she hadn't thought possible. She liked Levi a lot. Yet a part of her wouldn't let her feel connected. He was perfect, perfect for anyone but her. There was no way she could allow herself to feel more than friendship. How could she want or ask for more when Levi had planned to leave Kentucky in a few weeks. Falling in love with him would prove disastrous. However, what she was willing to do was sleep with him, something she'd refused to consider before. She smiled. After all, Levi had told her that she was the one who was in control of their relationship.

They were adults—consenting adults—and when it ended, both of them would be left with memories despite the promise of no happily ever after. Levi would return to New York and she would continue on with her life just like before.

"Hello, Miss Dee," she crooned when the cat quietly came

into the room. For some reason, Miss Divine was more aloof
than usual. She hadn't gotten out of her bed when Angela cleaned
the litter box or when she filled the filtered-water fountain. She
didn't even move when Angela put some cat treats in her bowl.

Angela picked up the cat, placing her on the quilted throw
in her lap. She turned off the television and picked up the tape
recorder mic. Recording her thoughts helped when she sat down
to write. "Saturday, April thirtieth—untitled romance novel
number four. Unnamed hero is a wealthy, widowed doctor with
an eight-year-old daughter. Unnamed heroine is a teacher hired
by the doctor to home-school his daughter. She's new in town,
unaware of the hero's reputation for quickly dismissing teachers. But the heroine is unfazed by his gruff manner because she
needs a job that includes room and board."

Angela pushed the pause button and composed her thoughts.
"The hero is not just the only doctor in town, he's also the fore-
most collector of African-American Civil War memorabilia."

She lost track of time as the ideas seemed to flow and she
was able to get them on tape. Excitement infused her as the plot
came together. Leaving the porch, she made her way to her office
and turned on her computer. By the time she'd transcribed the
tape and began filling in the details about her characters, Angela
knew this novel would be decidedly different from the others
she'd written.

Angela glanced up at the skylight. Streaks of sunlight had
broken through the clouds. Saving what she'd typed, she walked
out of the office and into the kitchen. She had to eat to keep her
energy up before returning to her novel.

Angelina Courtland was in what she called the *zone*. It was
similar to what racehorses experienced when their trainers put
on blinders. She was completely focused. Once she finished a
draft, edited and tweaked what she'd written, it would be sent to
her agent, who would submit it to a publisher.

Angela stepped onto the porch as she watched Levi's car
approach. A smile parted her lips when he stopped and got out
of the gleaming white sedan. Looking at him now forced her to

acknowledge what she hadn't wanted to admit. Although Levi was her friend, she wanted more from him.

She had with him what she hadn't had with any man in her life—trust and honesty. That was what had been missing in her relationship with Robert.

Her smile grew wider when Levi held out his arms and she walked into his strong and protective embrace. Circling her arms around his body, Angela closed her eyes and inhaled the scent of his aftershave, his laundered shirt and his body's natural scent. He looked and smelled delicious.

"How are you?" she whispered against the solid wall of his chest.

Levi rested his chin on the top of her head. "Good. And you?"

Easing back, she stared up at him. "Wonderful."

"I was waiting for you to call to tell me that your mother had canceled the cookout because of the weather."

"No way, Levi. Unless there's a tornado or earthquake, for my mother the show will always go on."

"If she had canceled it, then I would've made you hang out with me." Levi tightened his hold on Angela. "I'm looking forward to the time when we can spend more than a couple of hours together."

Angela tried to keep her emotions in check. Levi had expressed what she had been feeling since she awoke in the middle of the night. She'd awakened from an erotic dream that left her shaken and moaning in frustration. It had taken a while, but she'd managed to go back to sleep only to be awakened again by the same dream. This time she saw the face of the man in bed with her. She saw Levi smiling at her.

"I need you." The admission had slipped out.

Levi expelled an audible breath, not sure of what he'd just heard. Maybe he'd imagined Angela telling him she wanted him because he wanted her. They'd known each other a week, and never in that time had she given him any indication that she wanted more than friendship.

"Do you realize what you're saying?"

Tilting her head, she met his piercing gaze. "I know exactly what I'm saying."

"You know this will change everything we'd agreed to."

She nodded. "What we'd agreed to was no marriage and no babies, Levi, and that means you're going to have to use protection until I go back on the Pill."

"Are you sure?"

A trembling smile touched her lips. "Very sure."

Levi couldn't believe he was questioning a woman who he'd wanted to make love to within hours of meeting her. Was he getting old? Or had he been without a woman for so long that he'd become quite comfortable with his self-imposed abstinence?

"I'm not into gratuitous sex," he said, stalling long enough to give Angela a chance to withdraw her offer.

"Neither am I, Levi. Not having sex for five years should tell you that."

He decided to try one more approach. "Are you asking me to make love to you to get back at Robert?"

Angela pounded his chest with her fist. "Let me go!"

"Angela!"

She hit him again. "I said let me go!" He released her, his arms dropping at his sides. Her eyes flashed fire as she took a backward step. "I wouldn't sleep with you if you were the last man on the face of the earth!"

"But I would sleep with you even if there were a million women asking me to make love to them."

She froze. "What are you talking about?"

"Do you think I don't want you, Angela." He held up a hand to silence her. "Hush, sweetie, and let me finish," he said when she opened her mouth to interrupt him.

Angela blinked back the angry tears that had flooded her eyes. "You use that word rather loosely don't you?" she said, ignoring his warning.

"What word?"

"Sweetie."

"I've been told it's perfectly acceptable for women in Louisville to call anybody, and that includes children, men or other women *sweetie* or *honey* as long they use the Southern accent. Which one do you prefer? *Sweetie,* or *honey?*"

Her eyelids fluttered. "I don't mind being *honey.*"

"I guess that makes me your sweetie. As I was saying I want to make love to you, but it's not going to be all about sex."

Her eyes were as large as silver dollars when she met his penetrating gaze. "What is it going to be about?"

"Protecting your reputation."

She gave him a quizzical look. "I don't understand."

Levi cupped her chin gently in his hand. His free hand smoothed back the hair she'd tied in a ponytail. "Gossip, Ang. There's going to be a lot of talk about us. Remember, you have a reputation for dating a lot of guys, and some might think you've slept with them."

"But I didn't!"

"I know that and you know that. But does everyone else?"

Angela pursed her lips tightly. "I doubt it."

"That's exactly what I'm talking about. Once you strip away education, money and the other trappings of society, all that's left is your reputation. I'm certain you heard what the mayor's wife said about you going out with losers."

"She didn't say they were losers, Levi."

"If she said you'd wasted your time, then they were losers." Lowering his head, he brushed his mouth over hers. "Enough talk. I want you to pack an overnight bag and leave it in the trunk of my car. I want you to be ready whenever we decide to have a pajama party."

Angela repressed a giggle. "You want me to sleep at your place?"

"Yes. You can bring Miss Divine if you want."

"No. Miss Dee can stay home."

"Jealous?"

"Heck, yeah. I don't believe in threesomes." As soon as the word slipped off her tongue Angela was reminded of the two people who'd changed her and her life.

"I can always close the bedroom door," Levi suggested.

"I can close the door and she'll stay out. That's not going to happen with you, Levi. Whether you want to believe it or not, my cat has you wrapped around her little paw."

Levi let out a hearty laugh. "Let me go in and see my baby while you get your bag."

He found the cat in the room Angela had set up as her home office. Miss Divine was more than content to let him hold her. Levi glanced around the room that was bathed in sunlight from the skylight overhead and the French doors. There were two walls of built-in bookcases that were crowded with hardcover and paperback books. There were literally hundreds of romance novels. Every title seemed to include the words *mistress* or *passion, baby* or *ecstasy, secret* or *embrace*. It was apparent Angela was a romantic. It was easy to imagine her sitting in a deep, comfy club chair with her feet resting on a footstool, reading a romance novel. Her life was so uncomplicated. She watched movies, read, worked in her gift shop then returned to an elegantly decorated home.

A large screen monitor all-in-one PC, a printer and a stack of news and fashion magazines were arranged atop the surface of the L-shaped desk. Walking over to the fireplace, Levi studied the family photographs on the mantel. There was a class photo of Angela in the first grade. Her tongue stuck out through the space from her missing front teeth. There were other pictures of her as a teen and when she'd graduated from college.

His gaze lingered on one of her mother with another woman who looked like her twin. Levi wondered if the woman was Angela's Aunt Nicola. His question was answered when he studied a photo of Angela and the woman standing in front of the Eiffel Tower. The older woman did not look like the other two.

"The woman in the photo with my mother is Traci's mom. They're identical twins in every sense of the word." When Levi turned around, Angela saw Miss Dee cradled to his chest. "I gave Miss Thing clean water, food and I cleaned her litter box, so she should be quite content being left alone until I get back.

"Are you sure you don't want to bring her with us?"

"Put the cat down, Levi. Besides, my mother doesn't like cats."

Levi kissed Miss Divine's head. "Mommy's a meanie."

"Yeah, right," Angela drawled as she turned and walked out of the room. "When you have children it'll probably be like the inmates running the prison."

"Not if their mama is the warden," Levi said as he followed

her out of the room. He set the cat down and picked up the overnight bag Angela had left by the door. After Angela turned on the alarm and locked the door, he took her hand and led her to his car.

Chapter 11

Angela pointed to a late-model SUV with North Dakota plates parked in an area set aside for parking. "That's Ryder's truck. He's probably going to stay in Louisville until after the race."

Levi maneuvered alongside the Lincoln MKX and turned off the engine. Bright sunlight shimmered on the three-story house where Judge Benton and Dianne Chase had raised their children. He'd driven past a tennis court, a covered inground pool and a five-car garage.

"Your parents have enough land to build a nine-hole golf course."

Angela rolled her eyes, while shaking her head. "Please don't let my mother hear you say that."

"Why?"

"Because Daddy has been talking about doing just that for the past three years. All he needs is an ally to second what has become his obsession. But before the architectural landscaper can draw up the plans, my parents will be headed for divorce court."

Levi got out and came around to assist Angela. He'd grown up in a Miami beachfront home on a half-acre lot, while Angela and her brothers were raised in a mansion with at least five acres as their playground. It was obvious the Chases were wealthy.

"Everyone is probably around the back," she said, grasping his hand and pulling him along with her.

"Wait, baby. "I have to get the kegs out of the trunk."

"Don't worry about that, Levi. Give me your keys and I'll get someone to do that for you."

Reaching into his pocket, Levi gave Angela the keys to his

car and a sidelong glance. She looked incredibly feminine with a mass of curls framing her face. It had become a struggle not to stare at her bare legs in her slim black knee-length skirt that she paired with a white tank top.

The sound of voices, laughter and the distinctive aroma of grilled food greeted him as soon as Angela led him into an expansive outdoor kitchen. Stainless-steel burners, several outdoor grills, a pizza oven, a smoker, a refrigerator, bar and outdoor sink and a fireplace provided the perfect setting for family entertaining. A large tent covered the area, protecting those standing and sitting at tables from the hot sun. He spied Benton Chase, wearing a bibbed apron stamped with *Pit Monster* manning the grill.

Waving a pair of tongs, Benton beckoned them closer. "Welcome, son. Come on over and get something to eat. Jared, fix your sister's boyfriend something to drink. Make it the Chase special."

Angela caught Levi's arm, stopping him. "Be careful," she warned. Her voice had lowered to a whisper. "They're going to give you something that'll singe your hair."

He patted her hand. "Don't worry, baby. I won't embarrass you."

She kissed his cheek. "First let me introduce you to everyone before you manage to lose a few brain cells after you down a few of those so-called Chase specials."

Dipping his head, Levi pressed his mouth to her ear. "Do you really think your man can't hold his liquor?"

She rested a hand over his heart. "No, no, sweetie. It's just that I want to warn you just in case I have to become the designated driver."

"I'll be all right. I know when to stop. I start work at the hospital tomorrow."

Angela cut her eyes at him. "Okay, Big Time."

"That's the second time you called me that."

"What?" Angela asked.

"Big Time. When I was an intern, the police brought a pimp into the ER after one of his girls decided to open up his belly with a straight razor after he'd sliced her face. His street name was Big Time, and the word on the street was he was obsessed with the Clint Eastwood movie *Unforgiven*."

She grimaced. "What happened to him?"

"He didn't make it. I heard from some of his *associates* that every prostitute in North Philly turned out to celebrate his passing. There were so many flowers you would've thought it was either a Mafia wedding or you'd entered Longwood Gardens."

"Damn," Angela drawled. "I'll never call you Big Time again."

Moving his head ever so slightly, Levi pressed a tender kiss to her temple. "Thank you, baby."

"Can't you two wait until you're home to do that?"

Angela eased out of Levi's arms, turned and smiled at her brother. "Jealous, Ryder, since all of your girlfriends have hooves and horns?"

Ryder Chase approached his sister, picked her up and swung her around until she pleaded with him to stop. He set her on her feet. "You're looking good, Sis. And I think you've put on a little weight." He offered Levi his hand. "Ryder Chase."

Levi shook his hand, staring at the ornate buckle on Ryder's belt depicting a bucking bull. "Levi Eaton."

Within seconds he was surrounded by three other Chase brothers—Jared, Langdon and Duncan—and the resemblance among them was remarkable. They could've been quadruplets if Duncan hadn't had so much gray. All four were younger versions of their father.

Angela watched her brothers staring at Levi. "Don't even start. Levi hasn't eaten."

Jared took off his baseball cap and fanned his face. "I don't believe your man needs you to protect him, Ang. Do you, Doc?"

Levi smiled. "You've got that right."

"If that's the case," Langdon said, grinning, "then we'll see how you'll fare with our famous Kentucky bourbon."

Jared winked at Levi. "Duncan told us you live in New York where everyone orders fruity cocktails in pretty colors. Down here it's whiskey, bourbon or mash. Lang and I bought several bottles of one hundred-proof bourbon whiskey at auction last month. Care to join us when we sample it?"

"I'm game."

Angela caught Levi's arm. "Levi, don't."

He winked at her. "It's okay, baby."

She stomped her foot like a child as her brothers led Levi into the house. She was still in the same spot when her mother joined her. "They're doing it, Mama."

Dianne wrapped her arm around her daughter's waist. "You're going to have to trust Levi, sweetie. I'm certain he'll know when to stop."

"But do *they* know when to stop? You remember what they did to Robert? He wasn't able to get out of bed for days."

Dianne saw the distressed look on Angela's face. "You really like him, don't you?"

"What are you talking about, Mama?"

"Don't insult my intelligence, Angela. You know quite well I'm talking about Levi."

Angela knew it was useless to lie, because she'd never been able to keep anything from her mother. "Yes. I like him."

"How much?"

She closed her eyes. "A lot." When she opened her eyes she saw her mother's expression. "Yes, Mama. I like him very, very much."

Dianne's shocked expression softened. "So, do you plan to keep him?"

"It's not about keeping anyone. He's only going to be here a few more months, then he's going back to New York." Angela took her mother's arm and led her to one of the love seats. She explained how Levi had agreed to volunteer at the clinic for six months. "I guess you can say this is my payback for all the guys I messed over."

Dianne patted Angela's hand. "You will not have a pity party, Angela Maxine Chase. Not today."

She knew her mother was upset whenever Dianne called her by her full name. "I'm sorry, Mama."

"You're a Hitchcock woman and you know we don't cut and run. What Robert Gaskin did to you was unconscionable, but life goes on. I'm not one for revenge, but he's getting it in spades from Savannah."

"How do you know this?"

A mysterious smile tilted the corners of the older woman's mouth. She patted her short coiffed hair. "I have my sources."

"I don't want to know your source, but please give me the details."

Dianne turned and gave Angela a long, penetrating stare. "I heard she's pregnant again, but the baby's not Robert's. In fact, the first one wasn't his, either."

Angela's jaw dropped. "Damn-n-n! So, he's raising another man's children."

"It appears that way," Dianne said smugly. She patted her daughter's hand again. "Now, back to you and Levi. How serious are the two of you?"

Angela stared at the terracotta flooring. "We're friends."

"Friends?" Dianne repeated.

"Yes, friends. But without benefits."

At least not yet, she mused, thinking about her overnight bag stored in the trunk of Levi's car. Angela didn't know whether it was reluctance on his part, but Levi still hadn't indicated that he wanted to take their relationship to another level.

He talked about being old-fashioned and not engaging in gratuitous sex and she admired him for that. It meant he didn't jump into bed with every woman who smiled at him. What Angela had to resolve were her own feelings that she didn't just want Levi to make love to her as much as she needed him to make love to her. She needed to experience lovemaking that was deep and sexually fulfilling.

"Maybe it's good that you're not sleeping together." There was a wistful tone in Dianne's words.

"Why would you say that, Mama?"

"If a man continues to date a woman and not sleep with her, then it means not only does he respect her, but he also likes her."

"Is that what happened between you and Daddy?"

Leaning back against the cushion, Dianne closed her eyes. "Even though your father and I grew up during the sexual revolution, we didn't sleep together until we were engaged. Your dad wasn't my first, but he certainly was the best." Her mother lowered her gaze. "The baby-making sex was incredible, so much so that we had five children. I would've had six if we hadn't run out of bedrooms. And you know how much I love this house."

"Mama!" This was a Dianne Chase Angela was totally unfamiliar with. Of course they'd had their mother-daughter sex talk the year she turned eleven. But never had her mother revealed her own sexual experiences.

Dianne sucked her teeth, something she never would've done if her mother had been alive. "Don't mama me, Angela. You're a grown woman, doing grown woman things, so close your mouth."

"TMI, Mama."

"No, it's not too much information. I wish my mother would've talked to me the way I'm talking to you. And if and when you have a daughter, I hope you'll do the same."

Angela gave Dianne a warm smile. "You never cease to surprise me."

Dianne kissed her cheek. "Now I need you to surprise me before I get too old to bounce a grandbaby on my knee."

"Mama, you have four sons, so you can't put all the pressure on me."

Shaking her head, Dianne said, "I've given up on them."

Angela understood where her mother was coming from. Only Duncan seemed to be involved in a relationship. Ryder lived too far away for anyone to know who he was dating and Langdon and Jared were obsessed with their distillery.

"By the way, where's Myla?" Angela asked.

"Duncan said she's coming later. Ryder is as close-mouthed as a clam about the women he's seeing and Langdon and Jared only date women with names like bourbon or whiskey."

Angela laughed as she stood up and went over to greet Traci's parents. She thought her mother's twin was overdressed for a cookout, but had to admit she looked stunning in apple-green silk. Angela went to look for the groundskeeper to tell him to retrieve the kegs of beer from the trunk of Levi's car and bring them to the patio.

The patio was filled with Hitchcocks and Chases, eating, drinking and laughing when Levi emerged from the house, grinning from ear to ear. Langdon and Jared patted his back as if he'd scored the game-winning basket.

Angela sat up straight, but didn't get up to go over to Levi as he filled a plate from the buffet prepared by a local caterer. Dianne turned to look at Angela from behind the lenses of her sunglasses. "He's walking straight, so that means he survived."

"I'm glad, because I was prepared to be the designated driver." Angela pulled her feet up with Levi's approach, scooted over and made room for him to sit beside her. "How are you feeling?" she asked as he cradled a forkful of dirty rice. He'd filled his plate with shredded pork, grilled zucchini, sliced tomatoes and mozzarella and roasted peppers.

Levi gave Angela a lopsided grin. "N-ice." He'd drawn out the word so it sounded like two syllables. "Did you eat?"

She nodded. "Yes. Too much."

He swallowed a mouthful of rice. "I like your brothers."

"So do I. But if they had gotten you toasted there would've been hell to pay."

"I only had two shots. Langdon and Jared had at least four each."

"Knowing Lang and Jared, they'll probably stay over tonight, so there's no way you can go toe-to-toe with their hollow legs." She shifted again, attempting to find a more comfortable position. "I'm going to take a nap. Wake me if I sleep too long."

Levi enjoyed the warmth and the soft curves of the body curled alongside him. It had taken Herculean strength to temper his feelings around Angela, but remaining physically unaffected was becoming extremely difficult.

He wanted her—and he had wanted her almost as soon as they'd met. His attraction to her had been so immediate, so unexpected, that Levi had taken great pains to avoid touching her as much as he wanted to. He used every possible excuse to keep her at a distance—friendship, being old-fashioned and not having sex too soon. That excuse had been only half-true, since he'd had a few one-night stands, sexual encounters that he'd rather forget.

His real reluctance to get close to Angela had a lot to do with his friendship with Duncan. He'd always made it a practice not to become involved with women related to people he worked with. If the relationship soured, he might still run into them occasionally. For Levi a clean break always worked out better.

Angela had admitted that she needed him. But he didn't want her to just need him. He wanted her to *want* him. He wanted Angela to want him as much as he wanted her. He was even thinking about a long-distance relationship. Levi glanced at the woman whose body was pressed beside him and smiled. She looked serene, angelic. What Levi didn't want to admit was that his feelings for Angela Chase surpassed mere attraction. He was falling for her—*hard*.

Why her and not some of the other women in his past? There were some who were more beautiful, sophisticated, worldly, but they couldn't come close to this sexy Southern belle.

Angela sat on the cushioned wicker love seat with Levi in the enclosed terrace of her home, her bare feet resting on his thighs. Miss Divine had curled up next to Levi and promptly went to sleep. Crickets serenaded the night with nature's symphony of song. The sun had set and the only light came from a half moon and from the streetlamps along the paths and the windows in a house in the distance. She moaned slightly when he massaged her instep, then each toe.

Closing her eyes, she smiled. "That feels wonderful."

Levi's soft chuckle caressed her ear. "Foot rubs are free, but I charge for a full-body massage."

She moaned again as a shiver shot from her large toe and up her leg. "How much is a full-body massage?"

"You won't be able to afford it."

Angela opened her eyes, staring at his distinctive profile in the shadowy darkness. "Why not?"

"The price is to be determined."

"I'm not a pauper, Levi."

"I didn't say you were, but it still may be more than what you're willing to give up right now."

"Tell me what it is and I'll let you know."

There was a long pause, and only the sounds of crickets and

other insects broke the uncomfortable silence. "Come with me when I return to New York."

Angela froze. Nothing moved, not even her eyes as she stared at Levi. How could a man she'd known little more than a week ask her something so preposterous?

"And do what, Levi?"

"Live with me. Become my companion, my live-in girlfriend."

She pulled away from him and hugged her knees to her chest, struggling not to lose her temper. Angela had thought that Levi was different, but apparently she had made a mistake.

"A live-in girlfriend is nothing more than a kept woman." Levi chuckled again, incensing her. "You think that's funny, Levi?"

"You're a bundle of contradictions, Angela," he countered. "You say you want to be like your Aunt Nicola—who just happens to be a kept woman—yet when I present you with the same arrangement you act as if I'd offered to sell you as a sex slave. Which one is it? Do you want to be a free spirit, or do you want to live your own life and determine your own destiny?"

"My own destiny, of course."

Moving closer to her, Levi pressed her body to the cushions. "We begin tonight. No secrets or pretenses. We're going to live our lives on our own terms."

"And that means?"

"We're going to continue to date because I want to see you as much as I believe you want to see me. And it has nothing to do with showing up your ex. We're going to make love, Angela, but only when it's right for both of us. It will not be because we're horny. It will be because we want and need each other." He leaned closer, his mouth a hair's breadth from hers. "If there's anything I've left out then please let me know now before I make love to you because I want you, Angela Chase."

Angela was certain Levi could feel her heart beating. She'd tried to control her emotions whenever she was with Levi but had failed—completely. He epitomized her perfect hero and all she had to do was open her mouth and tell him what she wanted and he would grant her wish just like that.

"I, Angela Chase, would like you, Levi Eaton, to stop talking and take me inside and make love to me because I *want* you. And wanting you has nothing to do with how long I've been without a…" Levi's mouth covered hers, thwarting her words and taking her breath away.

He took possession of her mouth in the same way he'd taken care of her at her cousin's wedding reception—with quiet assurance. His kisses were tentative, tasting her mouth as if he were savoring it. Levi kissed the corners of her mouth, testing, teasing until her lips parted.

"You are so incredibly sweet," he crooned, his tongue parrying and dueling with hers. "I could devour you right here," Levi whispered against her moist lips.

Struggling to breathe, Angela anchored her arms under his shoulders, holding on as if he'd become her lifeline. "Do you have protection with you?"

"Yes."

Angela's smile was charming and demure. "Thank you." She kissed his chin. "Let's go inside."

Levi kissed Angela again, and released her. "Go on in. I'll lock up here."

She slipped off the love seat, opened the door and entered the house. Her heart pounded like a frightened bird. Her palms were damp, and Angela wondered if she could go through with what she'd wanted within minutes of Levi walking through her front door.

She'd lost count of the number of romance novels she'd read over the years, but instead of penning her own tale of love and passion, she was about to embark upon her own with a man who'd come into her life, spinning her around and around until she didn't know who she was or what she wanted.

Angela climbed the staircase like someone in a trance, putting one foot firmly in front of the other. Grabbing the banister, she trailed her fingertips along the polished mahogany, emitting an audible sigh when she reached the second-floor landing.

"I'm a woman about to do a grown woman's thing," she mused, remembering what her mother had said. She walked into her bedroom and made her way to the en-suite bath. Angela wasn't about to deceive herself and pretend she was in love with Levi, because she wasn't. She also didn't want to delude herself

and believe he was in love with her, because he wasn't. They were two consenting adults that wanted and needed each other. She undressed, twisted her hair into a knot and covered her head with a shower cap.

Angela brushed her teeth, slathered on a facial cleanser, then stood under the warm spray of the shower and lathered her body with a scented bath gel. Working quickly, she'd managed to shower and get into bed within ten minutes.

Levi turned off the lights on the first floor, with the exception of the lamp in the entryway. He climbed the staircase, Miss Divine following him silently.

Light spilled from under the doorjamb of the bedroom at the top of the stairs. He knew it was Angela's bedroom when the cat began scratching on the door.

Reaching over, he picked up the tiny feline and retraced his steps. Angela had warned him about Miss Divine wanting to come in, and Levi now had to agree with her.

It was as if he'd wanted Angela for all of his life and he wasn't about to share her with anyone or anything—not even a four-legged ball of fur. He left Miss Divine in the laundry room. She scratched the pillow in her bed, turned around several times, then settled down and tucked her nose against her side.

Levi found the second-floor bathroom. He opened and closed drawers in the storage cabinet until he found a supply of tooth-brushes. A wall of mirrors made the all-white bathroom appear larger than it actually was. The Edwardian-style console, deep-soaking, claw-foot tub and pedestal sink boasted polished brass antique fixtures that had been chosen with a meticulous eye.

Putting his clothes on a cushioned bench, Levi brushed his teeth, then stepped into the shower stall with an oversize shower-head. Jars of liquid soap, shampoo, conditioner and bars of face and bath soaps lined a shelf in a corner of the shower stall. Turning on the water and adjusting the temperature, he went through the motions of washing his hair and body. There was no need to rush. He and Angela had all night to become familiar with each other. He knew sharing a bed would change them and their rela-tionship—forever.

Draping a towel around his hips, Levi opened the door to

Angela's bedroom. The light from the bathroom streamed into the room. He put the towel on a hook on the bathroom door, closing the door partially leaving the bedroom in near-darkness.

"What took you so long, sweetie?"

Chapter 12

Smiling and shaking his head, Levi left a condom on the bedside table, and then slipped into bed. "I couldn't come to bed smelling like stale bourbon."

Turning over, she pressed her face to his shoulder. "You do smell nice."

He nuzzled her neck. "And you smell delicious."

She blushed. "Thank you."

Levi pulled her close. "Why does it feel as if I've known you all my life?" he asked.

Angela gave him a gentle smile. "I don't know. There's a line from the *Curious Case of Benjamin Button* that says, 'Life isn't measured in minutes, but in moments.'"

"How true, baby," Levy whispered. "Every moment I've spent with you has been wonderful."

"Life isn't measured in minutes, but in moments." Levi thought about those eight words. They were simple, yet somehow prophetic. Could he possibly be falling in love?

Angela closed her eyes. "What's happening with us, Levi?"

"What are you talking about, Angela?"

"Why do I feel like this is a one-night stand? I've never had a one-night stand. Have you?" The questions were running together, tumbling out of her mouth.

Levi released her, leaned over and turned on the lamp on his side of the bed. When he turned back, he saw indecision in Angela's eyes. "Baby, baby. Where is this all coming from?" His heart turned over when he saw her eyes fill with tears. "You tell me that you want me to make love to you, and I will, but only if and when you're ready. We can share this bed tonight without doing anything. The choice is yours."

Angela's eyelids fluttered wildly as she tried to blink back tears. Her bravado vanished the moment she felt the warmth of Levi when he got into bed.

She forced a smile. "Will the choice always be mine?"

"Yes. It will always be yours."

"Don't you want any responsibility in this relationship?"

"Sure. I'll make certain you don't get pregnant. I'll even write you a prescription for a contraceptive."

"You must think I'm silly, don't you?"

Burying his face in her hair, Levi pressed a kiss to her head. "No. I understand your ambivalence. If we'd met for the first time several months ago, or even a month ago, we wouldn't be having this conversation. I'm not going to hurt you, Angela. That's not my style."

"It's not my style to sleep with a guy I've only known for a week."

"Wasn't it you who said life isn't measured in minutes, but in moments? We've shared several wonderful moments this week. I'm not saying this to talk you out of your panties, but…"

Angela giggled. "I'm not wearing any panties."

His hand moved up her leg, lingering on her bare hip under the revealing nightgown. "You wear clothes all day, baby. But the same way you take your makeup off to let your face breathe, you should do the same for your body."

"I suppose I'm not that uninhibited."

Levi's fingers tightened on her buttock. "Hang out with me and you'll throw caution *and* inhibition to the wind."

"Is it because you're a doctor and the human body isn't a big deal to you?"

"That's where you're wrong. Do you really think if I see you naked it wouldn't affect me?"

There was only the sound of Angela's breathing. "I wouldn't know."

"Maybe this will help you to make up your mind." Reaching for her hand, Levi placed it over his growing erection.

A heat wave swept over Angela's body as white-hot desire

burned to her core. The sensation began in her head and flowed down her body like slow-moving lava, making her tremble from head to toe. Moving her hand away from his hardening flesh, she buried her face against Levi's shoulder and moaned.

Her breath was coming so quickly she felt lightheaded. After years of denying her body's urges, denying her femininity, and denying the strong passion within her, the time to end it was now. Angela moaned when Levi massaged the tight muscles at the nape of her neck.

"Relax, baby," he soothed. "Close your eyes."

She complied, laying her hands by her side. Breathing slowly, she managed to relax until Levi straddled her body and removed her nightgown. Angela giggled when his erection brushed her mound. "What are you doing?"

"I'm going to help you to relax," Levi whispered in her ear, "then I'm going to eat dessert."

Eat! Her eyes flew open. She stared up into a pair of dark eyes filled with amusement. "You mean eat *me?*"

Levi's expression did not change. "Yes."

Suddenly she felt like a virgin about to experience her first sexual encounter.

"Are you always so honest?" she asked.

He smiled. "Always. I'm just like you, Angie."

"You called me Angie. My Aunt Nikki is the only one who ever called me Angie."

Burying his face in the crook of her neck, Levi pressed a kiss behind her ear. His hand feathered up her inner thigh. "Relax, baby," he repeated when his fingers traced the curve of her hip.

A rising passion spread like a lighted fuse surging through her body. Her mind went numb when Levi's lips replaced his fingers, as his tongue probed and his teeth tasted and nipped the delicate flesh at the base of her throat. Angela's body arched off the mattress as she felt the warmth bathe her core. Waves of ecstasy throbbed through every inch of her body with a pleasure that was pure and explosive. Arching higher, she gasped in sweet agony when she felt all of her defenses weaken when Levi's tongue licked her breasts in a circular motion that made her areolas pebble and her nipples harden.

His hands were magical, touching and massaging erogenous zones she hadn't known existed—under her arms, her shoulders and the base of her spine. His stroke elicited the kind of ecstasy that made her feel as if she was coming out of her skin. She anchored her arms around his body under his shoulders, and held onto Levi, entwining her legs with his. "Please," she uttered with all the strength she could muster.

"Please what?" Levi whispered, burying his face in the fragrant strands of hair spread across the pillow.

She swallowed a moan as the pulsing grew stronger and stronger. "Please make love to me." Angela knew she was pleading, but what she wanted and needed overruled any shame and embarrassment.

Levi raised his head, his gaze bored into hers. "Are you sure, Angela?"

Her eyelids fluttered. "More sure than I've ever been of anything in my life."

He kissed her—a kiss more passionate and deeper than any they'd shared. His lips caressed hers until she opened her mouth. Their tongues dueled with one another, demanding a response. Levi called and she answered when she suckled his lower lip, and then the top. He responded by nibbling her lip. The tip of his tongue grazed the roof of her mouth and she let out a garbled scream.

Rolling over to the bedside table, Levi reached for a condom. He opened the packet and quickly rolled the latex sheath down his erection.

A demure smile and outstretched arms were his invitation when he turned back to look at the only woman who had occupied his thoughts. He didn't know what it was about her that made him go back on his promise not to get physically involved during his six-month assignment.

He sank into her embrace and deftly reversed their position with a minimum of effort. Cupping her hips, Levi stared at Angela. She gave him a tentative smile that made his heart squeeze. The hair framing her small face made her appear much younger than thirty-two.

"I'll try not to hurt you. If you want me to stop, then please tell me."

Angela closed her eyes for several seconds. "That's not going to happen."

He reversed their position again, and began a slow dance of desire. Flesh to flesh, heart to heart. They became one with each other. He was a master cartographer, exploring and mapping the dips and curves of her lush, compact body. It was his turn to gasp and lose his breath when Angela grasped his penis and fondled him until he felt as if he was going to explode.

"No, baby, no!" Taking her hand, Levi parted her legs with his knee and guided his sex into her tight warmth. It took only a few seconds, though it felt like more, for Levi to embed himself completely inside her.

Perfect. The single word summed up everything about the woman he clutched tightly to his body. They were a perfect fit. Levi had known many women, but none of them had affected him like Angela Chase.

Levi and Angela's bodies moved in harmony as she arched to meet his deep thrusts. The scent of their lovemaking became an aphrodisiac, enveloping them in an intimate cocoon from which neither wanted to escape.

Angela felt herself falling, faster and faster. Her descent was into a world of sensual pleasure she'd hadn't known. Just when she felt the fluttering that made her realize she was going to climax, Levi slowed his rhythm to bring her back from the precipice. His hands were just as busy as his mouth, touching, kissing and caressing.

Writhing beneath him, her entire body felt heavy, swollen. Then it happened. A wave of ecstasy washed over her, buffeting, shaking and tearing her asunder. Without warning, she started to soar higher and higher until she floated back down to earth.

The first orgasms came, holding her captive, then another— this one stronger and longer than the previous one. Levi's hands cupped her hips, lifting her off the bed when the third one hit her. He felt his body coming with her. His growl of release collided with her moans in a moment of uncontrolled passion.

Levi rolled over, bringing Angela with him. He wasn't ready

to withdraw from her because he enjoyed the way it felt when their bodies were joined. He trailed tender kisses along her forehead, the bridge of her nose and then her mouth, savoring the pulsing feel in his groin and the sense of completeness that rendered him speechless.

"Did I hurt you?" he asked, tucking the curve of her body into the hard contours of his. Angela mumbled incoherently. "Was that a yes or a no?"

"No, sweetie. You didn't hurt me."

"I want…"

"Please don't talk, Levi," she said.

Pushing hair off her damp forehead, he kissed her again and pulled out. Slipping off the bed, he walked to the bathroom to discard the condom. Angela was sound asleep, snoring lightly when he returned. He turned off the lamp, slipped into bed, pressing his groin to her buttocks. Minutes later he joined her in the sleep reserved for sated lovers.

Angela awoke to find herself alone in bed. The imprint of Levi's head on the pillow next to her was a reminder of what had happened. Smiling, she stretched her arms over her head. A slight tightness in her groin was a reminder of what she'd shared with her lover.

Lover. She found it easier to think of Levi as her lover rather than anything more. Lovers came and went, while partners were more committed to a relationship than she and Levi were. She slowly swung her legs over to the side of the bed, and gingerly walked out of the bedroom and into the bathroom.

She spied the handwritten note taped to the mirror: *Had to leave early. Scheduled to be at the hospital at six. Will call you later. Sweetie.*

Angela removed the sheet of paper, rolled it into a ball and dropped it in the wastebasket. Combing her fingers through her hair, she pulled it away from her face. If Levi didn't call her, she wouldn't hold it against him.

She completed her morning ablutions and went down to take care of Miss Divine. The cat sprang out of the laundry room as if she'd been shot out of a cannon. Angela knew her cat was upset because she'd been locked in overnight. "Sorry about that girl."

She went still when she heard tapping on the windows. It was raining. The forecast was for rain on Sunday, and it was expected to last for several days. She hoped it would end in time for the Friday running of the Kentucky Oaks.

During Derby week, Angela went into the shop early to help Traci with the increased customer traffic from the tourists who descended on Louisville. The city always took on a festive atmosphere that culminated with "The Run for the Roses." Some locals took offense when broadcasters described the atmosphere as being like New Orleans during Mardi Gras, since the festivities were much more dignified. Bourbon flowed like water and mint juleps were the cocktail of choice.

Angela took care of Miss Divine, and then prepared breakfast for herself before the cleaning service arrived.

Cloistered in her office Angela waited for the cleaning service to finish. Her usual routine was to get up early to write, but the sounds of the vacuum cleaner and the background noise of the cleaning staff was distracting. She booted up her PC and went online. There was an email from her editor.

Good morning, Angela,
I love, love, love your latest proposal. I've been looking for something special for years, but didn't know what it was until I read this. It's the perfect contemporary romance novel. Let me know how soon you can submit the manuscript. Hope to schedule it for early next spring. I'll let your agent know.
Instead of sending it electronically, I want you to bring it to New York. The publisher will cover all expenses.
Best,
MJ

Angela stifled a scream. Miriam Jabin was a prickly old-school editor who eschewed telephone calls and face-to-face meetings and months ago had decided to communicate with her authors through email. Although Miriam had given up her pack-a-day cigarette habit, she still enjoyed her two-martini lunch.

Angela tried to slow her beating heart and compose her thoughts. A minute later she sent an email to Miriam giving her a projected submission date. She was going to New York! If she timed it right, perhaps she would be able to attend the World Series with Levi.

The telephone rang, and Angela picked it up on the first ring. "Hello."

"Good morning, love. How are you feeling?"

Angela's smile was dazzling. Levi had promised to call her back and he had. "I'm wonderful. How are you?"

"Horny," he whispered. "I'm sorry I couldn't stay for sec-onds."

Heat stung Angela's cheeks when she recalled what they'd shared. "Levi."

"What is it, baby?"

"I want to apologize for acting…"

"Don't you dare say it, Angela. The first time is always a little awkward. It will be different the next time."

"How different?"

He chuckled. "It will be even better. I spent the morning fill-ing out papers, being fingerprinted and photographed. I also have my schedule for the week. I'll be working twelve-hour shifts for the next four days. I'm off Friday, Saturday and Sunday. I'd like you to spend the weekend with me."

Her eyebrows lifted. "I'd love to spend the weekend with you."

"Do you think you can stay out of trouble until Friday?"

"I'll try, sweetie," she crooned, her smile growing wider and wider.

"I'd love to talk longer, but I have a meeting with the chief of staff. I'll call you tonight."

"Call me when you can, Levi. I'm not going anywhere."

"I won't let you go anywhere," Levi said.

Angela didn't have a comeback, and she didn't want to read more into his words because perhaps she didn't dare wish for her own happy ending.

"Goodbye, Levi."

"Goodbye, love."

Angela stared at the phone long after she'd hung up. As Angelina Courtland the word love spoke volumes. But as Angela Chase she knew it was an endearment used loosely: I love your hair. I love that dress. I'd love to see a movie.

Levi was real, while her characters were made up—figments of her imagination.

"Who or what has you glowing?" Traci asked when Angela walked into the Garden Gate Tuesday morning.

Angela executed a pirouette in a pair of black leather ballet flats. "My editor loves my latest proposal." She took her smock off the wall hook, putting it over her white blouse and cropped black slacks. "She wants me to come to New York."

"When are you going?" Traci asked, excitedly.

Picking up a plastic spray bottle filled with water, Angela spritzed the hanging plants. "As soon as I complete the manuscript."

"When do you think you'll finish?"

"Hopefully, before the end of the summer. I gave Miriam a September deadline, but I'm going to try for the end of August."

"What about Levi?"

Turning slowly, Angela stared at her cousin. She didn't know how Traci did it, but she always managed to look gorgeous whether in jeans or haute couture. She'd added an additional four inches to her impressive height with a pair of strappy booties. Although stunning, she was much too thin, thinner than she'd been when she'd worked as a runway model.

"What about him, Traci?"

"Aren't you going to make time for him?"

She went back to misting the plant leaves. Angela told Traci that Levi had agreed to assume the job as acting head of pediatrics at Clarke General for the next two months.

"Won't he have days off?"

"Yes, but he'll always be on call."

Traci waved her hand dismissively. "I'm certain he'll find time for you."

Angela wasn't ready to tell her cousin that they already *had* made time for each other. If he didn't spend nights with her, then she would stay over with him. "We'll work something out."

Traci picked up a set of coasters, gently wiping them with the duster. "Reggie and I had a heart-to-heart talk last night about reconciling—permanently.

Momentarily speechless, Angela put down the bottle and walked over to her cousin. It had only been a few months that Traci and Reggie had been dating again. Angela put the duster down on a table, and then grasped Traci's hands. Her fingers were ice cold.

"Talk to me, cuz."

Traci closed her eyes. "I'm pregnant."

Angela felt her heart lurch. "Are you sure?"

Traci chewed her lip. "Yes. I went to a doctor yesterday and he confirmed it."

"What are you going to do?"

"I'm going to have it, of course!"

"I'm not implying that you get an abortion, Traci. I should've said what are you and Reggie going to do?"

"We're going to get married—again. This time I know it's going to work."

A slow smile spread its way across Angela's face before it became a full-on grin. "Hot damn! I'm going to be an auntie."

"Technically, the baby will be your second cousin."

"Why are you messing with me, Traci? You know my brothers will never make me an aunt. So as my cousin slash sister, your baby will be my niece or nephew." They jumped up and down like they used to as children. "When and where are you getting married?"

"Next Sunday afternoon. The pastor at Reggie's church will officiate. I want you to stand in as my witness, and if Levi's off, then he can be Reggie's witness. You're the only one in the family who knows about the baby."

"Why doesn't Reggie ask his brother?"

"Because the man has diarrhea of the mouth. And if my mother caught wind of this she would want something akin to the royal wedding. I'm thirty years old, pregnant and because this will be my third marriage I'd have a complete breakdown."

Angela stared at Traci, completely baffled. "You're eloping, right?" The question was more of a statement.

"Yes."

She hoped her cousin was ready for the fallout when the word got out that she'd run off and married without telling the family. If Traci's mother had taken to her bed the first time her daughter had married Reggie she shuddered to think what her reaction would be when she found out Traci and Reggie had remarried and were expecting a child.

"I'm honored to be your witness, but Reggie will have to ask Levi about standing up for him."

Traci hugged Angela. "You're the best."

A grandfather clock in a corner chimed the hour. It was nine o'clock. Angela unlocked and opened the wrought-iron gate, then unlocked the outer door. The Garden Gate was open for business.

Chapter 13

Levi glanced around the table, meeting the gazes of two residents and three interns. The routine of making rounds had changed since he'd worked at a hospital. Usually patients were present when doctors made their rounds and would answer questions. But the current practice of making grand rounds involved reviewing patient cases, care and progress without the patient being there.

"Thank you doctors for being on time." A chorus of acknowledgments followed his statement. "Today will be a little like speed dating, because I have a meeting with the chief of staff at eleven." Levi opened a folder with updates from the pediatric patients' files. He'd set up a system whereby the department secretary made available daily updates of each file for himself and his staff.

"We'll begin with William Crenshaw." Levi saw movement out the corner of his eye. "Dr. Wagner, am I keeping you awake?" he asked when he noticed the woman nodding. When a medical student sitting next to the resident touched her shoulder she slumped over the table. Another resident sprang into action, easing Dr. Wagner to the floor.

Levi took over, searching for a pulse, then a heartbeat. Her pulse was faint, heartbeat barely audible. "Call the ER and tell them we're bringing her in!" He pinched the skin on the back of the tiny hand with visible pale blue veins. Dr. Gemma Wagner was severely dehydrated.

Lifting the petite woman as easily as he would a small child, Levi raced out of the small conference room and down the hall to the emergency room. Several nurses in the ER stood ready to treat one of their own doctors. He placed her on a gurney, then stepped back, watching as a nurse worked quickly to hook up an IV. The nurse gasped after she'd removed Dr. Wagner's white coat and pushed up the long sleeve of her tee. She pushed up the other one, and her jaw dropped in disbelief.

The nurse's eyes met Levi's. "Dr. Eaton, I can't."

He knew if they didn't get fluids into her she was going to die. "Pulling on a pair of latex gloves, he tapped the back of the drug-addicted doctor's hand with two fingers until he managed to find a vein. He inserted the needle, taping it in place, while the nurse placed an oxygen mask over Dr. Wagner's nose. The machines monitoring her vitals beeped loudly over the eerie quiet.

The attending ER doctor raced over. "What do you have?"

Levi pointed to the tracks dotting the inside of the young woman's arm. "She probably shot up just before rounds."

Dr. Morse shook his head. "What a waste. I can't understand why she'd want to ruin her career this way."

"Perhaps you're being a little premature, Dr. Morse. That's something the hospital board will have to address."

The bearded, ponytailed doctor who was a throwback to the '70s gave him an incredulous stare. "You're going to go to bat for her?"

Levi's impassive expression did not change. "Why wouldn't I support a member of my staff? I'm counting on you to take care of her."

Morse nodded. "She's one of us, so I'll make certain she gets the best possible care. We'll put her in the rehab unit and monitor her withdrawal."

Levi smiled for the first time. "Thank you. I'll stop by and see her later." Taking off the gloves, he dropped them in a receptacle. He'd temporarily lost what personnel records indicated was one of the most promising doctors in the pediatric unit. Her patients loved Dr. Wagner and she loved them. Levi knew it would be an uphill battle and it would take a minor miracle to convince the hospital's chief of staff not to fire the resident on the spot.

Levi returned to the conference room and was met with a barrage of questions from the other doctors. He reassured them that their colleague had been stabilized and that the prognosis for her recovery was good. Grand rounds continued, but Levi was distracted. He couldn't stop thinking about Dr. Wagner.

Levi stared at the pattern on the carpet in the waiting area outside Dr. Neil McGill's office. His secretary had asked him to wait because her boss was on a long-distance call.

"You can go in now, Dr. Eaton."

He smiled at the elderly woman. "Thank you, Mrs. Graham."

Neil McGill stood up when Levi entered the impressively decorated office. "Levi, I'm sorry to have kept you waiting." He motioned to a chair at a small round table. "Please sit down."

The office had a leather sofa and two oversize chairs and framed Impressionist reproductions. The lead crystal vase filled with flowers and Waterford paperweights were testament to the doctor's stature in the highly regarded facility. Seeing the crystal reminded Levi of the exquisite pieces in the Garden Gate.

Levi sat, his gaze fixed on a signed photograph of McGill with a former vice president. Levi crossed his leg as his gaze scanned the room settling on a reproduction of Georges Seurat's *A Sunday Afternoon on the Island of La Grande Jatte.*

"I heard about one of your doctors," Neil McGill said, capturing Levi's attention. His sharp penetrating gray eyes narrowed. "We've had doctors overdose before, but never while on duty in the hospital. We're not going to be able to sweep this under the rug, so I'd like to know how you would handle this."

Levi schooled his face not to reveal his annoyance. He'd been able to avoid this kind of political hot potato while working at the Maywood Junction clinic and in his New York practice. Neil McGill was no doubt trying to *pass the buck* and make Dr. Wagner's overdose someone else's problem.

Levi chose his words carefully. "If I give you my opinion will you consider it a final decision in the incident report?"

McGill ran a hand over his bright yellow silk tie. It was the hospital chief's turn to mask his feelings. Bringing Levi Eaton onboard to head the hospital's pediatric department had been a stroke of luck.

"I will definitely think about it."

"Think or consider?" Levi asked.

What he didn't intend to do was throw the young resident's career out the window because she was sick. Gemma Wagner had spent countless hours studying and sacrificing to become a doctor, and Levi intended to give her the opportunity to get clean and put her life back on track.

McGill knew when he'd been bested. Perhaps if he gave Dr. Eaton what he wanted, then Levi would give him what he needed. "Okay. I'll consider it."

Levi leaned forward, facing Dr. McGill eye to eye. "Suspend her for six months, with the mandate she voluntarily sign herself into a drug rehab facility. If she's able to remain clean, then bring her back provisionally as a resident. She also must agree to random drug testing. If she objects or comes up dirty, then she's fired."

Leaning back in the executive chair, the chief closed his eyes. Seconds ticked by before he opened them. "What you suggest is doable. But first I have to find out if she's been stealing drugs from the hospital. And if she has, then there's nothing I can do to protect her, because as head of the hospital I'm obligated to report it to the police."

Levi nodded. "Okay. I can live with that. What was your other reason for asking to meet with me?"

McGill narrowed his eyes. "You may not sound like a New Yorker, but you sure act like one."

"And that is?"

"Brash."

Levi's eyebrows lifted a fraction. "Should I take that as a compliment?"

The older man smiled. "Coming from me, yes, it is. It's exactly what I need from someone heading a department."

"Remember, I'm *acting* head of pediatrics."

"You don't have to be acting, Levi."

"What are you saying, Dr. McGill?" Levi asked, addressing his boss by his title for the first time.

"I spoke to John Pearson the other day and he's talking about not coming back once his leg heals. He claims it's a sign that he needs to slow down, do some traveling *and* enjoy his grandchildren."

Levi was momentarily speechless, unable to respond to Dr. McGill's offer to make him head of Clarke General Hospital's department of pediatrics. It was unheard of that someone his age would head a department—even at a small rural county hospital.

How many thirty-six-year-old doctors do you know who become head of a department? Duncan's query floated in his head. Even Angela had asked whether he would be willing to relocate to Kentucky, and his answer had been yes, but only if there was something worthwhile. He hadn't known at the time that she was also part of that equation.

Taking over as head of pediatrics was a huge offer, but there was still the issue of his investment and involvement in his New York practice. "I'm honored that you would even consider me for the position, but I can't give you an answer right now."

"When do you think you can let me know?" McGill asked.

"It will have to be after I talk to my partners in New York."

"When do you think that'll be?"

Levi had to give it to Neil McGill. He was definitely pushy. "Wouldn't I have to be approved by the hospital board?"

McGill waved his hand. "Don't worry about the board. They'll accept whoever I put forward. Consider it a done deal."

Levi couldn't help smiling. "That smacks of cronyism."

"It's nôt what you know, but who you know, son. That is something my daddy told me and his daddy told him." He tapped his forehead. "That's something you should always keep in mind when it comes to getting whatever it is you want."

"I'll be sure to remember that."

There wasn't much for Levi to think about. He'd had only one immediate goal: becoming a doctor. Long-term, he'd wanted to purchase property, get married and become a father. He'd accomplished two out of three.

He and McGill talked about the upcoming Derby. The older man admitted that he owned a stake in one of the horses in the race and invited Levi to share his box at Churchill Downs.

"Thanks for the offer, but Judge Chase has invited me to sit with him."

"He's a good family man and a very fair judge. That's a rare combination nowadays. I've been trying for years to get Duncan to come and work for Clarke General, but he won't leave his clinic. "

Levi got up to leave before Neil McGill decided to go through the Chase family tree. "The folks who live in Maywood Junction really need his services, and right now I have to see a patient who's scheduled to be discharged at eleven." Leaning over the desk, he held out his hand. "I'll think about your offer."

McGill shook his hand. "I'll wait to render my decision on Dr. Wagner until I'm able to talk to her."

"Thank you."

Levi left the office, nodding to the secretary on his way out. He'd told McGill he would think about his offer for a permanent position with CG. But what he didn't want to think about was how it would affect his relationship with Angela. What they'd shared was much too new to contemplate a future, and he wondered how long they could remain friends with benefits before he wanted more. He hadn't allowed himself to become too involved with any woman, since he knew he was only staying for six months.

Now, he was into the third month, and he *was* involved with a woman, and he'd just received an offer that was certain to change his life forever.

Levi knew Angela's "love me, love me not" feelings stemmed from her very public humiliation as a jilted bride. And despite dating other men she hadn't slept with any of them, something he realized the moment he penetrated her body. Levi had slept with enough women to know if they were sexually active or not.

Levi had felt an enormous amount of pride that Angela had found him worthy to make love to when she'd been unable to give herself to any man since Robert Gaskin.

Not only was he faced with the decision whether to accept the position as head of pediatrics, but also trying to convince Angela that it was possible for them to take their relationship beyond what it was.

Being realistic, Levi knew he wasn't in love with Angela, and that his attraction to her came from wanting to protect her. Eaton men were raised to love and protect their women and Angela Chase needed protecting. On the surface she seemed to be a successful secure woman in control of herself and her life. But she'd shown him another side of her personality that was plagued by fear and mistrust. He was fully aware that he couldn't undo the past, yet that wouldn't stop him from trying.

Squatting down in front of the young boy in the wheelchair, Levi shook his hand. He winked at the nurse waiting to wheel the child out to the parking lot. His mother had brought him to the ER after he'd complained of a bellyache. Tests had confirmed a ruptured appendix. He underwent emergency surgery and two days later was ready to go home. "I want you to listen to what your Mama says," he said in his best Donald Duck voice. "No wrestling with your brother until your incision is completely healed."

The seven-year-old laughed uncontrollably. "You sound funny."

"You sound funny," Levi quacked again.

"You sound like Donald Duck."

"I'm not Donald Duck. I'm Daffy Duck."

The boy sobered. "I watch the cartoon channel and Daffy Duck spits when he talks."

Levi pressed his mouth to the boy's ear. "It wouldn't be very nice if I spit, would it?"

"No," he whispered. "Do Scooby Doo."

Levi went through a series of characters that included Mickey Mouse and Bugs Bunny. A small crowd had gathered to watch him interact with the boy who squealed in delight. Levi stood when the child's mother approached. Her son had inherited his mother's rust-colored hair and freckles.

She extended her hand. "Thank you, Dr. Eaton. Teddy was deathly afraid of doctors, so I guess that's why I waited so long to bring him in. Thanks to you he's changed his mind."

Levi took her hand, patting it in a comforting gesture. "A child's first introduction to a pediatrician usually involves a needle and pain, so it stands to reason that they would be afraid. I'm glad we've been able to allay his fears about doctors."

She planted a kiss on his cheek. "Thank you again."

He managed a tight smile. "You're welcome. Goodbye, Teddy."

"Goodbye, Dr. Eaton," the boy called out as he was wheeled out of the hospital.

Levi heard laughter and giggling, and when he turned he saw a trio of doctors grinning at him. "Careful, Eaton," warned an orthopedist, "or you'll find yourself changing your specialty from pediatrics to gynecology."

He frowned, deciding not to respond to the quip. If bedside manner had been a course, he would've received an A-plus. Putting a patient at ease was as important to him as treating the cause of the disease.

Walking toward the elevator, he stepped in and punched the button for the fourth floor. The door closed and the car rose smoothly, stopping at his designated floor. Levi nodded to a uniformed officer sitting outside the room of a prisoner who'd been brought in the night before for attempting to rob a gas station. Unfortunately the career criminal hadn't anticipated the owner pulling his own gun and had sustained a gunshot wound that would've ended his life if the bullet hadn't been a few centimeters from his heart.

"How's it going?" Levi asked, nodding to the officer.

The officer smiled. "It beats directing traffic."

Levi chuckled. "I hear you." He walked to the end of the hallway and pushed open the door to Gemma's room. The nurse sitting in the corner jumped up when he entered.

He motioned for her to step outside the room. "Is she lucid?"

"She's in and out."

"Do you mind standing out here while I go in and talk to her?"

The nurse flushed a bright red. "Of course not, Dr. Eaton." She wasn't used to doctors asking her permission but instead barking orders.

Levi returned to the room and stood at the bedside, staring at Gemma and wondering why he hadn't noticed her gaunt appearance before. He traced the back of her hand with the IV. "Gemma." Her eyes opened, staring blankly up at him. Levi smiled. "How are you feeling?"

Her eyelids fluttered before she closed her eyes again. "I'm okay. They gave me something so I wouldn't…wouldn't feel the full effect of detox."

Leaning over, he rested a hand on her shoulder. "I'm going to do what I can to keep you from being fired, but you're going to have to do something for me."

A crooked smile twisted her pale mouth. "You want me to go to rehab." Her inky-black hair and eyes made her face appear translucent.

His fingers tightened on her delicate body. "You know the drill, Gemma. One slip up and you'll never be able to practice medicine in this state again. Now, I want you to be honest with me."

Gemma exhaled an audible breath. "What do you want to know?"

"Did your drugs come from CG?"

"No."

"I hope you're not lying to me, Dr. Wagner."

She stared directly at him. "I'm not lying. I swear to you I'm not lying," she repeated when Levi gave her a questioning look. "My boyfriend gets them for me."

"Where does he get them?"

"From some guy who lives in Russell."

Levi knew enough about Russell to know it was west of downtown Louisville. "You're going to have to cut your boyfriend loose if you want to get clean, Gemma."

"I know."

"No, you don't know. Because the minute you go back to him you'll be using again."

"I can't leave him."

"Why not?"

Levi listened, stunned when the resident told her that he had paid for her to attend medical school. He had turned her on to heroin to control her.

Levi knew he was fighting a losing battle, because Gemma wasn't willing to leave her dealer.

He withdrew his hand. "I'm sorry, Gemma. I'm not going to risk the lives of the patients in this hospital by allowing them to be treated by a junkie. I'll let Dr. McGill know that I'll file the necessary paperwork to release you from your residency obligation at the hospital. I wish you luck whenever you decide to get clean."

Levi walked out of the room, feeling as if the world was on his shoulders. He'd hoped to help her, but it was obvious she wasn't willing to help herself.

He returned to his office and sat down staring into space when his cell phone rang. Plucking it off his belt, he looked at the display with Reginald Goddard's name. "What's up, Reggie?"

Levi listened, stunned when Reggie asked if he would stand in as a witness along with Angela when he and Traci tied the knot for a second time Sunday afternoon.

"We're doing this on the down-low, so I'd appreciate it if you wouldn't mention it to anyone."

"Like doctor-patient confidentiality."

"Just like that, brother."

"You've got my word. I won't say anything."

This would be the second wedding he would attend with Angela. It appeared as if her cousins were getting married even if she wasn't inclined to. Levi couldn't understand why she loved reading romance novels yet she'd set up roadblocks to her own happily ever after. Levi knew he wasn't perfect and never had professed to be. However, he was confident he would be a good husband and father. After all, he had a good teacher in his father, Solomon Eaton.

Chapter 14

"Good grief, baby! How many outfits are you bringing?"

Angela stared at the clothes spread out on her bed. "I haven't decided what I want to wear to the race and that will still be appropriate for Priscilla Turner's post-Derby party. And don't forget we're witnesses for Traci and Reggie's wedding. I have to wear something nice, because I plan to take them out afterward."

Levi crossed his arms over his chest. "Do you go through this every time you attend a social event?"

She refused to look at Levi. "Yes."

Turning on his heels, he headed for the door, stopping to pick up a hatbox and a large tote. "I'll wait for you downstairs."

Angela knew Levi was in a funk. He'd called to say he would pick her up at seven. But by seven, she still hadn't decided what she wanted to pack for the weekend celebrations. Biting her lip, she reached for a garment bag and filled it with three dresses and a conservative suit and zipped it. Anchoring the strap of the garment bag over her shoulder, she flicked off the wall switch as she left the bedroom.

Levi met her halfway down the staircase, taking the bag from her. "I put Miss Divine in the car."

When Angela had mentioned boarding the cat for the weekend Levi had overruled her when he said to bring her along. She wasn't certain how her pet would adjust to a new environment, so she'd decided to bring the crate instead of the pet carrier.

She locked up the house and got into the car, turning around to look at the cat pacing back and forth in the crate. "Settle down, Miss Dee. We're not going to the vet."

Levi slipped in behind the wheel. "You're going to Daddy's

house for the next few days. And you can have the run of the place. That means you can jump up on the chairs."

Angela buckled her seatbelt. "I said it before and I'll say it again. When you have a kid it'll be a wild child."

"No she won't. You can't stifle a child's spirit or creativity, Angie."

"Don't you believe in boundaries? Children who grow up without boundaries have problems."

He started the car, shifting into gear. "Of course I believe in setting limits. I'll raise my children the way I was raised and I don't think of myself as a wild child." Miss Divine let out a plaintive meow. "Now see what you did. She thought you called her wild."

"I thought you were Dr. Eaton, not Dr. Doolittle."

"I bet you didn't know I can talk to animals."

"Yeah, right."

Leaving Magnolia Pines, Levi pushed the gas to accelerate the car, eating up the road. "I can, Angie. I know when they're frightened or when they want something."

A hint of a smile tilted the corners of Angela's mouth. "Don't tell me my man is something of an animal whisperer."

Levi gave her a quick glance. "I'm your man?"

She flashed a sexy moue. *"Sho 'nuff."*

"I like being your man."

Angela sobered. "Am I really your woman, Levi?"

"What would I have to do to prove to you that you are? Propose marriage?"

"No… I mean you don't have to propose. I'll take your word for it."

Resting his right arm over the back of her headrest, Levi touched the soft curls falling around her face. "You're going to have to learn to trust me, Angie, because what you see is what you get."

"I like what I see," she said in a quiet voice.

"Do you trust what you see?" Levi countered.

She stared out the side window at the passing landscape, replaying Levi's query in her head. He'd asked about trust when it had become an everyday struggle for her to learn to trust again.

Angela trusted her parents, her brothers, Traci, her aunt and close relatives, but everyone else was suspect.

She'd wanted to trust Levi because they'd slept together. If he'd asked her if she'd trusted the men she'd dated the answer would've been an easy one. No.

"I'm trying, Levi."

Angela hadn't lied to Levi. It was easier for her to offer him her body than her heart. And she'd learned the hard way that trust in a relationship was more important than love. People fell in and out of love every second of the day. But trust had to be earned.

Lowering his arm, he rubbed her knee. "Okay, baby. I know it must be hard for you to trust any man after what you've gone through, but not all of us are SOBs."

"I know that. Just one man in particular."

"You're giving him too much energy, Angela. He's your past."

"You're right, Levi." She mimed zipping her mouth. "His name will never pass my lips again."

"Good for you. Have you decided which horse you're going to bet on?"

"Yes. What about you, Levi?"

He turned off onto the road leading to his townhouse. "I'm going with Sweet Southern Knight."

His choice shocked Angela. "The odds on him are thirty-to-one."

"That's why I like him. I usually go for the longshot."

"I'm a little more scientific," she admitted.

"How's that?"

"I put all the names of the horses in a hat, shake them up, and pick one. I do the same with the jockeys. I repeat the process until I'm able to match the jockey with a horse, and that's who I bet on."

Levi laughed until his ribs hurt. "I don't believe you."

"You don't have to, Levi. I've managed to pick two winners in eight years, so I'm not doing too badly. There was a time when I'd bet on the Oaks, but two races in two days has lost its appeal."

"What is the difference between the Oaks and the Derby other than one is run on Friday and the other on Saturday?"

"The Oaks is for three-year-old fillies. That's why it's called

"Lilies for the Fillies." The length of the Derby race is one and a quarter miles. But the Oaks is one and an eighth. The purse for the Oaks is one million and the first-place winner gets six hundred thousand. A silver Kentucky Oaks trophy is presented to the winner along with a large garland of lilies."

"How do you know so much about horseracing?"

"My paternal grandfather loved horseracing. He used to take me to the stables to watch the farmhands groom and exercise the thoroughbreds. He was such a racehorse enthusiast that he would follow the races. If it wasn't Saratoga Springs, then it would be the Preakness at Pimlico or the Belmont in New York. It drove my grandma crazy because she'd believed he was gambling. And for her, gambling was an unforgivable sin. I never knew him to bet on a horse. It was just that he was fascinated by them."

With all the talk about horses and races, they barely noticed how quickly they'd reached Levi's apartment. Levi drove up to the gatehouse, and drove through once the barrier automatically lifted. The shadows cast from the setting sun off the rooftops of the chalet-style townhouses reminded Angela of postcards of Alpine resorts. The only thing missing were snow-covered mountain peaks.

"These look new," she remarked.

Levi pulled into his reserved parking space and shut off the engine. "They are. They were built to accommodate additional staff once the hospital expanded. I'll bring the cat and the bags up," he said, exiting the car.

He helped Angela out, holding on to her hand as he unlocked the door leading to his apartment. "I get to live in the penthouse apartment." They walked up the staircase and he unlocked another door.

Angela stepped into a living-dining room with gleaming wood floors. She slipped out of her shoes, leaving them on the thick straw mat outside the front door. Turning, she smiled up at Levi watching her. "May I have a look around?"

Dipping his head, he kissed the end of her nose. "Of course. *Mi casa es su casa,*" he said.

Angela wondered if he meant that his house was her house literally as she walked past a galley kitchen with granite countertops, white cabinetry and stainless-steel appliances. She opened a door opposite the kitchen to find a stackable washer-dryer unit. There were two bedrooms, one with a full bath and the other with a shower stall. Both bathrooms were accessible from the bedrooms.

There was something about the furniture that reminded her of a dormitory. It wasn't fancy, but it was functional. It took several minutes before she realized what was missing: a woman's touch. It needed framed prints, plants, colorful throws, pillows and area rugs.

She peered through the half-open blinds in the larger of the two bedrooms. Sliding doors led out to a balcony that overlooked a parking lot. Light shone through the windows of the hospital that was a short distance away.

Sterile. That's the word that best described the space where Levi lived when he wasn't at the hospital. When Duncan bought a house outside Maywood Junction he'd asked her to help him decorate it. Her brother had given her his credit card and told her to buy whatever she thought he needed to make his house a home. He had no patience for or interest in going from store to store to purchase beds, sofas, tables, chairs and accessories that gave a house its personality.

"I'm going to put Miss Divine in the smaller bedroom."

Angela turned to find that Levi had come into the room without making a sound. Her garment bag was slung over his shoulder as he cradled the crate to his chest. "Okay. Is there anything you want me to do?"

"No. Just relax. As soon as I bring your other bags up I'll start dinner."

She smiled. "What's on the menu?"

"We're having Italian tonight—chicken Francese, linguine with garlic and oil and a green salad."

"It sounds scrumptious. Do you need me to help?"

He shook his head. "No, baby. I've prepared everything. It just has to be cooked."

"Can I at least set the table?"

Levi gave her a look parents usually reserved for their children when they were at their wit's end. "Don't you know how to sit down and relax?"

"Of course, but I'm not used to sitting around doing nothing."

"You sit around doing nothing when you watch your movies."

Closing the distance between them, Angela slipped the garment bag off his shoulder. "I jot down notes whenever I watch a movie."

This week she'd altered her writing schedule to increase the number of hours she worked at the Garden Gate to accommodate the tourists who were in town for the Derby. Instead of using her desktop, she'd brought in her laptop in to the shop, and whenever there was a lull she went into the small office at the rear of the shop to write.

"I'm going to hang my clothes up in the other bedroom," she said to Levi.

It took Angela less than fifteen minutes to unpack the garment bag and her tote and leave her toiletries in the en-suite bath in the smaller bathroom.

Miss Divine refused to leave her crate even when Angela tried coaxing her out with a treat. "Whatever," she drawled, closing and latching the door. Dimming the recessed lights, she went into the bathroom to wash her hands and when she emerged she saw that her cat had curled her body into a tiny ball.

Angela walked into the kitchen, stopping when she saw Levi standing at the stove in a pair of jeans, a white tee and leather flip-flops. She extended her right hand. "Here's a little housewarming gift."

Drying his hands on a towel, Levi took the gaily wrapped box. "You didn't have to do this. After all, I'm only going to be here a couple of months."

Resting her hip against the countertop, she studied his lean face. "It doesn't matter, Levi. It's still your home even if it's only temporary."

He untied the bow and peeled away the gift-wrap paper. His eyebrows lifted when he took out a quartet of crystal candleholders for votive candles.

Levi stared at Angela as if seeing her for the first time. She was the first woman who'd given him a gift. Usually he was the one to do the gift giving. He took a step, pulling her gently against his chest. "Thank you. They're beautiful. Whenever I look at them I'll think of you."

Closing her eyes, Angela wanted to tell Levi that she would never forget him, even if she lived to be an old spinster with half a dozen cats. By that time, she would be too old to care about them leaving pet hair everywhere.

"You're not going to be that easy to forget, either," she whispered against his shoulder.

Cradling her face, Levi made love to her with his eyes. "Come on, baby. Let's not get all weepy. Isn't that what happens in your romance novels?"

She nodded. "Sometimes."

"I'm not leaving now. So let's enjoy the time we have together."

Angela nodded again as she struggled to keep her emotions in check. She didn't want to acknowledge that her feelings for Levi had gone beyond merely liking him. Every time they were together, her feelings for him deepened and she couldn't help imagining herself falling in love with him. Yet she was well aware of the consequences of falling in love with Levi.

After he'd told her he lived in the suburbs of New York, she'd gone online to search for Mamaroneck. She read that it was a bedroom community for commuters who worked in Manhattan. Easy access to the city meant nights on the town with his friends and hot dates with women, who were probably lined up at his door. In other words, it was a hop, skip and jump from one of the most exciting and romantic cities in the world.

And it was obvious Levi did not have a problem attracting the opposite sex. He was a trifecta—looks, brains and money.

Angela had given herself a pep talk. She wasn't going to fall in love with Levi Eaton and she wasn't going to fall apart when he left Louisville. And, he was going to leave, but this time she wouldn't be blindsided.

Anchoring her arms under his shoulders, she hugged him tightly. "I promise not to get weepy if you promise to show me a good time."

A chuckle rumbled in his chest. "I can't carry a tune worth a damn, but I'm going to try and sing, "Time of my Life.""

Angela patted his shoulder blades. "Don't worry. I'll sing it for both of us." She pulled back from his embrace. "Where do you keep the dishes?"

Levi pointed to a cabinet. "You'll find what you need in there. You can take out two wineglasses. They aren't as nice as yours, but they'll do."

He didn't know what made him bring up leaving Kentucky since it was a subject he didn't want to think about. His relationship with Angela was so effortless that there were times he thought he was imagining it.

There were no demands from her wanting to see him, and she didn't blow up his phone like some women he'd been involved with. The only time she called him was when he left a voice-mail message.

Her initial reservations before they made love had been put aside. When he'd asked her to spend the Derby weekend with him she'd willingly accepted. She, more than any other woman he'd met, complemented him and his lifestyle.

Levi turned on a radio on the countertop, tuning it to a station that featured pop and old-school jams. He and Angela moved around the kitchen like a couple who'd choreographed their dance moves. She set the table in the dining area and lit the candles. He dredged the seasoned chicken cutlets in flour and an egg mixture to create a light batter, and sautéed them until they were thoroughly cooked. Then he transferred them to a warm platter.

He tested the linguine, and drained off the water to serve it *al dente.* The fragrant aroma of sautéed garlic and fresh herbs in olive oil filled the kitchen.

Angela rested her elbows on the waist-high counter separating the kitchen from the dining area, watching Levi as he prepared the food for their dinner. He stepped away from the stove, and opened the refrigerator to take out a clear bowl filled with salad greens, a cruet of vinaigrette, and a chilled bottle of Pinot Blanc.

Levi plated the chicken with a savory lemon-and-wine-infused chicken stock topped with chopped flat-leaf parsley, and placed the linguine in garlic and oil in a large pasta bowl. He put the dishes on the dining room table, and pulled out a chair for Angela to be seated.

"Dinner is served."

Her gaze swept over the table. "I can't believe you cooked everything in less than a half hour."

He turned off the lights in the kitchen, dimmed those in the living room and then sat down opposite her. "It would've taken much longer if I hadn't prepared everything beforehand." Uncorking the bottle wine, Levi filled both glasses. He held his glass aloft. "To my beautiful Southern belle."

Angela lowered her eyes as a demure smile softened her lips. "Thank you." She raised her glass to make her own toast. "To the perfect hero for any romance novel—on and off the page."

Levi took a sip of wine, his eyes crinkling in a smile. "I'm going to have to read one of your dirty little novels to find out just what the attraction is."

"They're not dirty, Levi."

"Do they have love scenes?"

"Yes, but—"

"Then they're dirty."

She wrinkled her nose. "I think *naughty* would be a better word."

Levi picked up the salad tongs. "I like *wicked* better."

There was very little conversation as they ate and listened to music. Angela realized what had been missing in her life—a gentle peace, and the man sitting opposite her was responsible for that.

You have to kiss a lot of frogs before you find your prince, she thought.

Levi sat up in his bed, his back supported by a pile of pillows. They'd finished dinner, followed it with a dessert of fresh berries and coffee. He invited Angela to share his shower, but she declined. The object of his musings walked into the bedroom in a pale blue silk robe, after taking her shower. Smiling, he pulled back the sheet and lightweight blanket as she slipped out of the robe, leaving it on the chair.

"That's what I'm talking about," he crooned when light from the bedside lamp slanted over her slender curvy body.

The heat from Levi's hungry gaze rose as his eyes traveled from her face to her breasts, her belly and settled between her legs. She slipped into bed beside him, his hand grazing her thighs.

Rising slightly, Angela pressed her mouth to his ear. "I'm on the Pill."

He went still. "I told you I would protect you."

She smiled. "You told me you would write a prescription. Don't look at me like that, sweetie. When you said you'd protect me I believed you. But taking the Pill will make our lovemaking more spontaneous."

Combing his fingers through her hair, Levi held it away from her face. "So you like spontaneity?"

Angela moistened her lower lip with her tongue, bringing Levi's gaze to linger there. "I love spontaneity."

"What about foreplay?"

"I like that, too."

His gaze met and fused with hers. Levi's right hand skimmed her body, grazing the backs of her thighs. He continued his slow, deliberate journey, with his fingers splayed over her mound.

Levi's gentle touch sent tremors of desire racing through Angela. His hand continued its exploration, sweeping over her belly and breasts. Her entire body was on fire, simmering with heat.

"Levi," she moaned. Whatever else she wanted to say was left unspoken as his hand came up, and his thumb touched her chin. Exerting the slightest pressure, she opened her mouth.

His tongue traced the outline of her mouth with an agonizing slowness before it slipped through her parted lips. His tongue worked its magic, moving in and out of her mouth and precipitating a familiar throbbing between her thighs. She'd become a lump of soft clay with Levi Eaton as the sculptor. He could mold her into whatever shape and form he desired.

Angela couldn't get close enough to him as she pressed her swollen, aching breasts to his chest. She was on fire—everywhere. It was her turn to be a sculptress, her fingers feathering over the solid muscles in Levi's broad chest.

"Angie. Oh, Angie," Levi chanted hoarsely. He couldn't stop touching her, couldn't believe the silkiness of her skin, the clean sweet scent of her body. He touched her breasts, squeezing gently as if testing the ripeness of fresh fruit. Slowly, his mouth replaced his fingers, his lips molding to her breasts.

Gasping, Angela arched her back. Her nipples pebbled in hardness against the ridge of Levi's teeth. Writhing beneath him, she couldn't stop the moans from escaping her lips.

Levi, his mouth fastened to one breast then the other, uttered a silent admonishment so that he could prolong the foreplay. His body was on the verge of exploding.

He'd fantasized about Angela Chase from the first moment he saw her, and knowing he was going to relive that fantasy pushed his libido into overdrive. He trailed a series of slow, slippery kisses down her neck, chanting her name as he tasted every inch of her flesh. Lingering between her legs, he licked and suckled like a starving newborn.

"Levi," she answered, whispering his name.

Levi responded by grasping his penis and pushing it slowly into her tight, warm, wet folds until there was no more room. They were joined flesh to flesh, man to woman, lover to lover. He kissed her deeply, his tongue keeping the same rhythm as his thrusting hips, and giving Angela a taste of herself. He heard Angela's gasps of pleasure, and his own groans as they crested, their bodies entwined so that they ceased to exist separately and became one with the other.

His passion rose to meet hers as he buried his face between Angela's neck and shoulder and exploded inside her. Heat seared his brain, singed every inch of his body as he surrendered his essence as liquid ecstasy poured from him, bathing her with love.

Levi couldn't deny the emotions holding him captive as he waited for his breathing to return to normal. Still joined, he reversed their position. He kissed her hair. "Are you okay?"

Angela moaned.

"Is that a yes or a no?"

"That's an unequivocal yes," she said, still gasping for air. "What are you doing to me, Levi?"

"Loving you, baby."

Her hand curled around his neck. "I don't want you to ever stop loving me."

He froze. Did Angela realize what she'd just said? Was she asking for more, or had she meant that she didn't want him to stop making love to her?

"I promise to never stop making love to you."

Angela settled her legs between his and she shifted into a more comfortable position. "Thank you, sweetie."

He closed his eyes. He had his answer. Angela was not talking about him loving her, but their lovemaking. He cursed Robert Gaskin. He cursed the man who had walked out on Angela, leaving her unable to trust and emotionally scarred.

A sense of renewed strength came over Levi. He had time—at least eight weeks to repair the damage. After all, he was a doctor—someone trained to heal. This time he would be trying to heal a broken heart.

Chapter 15

Levi studied the baseball scores in the sports section of the paper. His beloved Yankees had swept a three-game series from the Boston Red Sox.

His head popped up when he saw movement out the corner of his eye. Putting aside the newspaper, he stood up and held out his arms. He wasn't disappointed when Angela hugged him.

"Good morning, love."

Tilting her head, Angela gave him an inviting smile. "Good morning. How long have you been up?" It was minutes before seven and Levi had showered, but hadn't bothered to shave. Today he wore a pair of black jeans, matching Timberland boots and a long-sleeved white shirt. Miss Divine lay on the sofa next to him, licking her paws.

Dipping his head, Levi touched his mouth to hers. "I usually wake up around five."

Angela pulled out of his embrace, making her way into the kitchen. The coffeemaker had finished its brewing cycle. "What do you want in your coffee?"

"A little milk, no sugar." Levi stared at Angela as she moved confidently around the kitchen. They worked well in the kitchen, got along well outside the kitchen, and were acutely attuned to each other in bed.

"I see you got the princess to leave her castle."

Levi glanced at the cat. "She told me she didn't like being on house arrest, so I let her out, cleaned her crate and gave her water."

"What else did baby girl tell you?"

Levi winked at Angela. "A few other things that I won't repeat."

"Yeah, right."

"Did I tell you that I wanted to be a vet?"

Angela turned and met his eyes. "No, you didn't. What made you change your mind?"

"Snakes."

"You don't like them?" she asked.

"I'm afraid of them. The first year my family moved to Miami I was out in the backyard and a snake slithered over my bare feet and I was so frightened I couldn't move. The incident scarred me for life. Whenever I go to the zoo I make certain to skip the reptile exhibit."

"So, you became a doctor, instead."

"It was the next best thing."

"You say that as if it's so easy to become a doctor or a vet."

"The choice was easy for me because I love taking care of sick people and animals. What do you want for breakfast?" he asked, changing the subject.

Angela stared at him over her shoulder. "I'm going to pass on breakfast until later. The days I go into the shop I normally don't eat anything until eleven. Then I eat again when I get home around seven."

"You don't eat in between?"

"I usually have fruit. Don't look at me like that, Levi. I don't have an eating disorder."

"I would've thought so until last night."

"What about last night?"

He gave her a lecherous grin. "You're just right—a handful *and* a mouthful."

Angela's hand trembled slightly when she picked up the carafe and filled two mugs with steaming brew. The blush that began in her face spread to her chest. "That's too much information, sweetie," she whispered.

Levi approached her and forcibly pried her fingers from the handle of the carafe. "Did I embarrass you?"

Angela shook her head. "No."

His eyes brimming with tenderness, Levi pulled her into the

circle of his embrace. "I don't want you to ever feel uncomfortable with me. What we do in private is just between us. I'll never do anything that will compromise your reputation."

"I know that, Levi."

He kissed her nose. "We can go out for brunch. By the time we come back and get dressed it'll be time to get ready for the race. I've reserved a driver to take us to the track and then bring us back after the party."

She kissed his stubble. "You're definitely a keeper."

Levi looked at her. "Were you thinking of trading me in?"

Angela's expression changed, becoming serious. "No, Levi. Don't forget you're the one who'll be leaving Louisville, not me."

"What if I decide to stay?"

The seconds ticked off as they stared at each other. "Would you, Levi?"

He smiled, the warmth of the gesture not quite reaching his eyes. "If I had something to stay for."

Her heart stopped and started again in a rapid rhythm. "Would you stay for me?"

"Would you want me to stay for you?"

She lowered her eyes. "I'd love you to stay for me, but the decision will have to be because you want to stay because it would be the best for you and your career."

"So you want to take yourself out of the equation?"

Angela glanced up. There was something in Levi that frightened her, and at no time since she'd come to know him that had he ever frightened her. "This is not about me, Levi. It's what is best for you."

"What if you are what's best for me?"

Suddenly Angela felt as if she were in a runaway roller coaster, going around and around, up and down until the cars crashed or jumped the track.

She bit her lip to stop its trembling. "I… I… Everything is moving much too fast. We hardly know each other."

"How long did you know your ex before you agreed to marry him?"

"I thought we weren't going to talk about him."

"I didn't mention his name, Angie. Please answer my question."

She turned her head, staring at the flat-screen on a table in the living room. "We dated for a year, then we were engaged for a year."

"In other words, you were together for two years and you still didn't know the sonofabitch. And you probably thought you knew your maid of honor, and you didn't really know her, either."

Angela's gaze swung back to Levi. "You say all of that to say what?"

"Why can't we be like the lovers in your romance novels? Don't they pretend to be a couple or have marriages of convenience? And don't forget the secret babies."

"I thought you didn't read romance novels," she said in surprise.

"I saw the titles on your bookshelf. I have to assume you read the books because of the happy endings." He took her face in his hands. "You are past due and more than deserving of a happy ending, baby."

Angela looped her arms around his waist. She knew Levi was right. She was long overdue for a happily ever after.

"So, you're going to become my hero?"

Levi buried his face in her hair. "I thought I was already your hero when I agreed to protect you from the villain."

"You're right. You are my hero."

He wove his fingers through her hair, gently massaging her scalp. "And what are you? Lover, paramour, courtesan or concubine?"

"I'll be any of the aforementioned except a kept woman."

There came a beat. "Kept women aren't guaranteed happy endings."

The chiming of Levi's cell phone shattered the sensual spell that had wrapped around Angela like a comforting blanket. He released her, excused himself and walked to the coffee table to answer the call.

Angela found the boxes where her parents sat with Langdon and Ryder, while Duncan and Jared sat with the district attorney and his wife. She hugged her father and brothers as she made her way to her seat. The day was perfect for a horse race. Under a cloudless blue sky with a warm breeze, the dirt track was dry and supposed to be very fast. She sat next to her mother, leaving the seat next to her for Levi.

Dianne Chase pressed a hand to her bosom. "Oh, my word!" she whispered. "You look gorgeous."

"Thank you, Mama."

Angela had finally settled on wearing a silk and linen sheath dress with capped sleeves and an asymmetrical neckline in a bright sunny yellow. The wide, black patent-leather belt around her waist matched her peep-toe pumps. She'd styled her hair in a ponytail with a wide-brimmed hat with a wide black grosgrain ribbon band.

"Where's Levi?" Dianne questioned.

"He's placing a bet." She stared at her mother. She was stunning in an electric-blue silk pantsuit and blue and white spectator pumps and a matching pillbox hat. She glanced up, smiling when an usher showed Levi their box. "He's coming now."

"Oh, my word!" Dianne drawled. "He looks so handsome."

"Yes, he does," Angela said in agreement. Levi had decided to wear charcoal-gray slacks, a white buttoned-down shirt, navy blazer and matching silk tie. She smiled when he shook hands with her father and gave each of her brothers a rough bro-hug.

"Where's Myla?" she asked Dianne. She'd expected to see the very pretty schoolteacher at Duncan's side.

"Don't say anything to Duncan," Dianne whispered, "but I think she broke up with him."

"Why?"

"I heard some nonsense that he doesn't spend enough time with her. For heaven's sakes, the man's a doctor and he can't control when his patients need him. I hope you and Levi don't have those problems."

"No, but we'll talk later." She met Levi's eyes. He winked at her when he dipped his head to kiss Dianne's cheek. "You look gorgeous."

Dianne touched the pearl stud in her ear. "Thank you, Levi.

I must say you're looking rather dapper yourself. I hope you and Angela are coming to Prissy Turner's party after the race."

He nodded. "We plan to stay for a little while."

Dianne patted his hand. "Good for you. I'm so glad Angela has you to take her out."

"Mama, please let Levi sit down."

"Move over and let him sit next to me," Dianne ordered.

Angela and Levi exchanged a look. She lifted her shoulders, and because she hadn't wanted to cause a scene she shifted to her right, leaving a seat for Levi between her and mother.

Levi folded his long frame down between the two women. Reaching into his jacket pocket, he handed Angela a betting slip. "Please put this in your handbag."

She glanced at the slip. He'd bet a hundred dollars on Sweet Southern Knight to win. The odds were thirty-three-to-one. "You only bet on one horse?"

"There can only be one winner."

Angela pressed her shoulder to his. "What are you going to do with the money if you win?"

Levi curved an arm around her waist. "I'll give it to you and you can decide what you'd like to do with it."

"If he does come in first, then I'll donate the winnings to Duncan's clinic."

"You would actually do that?"

"Yes. The clinic needs the money more than I do. Duncan says his funding may be cut next year because of the economy."

"Has he thought about doing some fundraising?" Levi asked. "Everybody's feeling the pinch nowadays."

Ducking his head, Levi kissed her cheek. "Do you know that you're incredible?"

Angela rested her hand on his thigh. "You keep talking like that and I'll wind up with a swelled head."

"If you don't move your hand there's going to be another swollen head," he said in her ear.

She snatched her hand away from Levi's thighs as if she'd been burned.

"Oh—" Angela swallowed the expletive when she spied Robert leading an obviously pregnant Savannah to a box several rows below them. She knew the Gaskins didn't have a box and assumed they were sharing it with a season box-holder, who'd paid a pretty penny for the privilege of occupying a six-seat area on the third tier of the grandstand.

"Why does he feel the need to bring that loose heifer with him? Instead of betting on the race I'm certain a lot of people are taking bets as to who's her baby's daddy," Dianne spat out.

Angela leaned around Levi. "Careful, Mama. Your horns are showing."

Dianne blew out her cheeks. "They were lucky they left Louisville when they did, because I was ready to take out a hit on them."

Benton Chase dropped an arm over his wife's shoulders. "Calm down, baby. Neither of them are worth you getting upset about. Remember, we came here to enjoy ourselves."

Thank you, Daddy, Angela mouthed when her father winked at her. She managed to suppress a groan when she overheard Ryder whisper a savage curse in the same breath as Robert's name, wondering if or when it would ever be over. Robert and Savannah moving back to Louisville made it difficult for Angela to bury her past. The one thing she didn't want was for her brothers to confront Robert. Especially Ryder, who'd always had a hair-trigger temper.

She smiled at Levi when he reached for her hand, lacing their fingers together. Angela settled back to enjoy the race, dismissing any thoughts of Savannah and Robert.

Before attending his first Kentucky Derby, Levi had done some research. What surprised him was that an African-American jockey named James Lee had set a racetrack record on June 5, 1907, that had never been broken when he won the entire six-race card at Churchill Downs. Having been born and raised in Louisville, Angela had provided a bit more about the history of African-Americans in thoroughbred racing. Isaac Murphy, an African-American, was the first jockey of any race to win the Kentucky Derby three times. Also, a distant cousin of Angela's family had also been a jockey in the late nineteenth century. Horseracing, she claimed, was in her family's blood.

Levi felt the crowd's excitement before and after each race. Spectators came early, camping out on the one-hundred-forty-seven-acre national landmark. People had picnics and enjoyed musical jam sessions. It was New Year's Eve and the Fourth of July all rolled into one. Even though he had attended baseball, basketball and football games where fans went from avid cheerleaders to raging lunatics when opposing teams took the field, he hadn't expected that same kind of behavior from the wealthy, blue-blood crowd that attended the Derby. Between races he found it amusing to see horseracing society quickly reverting from Southern gentility to shrieking spectators.

Dianne touched Levi's sleeve, capturing his attention. "Benton suggested everyone come to the house for Sunday dinner. I hope this doesn't interfere with your plans for tomorrow."

Levi shook his head. "I'm sorry, but Angela and I have plans for tomorrow." He'd been sworn to secrecy about Traci and Reggie's wedding.

Dianne leaned closer and Levi dipped his head. "I'm sorry, too. It's not often that I get all my children together at the same time. By the way, I don't want you to think of me as a meddlesome mother," she said under her breath, "but I think you are perfect for my daughter. It hasn't been easy for her, but since she started seeing you, she's changed."

"She's not the only one who has changed, Mrs. Chase."

"Don't you dare Mrs. Chase me. Please call me Dianne."

Levi smiled. "Okay…Dianne."

Dianne sat back, looking like a cat that had licked the cream off the bottle of milk as she picked up a tiny pair of jeweled binoculars. "That's better, Levi."

Angela pressed her mouth to Levi's ear. "Watch it, sweetie, or my mother will ask for your full name and those of your parents so she can put a wedding announcement in the local paper."

Levi gave her hand a gentle squeeze. "There are worse things."

He heard the distinctive sound of her teeth coming together when she clamped her jaw.

"Cancer, lupus, MS, heart disease—"

"You've made your point, Levi," she interrupted. "Please don't think I'm against marriage. It's just not for me."

"Romance novel," he crooned. "Have you forgotten I'm the hero and you're the heroine and we're working toward the happy ending?"

"There's no way I can forget because you won't let me."

"What do you mean I won't let you?"

Angela gave him a direct stare. "I couldn't forget even if I wanted to. You're my fantasy hero come to life." Shifting on her seat, she leaned into him. "I didn't want to like you, Levi. I tried everything in my arsenal to send you packing, but like a boomerang you kept coming back."

Levi chuckled. "You didn't try hard enough."

Easing back, she raised her chin so the brim of her hat wouldn't touch his face. "I'm glad I didn't."

The smoldering flame he saw in Angela's eyes startled him. It was a silent invitation for him to make love to her, and he didn't want to be reminded of what they'd shared the night before—not now when they weren't able to do anything about it.

He blinked. "Tonight." Angela lowered her eyes and gave him a seductive look.

It took everything for Levi to turn his attention back to the racetrack instead of the woman beside him. He stared at the horses being led into the gates for the race before the Derby, but out of the corner of his eye he could still see the flawlessness of Angela's face, the sexiness of her high cheekbones, the straight line of the bridge of her nose, the way her nostrils flared slightly whenever she smiled and the sexy curve of her luscious lips. Those were the same lips that he'd kissed, nibbled and suckled.

"Do you have any plans for next weekend?" he asked her in a whisper.

Angela gave him a sidelong glance. "What are you thinking about, sweetie?"

"I'd like to take you away somewhere. We can stop in some little out of the way place, order room service and make love until we'll have to be resuscitated."

"We can't leave until after I lock up the Garden Gate."

"Whatever works for you, baby. Do you have any suggestions?"

Angela pursed her lips. "Bardstown's about an hour's drive from here and it's chock-full of historical sites."

"I'll go online and check it out. We probably won't get home until late Sunday night, so what are you going to do with Miss Divine?"

"I can drop her off with Langdon. He lives near Bardstown and has a couple of dogs and cats that will keep her company."

"Good."

Levi didn't tell Angela the reason he wanted to take her away from Louisville was to avoid having her run into her ex. It seemed as if Robert Gaskin showed up everywhere, and Levi wondered if Robert was keeping tabs on Angela.

A palpable excitement rippled through the crowd when the horses for the Derby were paraded onto the track. Even though there had been races all afternoon, none compared to the final race of the day. An uncanny stillness settled over the crowd when the jockeys in their colorful silks were hoisted onto the backs of the magnificent three-year-old horses. There was a commotion when one horse balked at being led into the starting gate. Another reared until one by one they were settled into their designated gates as an eerie hush descended over the track. After several anxiety-filled moments the gates opened and the horse sprinted out, their hoofs echoing like thunder as their riders fought for position.

Levi's heart was in his throat when he saw the purple and gold silks of the rider atop Sweet Southern Knight. The thirty-three-to-one longshot had moved up on the outside from eighth position to sixth, to fifth and then fourth. The dirt track was one and one-quarter miles, but seemed much shorter. For all the attention the race received it was only two minutes long.

Levi released Angela's hand and stood up when Sweet South Knight moved into second place. The noise was deafening and he found himself pounding on the front of the box as the longshot raced neck and neck with the favorite. What happened next was a blur. Sweet Southern Knight won the Derby by a nose, and Levi lifted Angela off her feet, his mouth covering hers in a smothering kiss.

"We won! We won!" he repeated over and over as her arms tightened around his neck.

Peering over Levi's shoulder, Angela met her father's eyes. He winked at her and she gave him a bright smile. Paper floated down the grandstand like confetti when spectators tore up their betting slips. Duncan, Langdon, Ryder and Jared swore under their breaths as their mutilated their slips.

Angela kissed Levi's cheek. "Please put me down." He set her on her feet. Angela took the slip from her bag, making a big show of it when she kissed it. "Take a good look at a winner, my brothers."

Duncan leaned over her, staring at the slip. "You bet on a longshot?"

"No. I bet on Mind Yo Bizness. This was Levi's slip, and now it's yours."

A slight frown creased Duncan's forehead. "I don't understand," he said when Angela handed it to him.

"Levi said if he won, he would give me the money. I decided to donate the winnings to the clinic. But it was Levi who'd placed the bet."

The three Chase brothers leaned over to get a look at the slip. "You've got it like that, brother?" Jared asked Levi.

Levi nodded, smiling. "I do all right."

Benton cradled Dianne's elbow. "I've seen enough racing for the day. We're going back to the house to change before heading over to Mayor Turner's place."

Angela looped her arm through Levi's. "We'll meet you there." She kissed her mother, then her father. "Later."

Levi held Angela's arm as he led her to the door. The number of people Priscilla had invited to her post-Derby celebration had swelled appreciably until they lingered in every room on the first floor, with the overflow strolling around the garden.

"How many mint juleps did you have?" Levi asked once they were seated in the rear of the Town Car. Angela laid her head in his lap.

She closed her eyes. "One."

"You're tipsy from one mint julep?"

"I'm not tipsy, Levi. I just feel a little queasy because all I ate were carrots and radishes."

Running his fingers through her hair, he leaned over and kissed her forehead. "I can't believe all Priscilla served was crudités. What happened to the Buffalo wings, ribs, dim sum, sweet and sour meatballs, crab puffs and Jamaican meat patties? I like veggies, but I need more than broccoli and cauliflower and a yogurt dip if I'm going to drink anything alcoholic."

Angela opened her eyes. "What are Jamaican meat patties, sweetie?"

His eyebrows lifted. "You've never had one?"

"No."

"A patty is flaky pocket filled with ground beef and spices. There are chicken patties, but I like the ones made with beef— the spicier the better. Poor baby. You've really been sheltered, haven't you?"

"No."

"Well, you have if you don't know what a meat patty is. When you come to New York I'm going to take you Katz's Deli for the best pastrami on the planet. Then we're going to Brooklyn. I found a little hole in the wall that makes the flakiest, spiciest meat patties in the city."

"What about Yankee Stadium?"

"Yankee Stadium will be a priority."

"And the Brooklyn Bridge?"

"That, too."

She gave him a lopsided smile. "Thank you, sweetie."

"The only place you're going now is to bed, and I'll personally tuck you in."

"I have to wash my face and brush my teeth first," Angela insisted.

"I'll help you with that."

"Did I ever tell you that you're a keeper, Levi Eaton?" She was slurring her words.

"Yes, you did, Angela Chase. Yes, you did," he repeated, staring at the partition separating them from the driver. Levi sighed. Angela wanted to keep him, but would she allow him to keep her?

The question nagged at him when he put her to bed, and it continued to nag at him when they met Traci and Reggie at the church the next day where they would exchange vows and become husband and wife for a second time.

Chapter 16

Angela held Traci's bouquet in one hand—a mix of roses ranging from pure white to deep purple—as the smiling bride held hands with the groom and pledged to love and cherish him until death.

Traci looked chic in a pale pink sheath dress and black silk-covered stilettos, knowing it was just a matter of time before the four-and-five-inch heels were relegated to the back of her closet in favor of more sensible shoes as her pregnancy progressed.

Reginald Goddard stared adoringly at his bride as he repeated his vows. His dimpled smile spoke volumes. He was in love with Traci. "I fell in love with you what seems like yesterday, but today I'm the luckiest man in the world because I get to stand before man and God to pledge all that I am to you until I draw my last breath."

They exchanged rings, and then the minister intoned the words that made them husband and wife before telling the groom he could now kiss his bride. The retired pro-football player wrapped his massive arms around Traci's waist, lifting her aloft and giving her a noisy kiss before he gently set her down on her feet.

Angela hugged Traci. "Congratulations, cuz."

Traci kissed her cousin's cheek. "Thank you, Ang. And thank you for standing up for me."

"You know I'd do anything for you, Traci." Angela barely had time to react when she found herself in a bear-hug embrace. "Congratulations, Big Daddy."

He planted a kiss on Angela's forehead, and shook hands with

Levi. "I kinda like Big Poppa." Turning, Reggie thanked the minister, and handed him an envelope.

"Let's go, Biggie Smalls. Your wife needs to eat, or she's going to faint," Angela said.

Levi stared at Traci. "You're pregnant?"

Traci blushed, a rush of color darkening her gold-brown face. "Yes. I'm two months."

Levi took a step and pressed a kiss to Traci's cheek. "Congratulations."

Traci, standing at eye level with him in her heels, smiled. "I hope you change your mind and relocate to Louisville so you can become my baby's pediatrician."

His expression changed, becoming a mask that made it impossible to read his thoughts. "It's not quite that simple."

"What can we do to convince you to stay?" Traci asked.

Angela took her cousin's arm. "Traci, I've made reservations at Ruth's Chris for four, and if we don't leave now we'll lose our table."

Bending slightly, Reggie picked up his bride and carried her out of the church to the parking lot. "We'll follow you guys," he said to Levi.

The restaurant, located on the sixteenth floor of Kaden Tower, offered breathtaking views of Louisville. Angela, Levi and the newlyweds ordered appetizers, salads, the restaurant's signature steaks, dessert and two bottles of sparkling cider because of Traci's condition.

After downing the mint julep on a practically empty stomach the day before, Angela knew it would be a while before she partook of anything alcoholic.

She'd ordered the calamari with a sweet and spicy Asian chili sauce, and Traci ordered the lobster bisque. Levi and Reggie decided on barbecue shrimp and shrimp remoulade.

The diamonds in Traci's eternity band sparkled from the sunlight coming through the restaurant's windows. "When do you plan on telling your parents that you're now a married woman?" Angela asked Traci.

Traci exchanged a look with her husband. "Tomorrow."

"Why tomorrow?"

"Because I want to enjoy my wedding night without hearing my mother complain. And you know your aunt, Ang. She'd think nothing of barging into my place or Reggie's to give us a piece of her mind. The only thing that would make her leave is if Reggie and I got butt naked and got busy in front of her."

Levi coughed, nearly choking on a mouthful of shrimp. Angela patted his back when he picked up a goblet of water. "Easy, sweetie."

Traci waved her hand. "Hang around long enough and you'll get used to my mouth."

Dropping an arm over his wife's shoulders, Reggie kissed her short curly hair. "That's why I love you, babe. You always call a spade a spade."

"I think she has some competition in that department," Levi drawled, recovering from his coughing jag.

"I know you're not talking about me, Levi."

He gave Angela an innocent look. "Did I mention your name, love?"

"Love?" chorused Reggie and Traci.

"Is there something going on that I should know about?" Traci questioned.

"No!" Levi and Angela said in unison.

"What are you going to do with your loft?" Angela asked her cousin, deftly changing the topic. Traci had purchased a loft in what used to be an industrial area of Louisville.

"I'm going to keep it. Reggie and I decided we need a place in the city and one in the country. We'll use the loft for entertaining friends, or when his family comes to visit."

Angela took a sip of cider. "Are you going to be available to cat-sit for me when I visit Levi in New York?"

Levi put his hand over Angela's. "She can't."

"Why not?"

"If you've ever read a kitty litter bag you'll see a warning that pregnant women should be careful because cat feces may carry a parasite that causes toxoplasmosis."

"What's that, Doc?" Reggie asked.

"If a pregnant woman contracts toxoplasmosis the parasite

can reach her developing baby, and the baby's immune system is not able to fend off the parasite. The result may be damage to the eyes and brain. The greatest risk is miscarriage."

Traci's eyes were large as silver dollars. "Really?"

Levi nodded slowly. "Really."

"Does this mean I can't come to Ang's house?"

"No. Just stay away from the litter box."

Reggie stared at him. "Thanks, Doc. You just may have saved *my baby.*"

"No problem. If you or Traci have any medical questions, please call me. You have my number."

The waiter came over to remove the appetizers and all conversation came to a halt. It started up again with the next course, this time the subjects were politics and sports. Reggie and Levi arguing good-naturedly about what team was better and who they believed would win the World Series and the Super Bowl.

Traci wanted to know about the Derby and Angela told her about the fashions, and also revealed that Levi had picked the winner, but donated the money to Duncan's clinic.

After dessert and coffee, Levi signaled for the waiter to give him the check. When Angela protested, he whispered, "Will you please let me be a hero."

Her Cheshire-cat grin faded when she felt Levi's hand on her upper thigh under the table. The opening to her wrap skirt had given him easy access. Angela managed to smother a gasp before Traci or Reggie became aware of what had happened.

When she woke that morning it was to Levi's erection pressed against her hips. She'd known by his soft snoring that he was still asleep, so Angela made certain not to move. She went back to sleep and when she woke again, she found herself alone in bed. Minutes later, Levi, shaved and showered, brought a tray into the bedroom where they had breakfast in bed. He revealed that it was something his father had done for as long as he could remember: preparing breakfast and bringing it to his mother on Sunday mornings. Once they had children he still made breakfast for his wife, but would take their sons out for brunch before they all attended church services.

Angela closed her eyes. "Wait until we get home, Levi."

Traci looked from her cousin to the man sitting next to her. "What's up, Ang?"

She affected a saccharine smile. "I told Levi I would pay for tonight's dinner, but it seems as if he decided to one-up me."

"Let the man be a man, Angela," Reggie said.

Levi winked at Angela. "Yeah, baby. Like Reggie said. Let me be the man."

She pushed her face close to his. "He said *a* man, not *the* man." Angela hadn't time to blink when Levi's mouth covered hers in an explosive kiss. It ended as quickly as it began, with her mouth forming a perfect O.

"*That's* what men do to keep their women quiet." The smug look on his face was one Angela would remember for the rest of her life.

"Damn-n-n!" Traci drawled.

Reggie stood up, reached into his pocket and dropped a large bill on the table. "That should take care of the tip." He extended his hand to Levi. "Thanks, buddy, for standing in as my best man and for dinner. Traci and I will return the favor as soon as the dust settles once we announce our marriage."

Levi shook his hand. "I was an honor to be your best man." Levi settled the bill and the two couples rode the elevator to the street level, parting ways in the parking lot and driving off in opposite directions.

Angela sat quietly, staring straight ahead through the windshield as Levi headed for Magnolia Pines. They'd stopped there to drop off Miss Divine before heading over to the church.

"Are you mad at me?" Levi asked, not taking his eyes off the road.

"No."

"Well, you look mad."

Angela looked at him for the first time since getting into the car. "You don't know me well enough to say that."

Levi gave her a quick glance. "How do you look when you're mad?"

"The same way I do now."

He smiled. "I don't believe it."

"Believe what, Levi?"

"Angry or happy. You're still beautiful."

She shook her head. "You're unbelievable…always the silver-tongued devil."

"No, baby. It's the truth. You're the most incredible woman I've had the pleasure of knowing. You have a special gift when dealing with your customers, you're incredibly loyal to your family, and you proved you have a heart as good as gold when you donated the Derby winnings to the Maywood Junction clinic. You say you don't need money, yet you still get up and go to work. And despite experiencing a very public humiliation, you didn't cut and run, but stayed," said Levi. "You're sexy whether you want to acknowledge it or not. Now that we're sleeping together I no longer go to bed with a hard-on, but that doesn't stop me from waking up with one."

"You had one this morning, but you were still asleep."

"Why didn't you wake me up, Angie?"

"I didn't want to bother you."

Signaling, Levi turned off onto the local road leading to Magnolia Pines. "If there's one time when I need to be awakened, then that would be it."

"Even after you've worked a double shift?"

Attractive lines fanned out around his eyes when he smiled. "It would be the best way to put me to sleep."

Her smile matched his. "We'll see."

"Yes we will, won't we?" he said mysteriously. Levi pulled into the driveway, parking behind Angela's Audi. He helped her out, holding on to her hand as they mounted the porch. Angela unlocked the door and Miss Divine was there to meet them. Tossing her keys in a crystal bowl on the entryway table, she slipped out of her heels.

She turned to face Levi. "Thank you for a wonderful weekend."

Cradling her face, Levi lowered his head. "I should be the one thanking you." He kissed her, easing her back until her body was pressed against the wall.

His right hand moved from her face, over her breast and still lower to the opening in her skirt. The fabric parted when his fingers slipped under the elastic of her panties, finding her wet, hot *and* pulsing. While his hands and fingers worked their magic, hers were busy undoing the buckle on his belt, and unzipping his pants.

Groaning, straining, they struggled to get closer while maintaining their balance. It was when she reached through the opening in his boxers to release his hardened sex that the dam broke. Her bare feet left the floor when Levi picked her up with one arm, pulled down her panties with the other and then guided his erection inside her. Her legs circled around his waist, and her arms around his neck.

The passionate cries and groans of their lovemaking only heightened their desire. Levi drove into Angela over and over, again and again until he felt as if his head would explode.

She was so wet, so tight, her flesh holding him captive like a glove a size too small. Cradling her hips, he felt the tremors of her orgasm. What Levi felt for the woman in his arms went beyond lovemaking. It was mating.

Angela moaned aloud with erotic pleasure that singed her body from head to toe. Her breath was now coming in desperate gasps that were a prelude to an explosive orgasm. Her body melted into Levi's, the runaway beating of her heart keeping pace with his. She was hot, then cold and then the heat returned.

Closing her eyes, Angela buried her face between his strong neck and shoulder. Everything that was Levi Eaton seeped into her and she knew he was special. That he was the one who would heal her heart and help her see beyond her past to a future with a man she could trust.

Angela gasped in the sweetest ecstasy that made her want to cry. And she did cry. When an orgasm shuddered through her body, she cried out her release.

Levi felt the contractions squeezing and releasing his straining sex. He quickened his thrusting, as love flowed from Angela like molten lava, melting around him as he felt his release inside of her. It was the first time in his life that the thought of fatherhood was so strong that he'd wanted to make love to a woman without protection.

Not only had he fallen hard for Angela, but he was also falling in love with her. A peace he had never known flowed through him as he lowered Angela until her feet touched the floor. He felt the tremors still shaking her body.

"Are you all right, baby?"

Angela snuggled against his chest. "I'm more than all right. That was wonderful."

Pulling back, Levi saw an expression of pure bliss on her face. "Was that spontaneous enough for you?"

She tiptoed and nibbled his lower lip. "It was more than I could've ever imagined." Angela closed her eyes, moaning in protest when he pulled out.

Levi adjusted his clothes. "I'm going home while I still can, because if I stay here I won't make it to work tomorrow."

Angela felt his loss even before he walked out the door. She knew she wouldn't see him again until Friday. But knowing they were going away for the weekend made his absence bearable.

She affected a bright smile. "I'll see you."

Dipping his head, Levi kissed the corners of her mouth. "I'll call you."

Angela stood at the door, watching as he walked to where he'd parked his car. She took a deep breath, inhaling the lingering scent of his cologne and her perfume mingling with the scent of their lovemaking.

She waved to Levi. She waited until the taillights disappeared from view, and closed and locked the door. Her back pressed against the door, she closed her eyes reliving the erotic encounter as warm tears pricked the backs of her eyelids.

Her mind burned with the memory of what she'd shared, and she knew unequivocally that she'd fallen in love with Levi Eaton. She blinked back the torrent of tears threatening to fall. Why, Angela thought, did she feel so empty instead of elation? Her promise not to become involved was shattered. And he wasn't some fantasy, or a figment of her imagination, but a real flesh and blood man who she wanted to spend the rest of her life with. She wanted what her parents had and what Traci and Reggie had. She wanted to be married *and* be the mother of Levi Eaton's children. Angela wanted her own happy ending.

Angela walked up the staircase to the second floor to shower and change her clothes. She wanted to remain optimistic about her relationship with Levi, but it wasn't going to be easy. He only had another seven weeks before he would leave Kentucky—forever.

If she could maintain the same pace in her writing, in seven weeks she would have completed her manuscript. She'd hoped her deadline would coincide with Levi's departure and they could travel to New York together.

Angela was looking forward to meeting her editor, eating a meat patty, visiting Yankee Stadium and walking across the Brooklyn Bridge. There was no doubt her first trip to New York would be one she would remember for the rest of her life.

Chapter 17

Levi couldn't bring himself to look at Dr. Gemma Wagner. It was as if she wanted to sabotage her career. She'd been summoned to meet with the chief of staff and the hospital board about her future.

She'd admitted to being a drug abuser but denied stealing drugs from the hospital. She refused to go into a rehab program, which left the board with no recourse but to terminate her hospital residency. Levi's head popped up when he heard the soft click of the lock as she walked out, closing the door behind her.

Neil McGill folded his hands together. "I'm sorry, Dr. Eaton, but you know the adage, 'you can lead a horse to water but you can't make it drink.' If Dr. Wagner would've agreed to go into treatment, we may have considered bringing her back based on your recommendations, but apparently she refuses to acknowledge she has a problem."

Levi pushed back his chair. He had lost one resident. "Thank you, ladies, gentlemen and Dr. McGill for taking the time to hear me out."

The door opened and McGill's secretary stuck her head in. "Excuse me, Dr. McGill. There's call on line three from the governor's office."

McGill turned and picked up the phone on the table. "Good morning, Governor Haskell."

All eyes were on the head of the hospital as his eyes grew wider, he nodded and scribbled something on the pad in front of him. "I'll assemble a team as soon as I can. Yes, sir, I understand. You're welcome."

He pressed a button, breaking the connection. "There was a

tornado near the Indiana border that hit several counties. There's been extensive damage to homes and businesses, including hospitals. The governor has called out the National Guard. And they need experienced doctors to help with the sick and injured. Dr. Eaton, can I count on you to help out?"

"Of course," Levi said.

"I need you to pack for at least two weeks. The state police will arrange to transport you and a team of doctors to the site where they're going to set up a field hospital."

"What time do you want us ready?" Levi asked.

"Two o'clock. Everyone will meet on the north end of the staff parking lot."

Levi left the room, and reached for his cell. He punched in the speed dial number for Angela. It took him less than a minute to tell her that he probably wouldn't see her for at least two weeks.

"I'll make up for our weekend when we get back."

"Don't worry about that, sweetie. You'll probably want to sleep around the clock when you get back. Remember, you have your family reunion at the end of the month."

He smiled. "Are you coming with me?"

"I wouldn't miss it."

"Thanks, babe. I have to go home and pack. I'll call you whenever I have some downtime."

"Send me a text, Levi, and I'll text you back."

"Okay. I miss you already."

"Same here. Be careful, Levi."

"I will. Bye, love."

There was a pause, then Angela's voice came through the earpiece. "Goodbye, darling."

Angela saved what she'd written on her computer, raced out of the office and into the kitchen to turn on the Weather Channel for information. She watched, transfixed, at the footage of the damage in the aftermath of the tornado that had hit two counties. She clasped a hand over her mouth when she saw an elderly woman wandering aimlessly around in the rain near what had once been her home.

"Oh, my word," she whispered through her fingers. It looked

as if someone had dropped a bomb, obliterating everything within miles. She said a silent prayer for the people who lived there and for the first responders.

Reaching for the phone, she dialed the number to the Maywood Junction clinic. "This is Angela Chase," she said introducing herself when the receptionist answered. "Is Duncan available?"

"He's with a patient. But I'll have him call you back as soon as he's finished."

"Thank you." Within seconds of hanging up the phone rang again and Angela picked it up. "Duncan?"

"Guess again?" asked a sultry feminine voice.

"Good morning, Mrs. Goddard. Did you tell your mother?"

"I just got off the phone with her. I told her Reggie and I had remarried and she was going to be a grandmother all in one breath."

"And…"

"Daphne Hitchcock Freeman was completely silent."

"No!"

"No lie, Ang. Then she started crying. Have you ever known my mother to cry? I take that back. She cries whenever she wants Daddy to do something she knows he's totally against. And my marshmallow father gives in every time. Once she stopped crying she said she's going to have a little something for the family."

"Little is something my aunt is not familiar with."

"I know that, Ang, and so do you."

"Are you going to give in to her?"

"I said no, but Reggie capitulated and said if it's only family, otherwise he'll personally shut it down. And you know my husband has enough thug in him to follow through with his threat."

"Where and when?"

"It'll probably be over the Memorial Day weekend. I know Aunt Dianne usually has a cookout that weekend, but Mom said she's going to talk to her and maybe they can host something together."

Angela grimaced. "I won't be able to make it." She told Traci about going to Philadelphia with Levi for his family reunion."

"Is there something you're not telling me, Ang?"

"No, Traci, it's not like that. I made a deal with him. Since he came with me to Yvette's wedding I agreed to go with him to his family reunion. I… Traci, I'll call you back," she said hearing the call-waiting signal and glancing at the caller ID display.

"You don't have to call me back. We'll talk tomorrow."

Angela tapped the call-waiting button. "Hey, Duncan."

"Hey, Ang. What's up?"

She told him about Levi's call and she was surprised when he revealed that a call had gone out to doctors all over the state for volunteers. "One of the hospitals took a direct hit and unfortunately there were fatalities. I sent the physician assistant, so right now I'm the only full-timer covering the clinic. I'd love to talk, but I have another patient. I'll call you later on this week. Love you, Ang."

Angela smiled hearing his trademark goodbye. "Love you back, bro."

Picking up the remote, she turned off the television.

I miss you already. Levi's words came back with surprising clarity. "I miss you, too," she whispered.

A soft meowing caught her attention and Angela turned to find Miss Divine standing at the entrance to the kitchen. She still avoided the kitchen, living and dining rooms, despite Levi's urging.

"Does Mama's baby want a treat?" The cat meowed in response. "Let's go get a treat, baby." She went into the pantry, opened a bag with the treats and handed one to Miss Divine, who held it in her mouth as she ran off in the direction of the laundry room.

Angela brewed a cup of tea, taking it with her when she went back to her manuscript.

Three days later she got a text message from Levi:

Delivered a baby 2day 4 the first time in 8 years. It felt good.

Congrats. How r u doing?

Tired, but good. And u?

Miss u

She smiled when she read: Miss u 2

Her fingers typed: Pls. take care. I don't know how 2 take care of a Dr.

:) Luv U

Angela closed her eyes, not wanting Levi to misinterpret what she meant. It was a term she used with her brothers whenever she spoke to them. Her sign-off signature was always love you, bro. So couldn't Levi say the same? Luv u back.

She waited for his response

Trying 2 get some sleep. Have 2 set up neonatal 2morrow

Later, sweetie

Later, luv

The texts came every two to three days. Some were light and funny and others were terse one-liners.

One week became two and then three. Angela didn't believe she could miss Levi that much. It wasn't as if they saw each other every day, but even when they were apart she somehow felt connected to him.

She'd tried to analyze her relationship with Levi, to rationalize her feelings by saying it was just sex. But if she was truly honest with herself, she'd know that wasn't it.

She was able to talk to him about any and everything without censoring herself. He'd always given her a choice in what she wanted to do, and in how she wanted their relationship to proceed. Levi was intelligent and generous—a rare combination that Angela found lacking in most of the men she'd dated. Was Levi Eaton a modern-day, real-life hero that every woman dreamed about? And here she had him.

Angela was resigned to the fact that Levi was going to leave Kentucky and resume his life in much the same way she would continue with her life. After all, she was grown, doing grown-woman things and able to handle the consequences.

Angela knew she loved Levi, and what's more she had fallen *in love* with him. But it was trust that had always superseded love. St. Augustine wrote, *Love is like a temporary earthquake. It erupts, then subsides.* When she'd come across those words she'd had an epiphany. It made her see what she'd had with Robert Gaskin wasn't love. He'd offered what she'd needed at the time, things she could've easily gotten from another man. But her immaturity and insecurity hadn't allowed her to see that.

Business had picked up at the Garden Gate and her summer hours began two hours earlier at noon. Traci managed her morning sickness by eating small meals. And when she felt fatigued, she would lie down on the love seat in the back of the shop.

Angela had begun bringing her laptop and jump drive to the Garden Gate. Whenever there was a lull in customers or when Traci took over the front desk, she raced to the back and typed a few pages.

The story seemed to pour out of her like a running faucet. The words came so easily, the characters were so real and the scenes so intensely vivid that fantasy and reality seemed to merge.

"Do you mind if I leave now?"

Angela glanced over her shoulder. Traci stood in the doorway with both hands shoved into the pockets of her smock. She was glowing. Her curly hair was longer, her complexion flawless, her face fuller. Her cousin had given up her vegetarian diet for one that included lean meat, chicken and fish.

"Of course not. Let me save what I've typed. How are you feeling?" she asked, tapping several keys.

"I'm feeling just a little tired today. It could be the weather."

Angela turned off her laptop. "Rain, rain, go away. Come again another day," she chanted.

Traci took off her smock, hanging it on a wall hook. "I thought you liked the rain."

"Only when I don't have to go out in it. I'm like Miss Divine. I don't like getting wet."

"How's the spoiled brat?"

"Spoiled," Angela confirmed. "Are you sure you're all right?"

"I'm just going to take a nap before I stop by and see my mother. She's driving me insane with this so-called wedding reception. If it wasn't for the baby, I wouldn't have told her that Reggie and I had remarried. I'll call you with the update."

"Give Big Poppa a kiss for me," Angela yelled as Traci made her way to the rear exit.

"I will."

Angela walked into the front of the shop and stared through

the plate-glass window. Passersby were dressed for the rainy weather. And what was worse was they hadn't had one customer all day. If it had been up to her, Angela would've closed early. But the Garden Gate was Traci's business and she was a minority partner.

She and Traci had talked about hiring a part-time salesperson to fill in once Traci went on maternity leave. Angela knew she would have to change her hours if only to open up and lock the shop every day. It would affect how much time she could spend writing. But family was family and Traci would do the same for her.

She turned around and made her way to the daybed, picking up a magazine. This was one time she wished that she was home, cloistered in her office. Later she would retreat to the back porch and watch a movie.

Angela was flipping through the pages of the magazine and had become engrossed in an article on luxury yachts when the doorbell chimed. A tall man in a bright yellow slicker and baseball cap walked in. It wasn't until he took off his cap and shook off the rainwater, that she realized who he was.

"Levi." His name was a breathless whisper.

One minute she was standing, staring up at a bearded man, and an instant later she was in his arms, her mouth fused with his. Everything about him came rushing back—his smell, the intoxicating taste of his mouth, the warmth of his body.

"When did you get back?" she asked in between kisses that burned her mouth.

Levi's smile spread amid his bearded face. "I came directly from the airport."

Unzipping the slicker, she ran her hands over his chest. "You lost weight."

"I lost a lot, baby—sleep being number one on the list."

Her hands went to his face. "Why didn't you go home?"

"I needed to see you first."

"You see me, Levi. Now I want you to go home and get some rest. I'll be by after I close up."

Levi glanced at his watch. "Maybe I'll crash on your daybed until you close."

Pulling his arm, Angela led him to the back. "No, you won't. I have a love seat that converts into a bed. You can crash there."

Levi slipped off the slicker and hung it on the hook next to Traci's smock. He ran a hand over his hair. It'd been weeks since he'd had a haircut, and he hadn't shaved since the day he left for Indiana.

"I'll do that," he said when Angela attempted to pull out the convertible bed. After unfolding the bed, Levi removed his boots, socks and damp jeans as she spread a sheet over the mattress and provided two fluffy pillows with matching pillowcases.

"Do you want a light blanket?"

Levi's eyes made love to the woman who'd occupied his every waking moment. He'd lost count of the number of cuts and gashes he'd sutured, tetanus and cholera shots. He'd delivered four babies—two were full-term and the other two preemies, who had excellent chances for survival once the neonatal clinic was up and running.

"Yes, please."

"Get in bed, sweetie."

Levi knew if he didn't sit down he would fall down. He didn't want to wait and drive back to Louisville, so he booked a flight on a private plane to fly back, and took a taxi from the airport to downtown Louisville.

He got into bed, sighing audibly. "I'm going home with you tonight, because my car is at my apartment."

Angela spread a handmade quilt over him. "When are you going back to the hospital?"

Levi's eyelids fluttered as he struggled to stay awake. "Not for a week. Remember, we're going to Philadelphia this weekend."

Sitting on the side of the mattress, Angela leaned over and kissed his forehead. "Go to sleep, sweetie. We'll talk once you wake up."

He opened his eyes. "You're not bailing on me, are you?"

"Never."

A dreamy smile parted Levi's lips. "Love you, babe."

"Love you back."

Within seconds he was asleep, his chest rising and falling. Angela felt a rush of emotion once she realized he'd come directly to her instead of going home. Did she dare hope that he loved her?

Levi slept for thirty-six hours, waking up when nature called. He drank lots of water, then went back to sleep. Having him under her roof had curtailed her writing and Angela made certain all evidence of her manuscript was concealed in a locked file cabinet. Perhaps she was superstitious, but she wouldn't even let Traci read any of her work while she was still writing.

As much as she'd wanted to tell Levi that she was bestselling author, Angelina Courtland, she didn't. Once she delivered the manuscript, she decided she'd reveal her secret to Levi, and tell him that she'd been invited to New York to meet with her editor and publisher.

Chapter 18

"I think your mother is angry with me."

Angela turned and stared at Levi's profile. He'd gotten a haircut and a shave and his smooth jaw seemed to glisten in the sunlight. "You're imagining things."

"You think so?"

"I know so, Angie. She kept giving me dirty looks and said that you needed to be with your family this weekend to celebrate Traci and Reggie's wedding."

"I did that already when we took them to Ruth's Chris."

"That didn't count."

"It didn't count because Dianne Chase wasn't involved in it, Levi. When I promised I'd go with you to your family reunion I had every intention of keeping that promise. I have twenty-five other weekends in the year to hang out with my mother."

Levi's hands tightened on the leather-wrapped steering wheel. "Maybe I shouldn't have told her that I'm in love with her daughter and I have no intention of taking her away from her family."

Angela slumped in her seat as if she'd been stung by a taser. The air whooshed out of her lungs. Had Levi said that he was in love with her?

"You shouldn't have told her what?" she asked, recovering her composure.

"I shouldn't have told her that I love you."

"Levi, you're in love with me?"

The corners of Levi's mouth tilted when he smiled. "Yeah, that, too."

Angela put her hand over his on the steering wheel. "I'm serious, Levi."

"So am I, Angela. What's the matter? You don't believe I love you?"

Her thumb caressed his long, slender fingers. His hands were strong, the hands of a healer. "I would've believed it more if you'd told me first instead of my mother."

Levi set the car on cruise control, and took his foot off the gas pedal. "I told you, Angela, when I sent you a text that I loved you. And it didn't take being away from you for three weeks for me to realize that. At first I thought it was about the sex, but I knew it went deeper than that. I'm not saying making love to you isn't wonderful."

She turned her head so he wouldn't see her smirk. "What are you saying, sweetie?"

"I'm in love with you, Angela Chase. Does that meet with your approval?"

The smirk slowly became a full grin. "I think it does. Now I have something to tell you."

"I'm listening, baby."

"I think I love you, too."

"You think?"

"Uh-huh. However, the jury is still out."

"What would I have to do to sway said jury?"

They shared a smile. "I'm certain I'll think of something before we get to the City of Brotherly Love."

"I'll have you know that the brothers from the city do know how to love."

Leaning over, Angela kissed the back of his hand. "You know you're confused."

"About what?"

"You love Philly, yet you sound like a Southerner. You live in New York, claim you like the Yankees, but you never talk about the Jets or the Giants. What's up with the divided loyalties?"

"Don't hate, baby, just because Kentucky doesn't have a pro team. It's like ya'll don't know nothin' except basketball."

"That's because basketball is a religion in Kentucky. Don't you hate, Levi. We have the Kentucky Derby."

"Did you forget that New York has the last leg of the Triple Crown. Triple Crown, not double crown, baby. So there!"

"Oh, no you didn't put your hands in my face!"

"My hands would like to be someplace else, but I'm certain we'd be arrested for indecency if I pulled this car over and did what I'd like to do."

There was an awkward silence.

"Do you want to stop and eat something?" Levi asked, breaking the uncomfortable silence.

Angela met his eyes. They were serious. "Sure."

"I'll pull off at the next exit."

He'd decided to drive to Philadelphia instead of flying because it was impossible to get a ticket for the holiday weekend. Philly was a little less than seven hundred miles from Louisville, and he figured with occasional stops he could complete the drive in less than twelve hours.

"I don't mind sharing the driving," Angela volunteered. "That is, if you'll let me drive your car."

"Why wouldn't I let you drive?"

"Some men don't like women driving their precious cars."

Levi frowned. "It not as precious as you are so you're more than welcome to drive. Besides, with both of us driving, we'll get there faster."

"When do you think everyone will get there?"

"My dad and mother came in last night. My brothers and their families are coming in tonight. The ones who live in West Virginia and D.C. are probably already there. The Texans won't be in until tomorrow morning."

"Why do you call them the Texans?"

"That's how they refer to themselves. It's like 'we Texans don't do this or that.' You don't know how that irks some of the other Eatons. But family is family, so we have to love them."

"Have you ever brought a woman to a family reunion?"

"Nope. You're the first."

"Did you tell anyone you were bringing a woman?"

"Nope."

"Surprise, surprise."

"Don't worry, babe. They'll love you."

* * *

Levi parked his car at the entrance to The Rittenhouse and was met by a valet. Within minutes their luggage was unloaded and he escorted Angela across the lobby of the five-star Philadelphia hotel. Griffin and Belinda Eaton-Rice were this year's family organizers and they'd selected the hotel for out-of-town relatives. Griffin, an entertainment and sports attorney who lived in Paoli, a suburb west of the city, had opened his home to his brother-in-law Myles and his family, who'd driven in from Pittsburgh.

As Levi checked in, Angela glanced around the luxurious hotel lobby with Art-Deco furnishings. They'd stopped once to eat breakfast and refuel. But once she was behind the wheel of the car, her focus was on reaching their destination as quickly as possible. Levi took over driving once they'd reached the Pennsylvania state line.

Levi handed her one of the cardkeys. "We're in the presidential suite."

"I won't feel like a first lady until after I have a bath."

Cupping her elbow, Levi led her to a bank of elevators. "There's a spa, salon and health club on the premises, so if you want to get your hair done or get a massage then just pick up the phone and make an appointment."

"What's the itinerary for tomorrow?"

"There's breakfast here at the hotel, then everyone's on their own until seven. Belinda and Griffin will host a welcoming dinner. Saturday is breakfast at the hotel and the rest of the day is free for everyone to tour the city. For those interested in baseball, Griffin purchased a block of tickets to the Phillies game."

Angela's eyes grew wider. "Who are they playing?"

"The New York Mets. Do you want to go?"

"Of course."

"Good. On Sunday we go to a church where Eatons have worshipped for years, followed by brunch at cousin Chandra's house in the Brandywine Valley that will probably last all afternoon and into the evening. We come back here Sunday to sleep and check out Monday morning and head back to Louisville." The elevator arrived at the designated floor, the doors opened and they exited the car. "Let me know if there's anything you'd like to see while we're here in Philly and I'll reserve a driver to take us around."

"I want to eat a Philly cheesesteak."

"Pat's or Geno's?" Levi laughed when Angela gave him a blank stare. As they walked along the carpeted hallway to their suite, he told her about the cheesesteak war that had been going on for more than thirty years.

"Which one is better?"

"No comment. I'll let you decide after you have both." He stopped in front their suite, inserted the cardkey, waited for the green light and pushed open the door.

Angela walked into a living room larger than the total square footage of some homes. A massive column divided the living room from the dining space. She smiled upon seeing a baby grand piano.

Levi took her hand. "Come check out the bedroom."

Gold-and-maroon-striped wallpaper was repeated in the canopy above the king-size, four-poster bed. Pulling away from Levi's loose grip, Angela ran to the bed and flopped back onto it. The firm mattress barely gave under her weight.

She extended her arms. "Come on, Levi, and test it." There was a knock on the door and Angela sat up.

"That must be our luggage."

Angela didn't move as Levi turned and left the bedroom to answer the door. She was still sitting in the same spot when he returned, placing their bags in a corner.

Slowly, methodically, his hands went to the buttons on his shirt, then the waistband of his jeans. "May I interest you in sharing my bath?"

Slipping off the bed, she curtsied gracefully. "Fancy you ask. I was contemplating the very same thing."

Levi undressed Angela, leaving her clothes on the bench at the foot of the bed. Then she undressed him. Hand in hand they made their way to the bathroom and standing under the warm spray of the shower, made love. It wasn't the frantic coupling of two lovers who'd been apart for far too long. But their lovemaking unfolded like there was no need to hurry. They would savor the sweetness of their mating over and over again.

Levi's mouth was everywhere, nibbling at her ear, tracing the column of her neck, her breasts. He moved lower to her belly, deliberately bypassing the juncture between her legs. His tongue traced a path from the bottom of her feet, up her legs to her inner thigh. Angela thought she was ready for him when he fastened his mouth to her mound, as the tip of his tongue teased her clitoris until it swelled to twice its size.

Head thrashing, tears washing away with the shower spray, Angela arched and screamed as the first orgasm seized her, holding her captive. A second followed, overlapping the first when he penetrated her. Cradling her hips in his hands, Levi lifted her higher and angled her body off the tiles as he thrust into her like a man possessed.

"No!" he bellowed when the tingling indicated he was about to ejaculate. He couldn't. He didn't want to. It was too soon. Slowly he pulled out, but not all the way.

Angela slipped out from under Levi. Puting her hands on his chest, she met his eyes. "Lie on your back." He quickly obeyed.

It was her turn to give Levi the pleasure he'd given her. Her mouth charted a course down his body from head to toe. Then she reversed course pausing as she lowered her head until she took in as much of his sex into her mouth as she could. If he'd worshipped her body, then she wanted to return the favor, suckling his erection.

"Stop, Angie," he pleaded. "Please stop or I'll come in your mouth."

Holding on to his shaft, her head popped up. "We can't have that, can we?" she whispered. Levi shook his head. She tightened her hold on his throbbing penis. "What do you want, sweetie?"

Levi managed to push to a sitting position, supporting his back against the wall of the shower stall. "Sit on me."

Angela straddled Levi and pressed her forehead to his. Smiling, she lowered her body until she took him inside her—inch by every hot, delicious inch. His hands cradled her waist, guiding her up and down over his erection.

Levi didn't know how long it went on. All he knew was that

the pleasure was mind shattering. When he finally did release his passion, his body felt as if it was floating higher and higher. But instead of crashing, he felt his soul melt away.

"I love you, I love you," he repeated over and over when Angela cried against his shoulder.

"I love you so much, Levi, that my heart hurts," she sniffled.

He smoothed the wet hair off her face. "Shush, baby. Love is not about pain, and I don't want to ever do anything to hurt you."

Angela shifted in an attempt to straighten her legs. Her calves were cramping up. "I hate to kill the mood, but if I don't get up I won't be able to walk."

Anchoring his hand on the floor, Levi managed to stand, bringing her up with him. "You forget the man who loves you is a doctor and I can take care of all your aches and pains."

"Ain't you somethin', Dr. Feelgood."

"Hell, yeah," he drawled, kneeling and massaging her legs and thighs.

"Levi."

"Yes, love."

"We're wasting water."

He glanced up at her. "You're right. Let's shower, then I'll order room service."

They took turns washing each other's bodies. After they dried each other off, they wrapped themselves in thick cotton robes, and sat on the bed and decided what they wanted for dinner. Levi called room service with their order, while Angela slipped into a pair of cotton lounging pants and tank top. Levi exchanged his robe for a pair of khaki shorts and a white tee.

The waiter arrived, setting the table in the dining area with silver, china and crystal before he set out their entrees. He uncorked a bottle of chilled champagne, half-filled a flute and handed it to Levi to taste.

Nodding, he smiled. "Excellent." Levi signed the check, gave the man a generous tip, and walked him to the door. "Please send someone to pick up the tray in a couple of hours. I'll leave it outside the door."

"Yes, Dr. Eaton."

* * *

Angela and Levi waited an hour after finishing dinner to go to bed. She lay in his embrace, listening intently as he told her of the three weeks he'd spent working twelve-and-sixteen-hour days at a mobile hospital where scores of injured people were brought around the clock. There were broken limbs, concussions, lacerations from flying glass and other injuries requiring immediate surgery.

He spoke of frightened children whose parents were missing, or abandoned pets searching for their owners. There were also those who'd suffered a break with reality, searching through the rubble looking for heirlooms and family photos.

Temporary shelters were set up to house those who had no family nearby, while fresh food and water had to be trucked in daily and distributed by the Red Cross. What had begun as a search and rescue mission became search and recovery. But there were miracles. Survivors were found under tons of rubble.

"It was as if someone had dropped a bomb, Angie. Unless you saw it for yourself there was no way to imagine the devastation caused by a twister. The hospital took a direct hit and most of the deaths were medical personnel—doctors, nurses, technicians. But their numbers paled in comparison to those injured."

"How many, Levi?"

"Thousands. The only ones who made it through unscathed were the newborns."

Shifting in his embrace, Angela pressed her face to his chest. "Do you ever get used to death and dying?"

A beat passed. "Never. And I don't want to."

"Why not?"

"I don't want to lose my humanity and compassion, which is what made me want to become a doctor."

"Are you a good doctor?"

Laughter rumbled in his chest. "I would like to think I am. At least the children believe I am, because I'm able to imitate their favorite cartoon characters. They love my Mickey Mouse and Donald Duck impressions."

"Really?"

"Yes, really."

"Do one for me."

Levi combed his fingers through her hair. "Not tonight. I'll do it tomorrow for the kids."

Angela smothered a yawn as her heart swelled with a love she hadn't thought possible. She knew that if she hadn't gone through what she did five years ago, her life would've been very different today.

Chapter 19

Angela was surrounded by three generations of Eatons ranging from infants to middle age. Someone had referred to her as Levi's girl and the label stuck. Levi was right about the number of young Eatons.

During breakfast she sat at a table with a group of women who were updating each other about what was going on in their busy lives. All agreed their major problem was juggling motherhood and career, and that made her aware of what she would be faced with if she changed her mind about marriage. Unlike Traci, who'd married three times by age thirty, Angela was still reluctant to consider taking that step.

Selena's nineteen-month-old daughter Lily Mia Eaton had crawled onto Angela's lap and whenever her mother or father tried to pick her up, she would cry. The little girl had a burnished-gold complexion, curly black hair and dark gray eyes—eyes she'd inherited from her maternal great-grandmother. Although the baby's namesake had been invited, Lily Yates had declined at the last minute because she'd come down with bronchitis.

Selena lifted questioning brows. "I don't know what's wrong with her. Normally she won't let anyone pick her up with the exception of me and Xavier, but there's something about you she likes."

Angela stared at the sleeping baby in her arms. "Maybe it's because she knows I like her." She smiled at the chocolatier. "She's adorable." The baby was adorable and feeling the warmth from the tiny body, and inhaling her delicate scent stirred Angela's maternal instincts. There had been a time when she'd fantasized about becoming a mother. But that time had passed. Now it was back and she knew it was because of Levi.

She wanted a baby.

Levi Eaton's baby.

Selena covered her mouth to stifle a giggle. "You wouldn't say that when it's time to put her down for the night. She will cry for her daddy until he comes into the room and sits with her until she goes to sleep."

"That's because she's daddy's little girl."

Angela glanced up, meeting Levi's penetrating stare, unable to read his expression. A ghost of a smile flickered across her face before she looked away.

Dr. Mia Chandler joined the group. She and her husband had checked into the hotel the day before and decided to sleep in late, ordering room service. Tall, slender and stunningly beautiful she was often mistaken for a fashion model.

"Where's Kenyon?" Selena asked Mia.

"I left him on the phone. He's trying to hook up with a few of his old military buddies who live in the area."

Selena leaned forward. "Xavier has already connected with three of his buddies from the Corps. He's trying to see if Griffin can get a few more tickets to the ballgame so they can all hang out together after the game."

Mia shook her head. "I smell trouble if they're going out after the game."

"The worst that can happen is they'll miss breakfast," Angela said.

"Try brunch," Mia and Selena said in unison.

Angela blinked. "It's like that?"

Mia and Selena shared a glance. "You'll find out once you marry Levi," the doctor crooned.

Angela's eyelids fluttered. "It's not like that between Levi and me. We're friends."

"Who's a friend?" questioned Holly Eaton.

"Angela and your son," Selena said to Levi's mother.

"Surely you jest, young lady," the older woman replied, then walked away.

Waiting until Holly was out of earshot, Selena and Mia dissolved into laughter. Mia touched the corners of her eyes with a finger. "You can fool some of the people some of the time, but you'll never fool my aunt. Everyone expected Aunt Holly to have a woman here to parade in front of Levi, but when he told her he was bringing someone she backed off."

Angela felt a lump in the middle of her chest. Had Levi asked her to come to Philadelphia because he knew his mother would try and set him up with another woman? "Should I assume I'm the first woman he's brought to meet his family?"

Mia touched Angela's shoulder. "No. We've seen him with other women at weddings, but you're the first to come with him to a reunion. And you're the first one we like," she added.

"Thank you. What was wrong with the others?"

"They were nothing like you." Mia turned to Selena. "What did you think of the one he brought to my wedding last year?"

"She had her nose so far up in the air it's a wonder she didn't drown whenever it rained."

Mia nodded. "They were divas. I saw where you'd signed up to go to the Phillies game. Levi's old girlfriends would've never done that. You definitely have what it takes to become an Eaton woman."

You definitely have what it takes to become an Eaton woman. Dr. Mia Chandler's statement was etched on Angela's brain like a permanent tattoo.

And she felt like an Eaton woman when she joined the women for an afternoon of pampering at the spa enjoying massages, facials, mani-pedis, waxing, haircuts and styling. The younger children were left in the care of their fathers or grandparents.

Later that evening, everyone drove to Paoli for a buffet dinner. Belinda and Griffin's twin teenage daughters, whom Angela discovered were actually their nieces, were the perfect hosts. Their young son chattered incessantly and Belinda remarked that he was his father's mini-me and no doubt would also become an attorney. The Rices had filled the inground pool, but no one ventured into the water because of the cool nighttime temperatures.

Saturday night, Angela was one of four women who attended the baseball game, the score seesawing back and forth until it went into extra endings. The group left the stadium in the four-teenth inning, half returning to the hotel and the others linger-ing behind to meet up with old buddies.

Levi didn't return to their suite until dawn, falling facedown on the bed fully clothed. It took Angela more than ten minutes to undress him and get him back into bed. She placed the Do Not Disturb placard on the door and rode down to the lobby to meet those going to church. When she returned, Levi had recovered enough to make the drive to the Brandywine Valley. She didn't ask him where he'd gone or what he'd done and he didn't volun-teer to tell her.

Brunch at the Tuckers was held outdoors with spectacular breathtaking views of the valley. There was something about the rolling hills in this region of Pennsylvania that remind Angela of Kentucky. She met celebrated playwright Preston Tucker, and talked to him about his plays. When she told him she was inter-ested in writing a play, he gave her great advice.

Over the weekend she was aware that Holly Eaton was watch-ing her, and Angela groaned inwardly at her approach. Angela moved over on the bench to make room for Holly. She reminded her of a suburban housewife with a man-tailored blouse, khakis, imported slip-ons and pearls. Holly had tied a rose-pink cardi-gan around her neck.

Holly patted Angela's hand. "My son seems to be quite taken with you, Angela."

"Well, the feeling is mutual. I'm quite taken with Levi. You raised a remarkable son."

Holly removed her hand, patted her coiffed, barely-gray hair. "How serious are you and Levi?"

"We're friends, Mrs. Eaton."

"That's what I keep hearing."

"It's the truth. I'm sorry if you want it to be more, but…" Angela's voice trailed off when she saw the disappointment on Levi's mother's face. "We haven't known each other *that* long."

Holly's expression brightened. "I see. But you do like him?"

"Very, very much."

Nodding, Holly said, "That's enough for me." She shocked

Angela when she kissed her cheek. "That's for giving Levi what he needs."

When the woman got up and walked away Angela wondered why Holly was so interested in Levi's love life. Had some woman broken his heart, or promised to marry him, and broken the engagement? Or perhaps Holly wanted to see all of her children married. She wanted to tell her that her odds were much better than Dianne Chase who had five unmarried children and no grandchildren.

The reunion ended Monday morning with everyone gathering at Lacroix at The Rittenhouse. Dr. Dwight Eaton, the family patriarch gave a short speech, thanking everyone for coming to Philadelphia and they didn't need an invitation to return any time. His face fell when he mentioned the obvious absence of his brother Raleigh and Raleigh's daughter Crystal.

Dwight adjusted his glasses. "I know my brother doesn't like reunions as much as he likes marriages." There came an explosion of laughter. "After all, the man is on his fourth marriage. Will some of you single folks please get married so I can get to see my brother again?" All eyes were trained on Levi who pretended indifference. "You young folks will have to get together to decide where next year's reunion will be. Do I hear a shout out for West Virginia or Charleston?"

Xavier raised his hand. "Selena and I will host it next year. Remember good people it's Charleston, South Carolina, not Charleston, West Virginia."

Amid hugs, kisses and tears the Eatons extended family promised to see one another the following Memorial Day weekend.

Levi and Angela didn't leave Philadelphia until early Tuesday morning to avoid the holiday traffic. Levi drove for six straight hours, then when they stopped to refuel Angela took over and drove the remaining five. They arrived in Louisville in the early afternoon. He dropped her off at her house.

"Are you really going to work?" he asked her.

"I have to, Levi." She brushed a light kiss over his mouth.

"Please go so I can shower and change. I'll call you later after I pick up Miss Divine from my mother."

He ran his finger over her cheekbone. "Try to get some sleep tonight."

"You, too."

She closed the door, raced to the bathroom to get ready for work. Angela knew Levi was right. She'd gotten very little sleep over the weekend, and after driving for five straight hours she was exhausted. But she'd promised Traci she would come in today and she always kept her promises.

Levi lay in bed, arms folded under his head, staring up at the ceiling. If he'd planned a perfect weekend, it couldn't have gotten any better than the one he'd shared with his family and Angela.

His mother had cornered him wanting to know his intentions when it came to Angela. Only Solomon Eaton had been able to get Holly to stop the interrogation. Levi had never been one to kiss and tell, and he wasn't about to break the rule now because his mother wanted to know about the woman who'd captured his heart.

Not only had he fallen in love with Angela but he also wanted her in his life—permanently. He wanted her as his wife and the mother of their children. But that would only happen if he took steps to make it a reality.

Levi sat up and retrieved his cell. He tapped several buttons. "This is Dr. Eaton. I'd like to speak to Dr. McGill." He waited for the secretary to patch him through. "Neil, Levi."

"I heard you did a terrific job. Delivered a bunch of babies, did you?"

Levi smiled. "It was four. You'd asked me whether I'd take the position as head of pediatrics and I told you I'd have to think about it."

"Have you thought about it, Levi?"

"Yes. I'll accept it."

"Hot damn! When you come in next week we'll discuss salary, benefits and perks. Thank you, Levi."

"You're welcome, Neil."

Levi ended the call, knowing he had taken the first step to cement his future.

"I want to know everything," Traci said when Angela walked into the Garden Gate."

"And I want to know everything that happened at your wedding reception first," Angela countered.

Traci patted the daybed. "Sit down and I'll give you all the details. First of all, it was like the Super Bowl. The only thing missing was the half-time entertainment."

"No!"

"Oh, yeah," Traci confirmed. "My mother got in touch with Reggie's mother and it was on. Half of his old teammates showed up—*again*—to wish us well. I was so embarrassed I didn't know where to hide my face. If I could have I would've disowned her when she made the announcement that all of her prayers were finally answered because she was going to become a grandmother."

"No, she didn't," Angela whispered.

"Yes, she did. Then she put on a performance that rivaled any of Meryl Streep's when she pretended to be overcome with emotion."

"Aunt Daphne should've become an actress instead of a math teacher. What did Uncle Frank say?"

"He played into the nonsense like he always does. All my dad has to see is one tear and he's like hot butter in my mother's hands. It was so embarrassing. I told Mama the Southern belle act is old-school, but apparently it still works for her because Daddy falls for it every time."

"Did anyone videotape it?"

"Of course. As soon as I get a copy I'll let you see it."

"Does it fall under the category of comedy or drama?"

"Neither. There's a new category for this one—*hot mess*," Traci spat out. "Enough about me. What happened in Philly? Did you get to meet Levi's parents?"

Angela gave Traci a rundown of the Eaton family reunion, recounting how Levi had become the pied piper when all the children gathered around him when he did impressions of cartoon characters.

"I don't remember the names of all the adults, but I wrote down the names of the children because Levi wants to buy gifts for each of them from us. The grandfathers got together and went golfing, the grandmothers got to bond with their grandchildren and the women my age bonded at a day spa."

"What about Levi's friends?"

"Of course it was sports. They went to a baseball game, then went somewhere after that and didn't get back until dawn."

Traci gave Angela an incredulous look. "You didn't ask Levi where he'd been?"

"No, Traci. He's not my husband."

"Even if he were your husband, wouldn't you want to know where he'd been and what he'd been doing?"

"No," Angela repeated. "I'm not going to run behind a man to check on what he's doing or who he's seeing. It's about trust, Traci. If I can't trust him, then I don't want to be with him."

"Do you trust Levi?"

She nodded. "I do."

"Do you love Levi?"

Angela was slower in answering. "I do."

"What are you going to do about it?"

"Enjoy the ride until it's time to get off."

Chapter 20

Angela did enjoy the ride. She had less than a month before things would come to an end, but instead of slowing down it came to an abrupt halt, nearly derailing when the wheels came off the track.

Traci placed an ad in the local paper for a part-time salesperson and the response was overwhelming given the economy. She interviewed scores of applicants and in the end hired a sixty-something-year-old man who'd worked as an appraiser for an auction house before being forced to take early retirement. His elegant appearance and sophisticated manner had become the bait whenever he was at the Garden Gate.

Angela cut back on her own hours, spending more time in her home office writing furiously to complete the manuscript. Levi had returned to the hospital and because he was short staffed he alternated working weekends.

The buzz of the intercom startled her early Wednesday morning. When she answered the call, the guard on duty announced Levi was there.

"Please let him in."

Saving what she'd typed, she went to open the door. Standing on the porch she watched his car's approach. A tender smile softened her mouth when he got out carrying a large white shopping bag.

"I brought breakfast."

Her smile widened. If he'd lost weight so had she. Traci had joked that while she was gaining Angela was losing, and she could only attribute the weight loss to drinking water and green tea while she was writing nonstop.

She tiptoed to kiss his stubble. "You are truly my guardian angel."

Resting his hand on her hip, Levi kissed her forehead. "I figured I'd hole up here for a while before I go back for the three o'clock shift change."

"Mi casa es su casa," she said, repeating what he'd said to her the first time she went to his apartment. She took the shopping bag and walked into the kitchen. "Where do you want to eat?"

Levi stared at her slim figure in a pair of jeans that didn't fit as snugly as they had when he first met her. There were hollows in her cheeks that weren't there before. "It's cool enough this morning to sit on the front porch."

"Front porch it is."

Levi looked around. "Where's Miss Divine?"

"She's probably in my office."

Angela reached in a cabinet under the sink for something to clean and wipe down the table on the porch. She'd put out two place settings, brewed coffee and had removed two large containers from the shopping bag, but Levi still hadn't come back out of the house.

She went inside looking for him. Levi stood at her workstation, reading her manuscript.

"What are you doing?"

His head popped up. An accusing look in his eyes rendered her motionless. "Why didn't you tell me you wrote novels?" Though spoken softly his words were as cutting as a knife.

"I couldn't," she whispered, finding her voice.

Levi placed the pages on a corner of the desk. "You couldn't because you didn't trust me with your secret. All your talk about trust and you still couldn't trust me, Angela."

Her lower lip trembled and she pulled it between her teeth. "I wanted to tell you."

"When!"

Angela jumped when the word exploded from him. It was the first time she'd heard Levi raise his voice. She closed her eyes, trying to compose herself. "I wanted to wait until I finished the manuscript and take it to New York. I would've told you then."

A muscle twitched in his jaw. "Would you have really told

me, Angie? Or would you have continued to hide things from me despite what we've shared? What we mean to each other?"

"I don't—"

He held up a hand, stopping her comeback. "Thank you for letting me know now before I was unable to walk away."

Angela stood, paralyzed by sadness as she watched the man she loved walk out of her house and her life. She refused to cry—not again. A wry smile twisted her mouth. This time she was prepared, because Levi had told her to her face that he was leaving.

"But heroes don't leave," she whispered to the silent room. *He's upset now, but he'll be back,* she told herself.

She took a step, picking up the pages Levi had read. Her legal surname and pseudonym were in the slug line on every page. There was no way she could've denied the manuscript was hers. Traci knew she was Angelina Courtland. Nicola Chase knew she was Angelina Courtland. And now Dr. Levi Eaton also knew she was Angelina Courtland.

Angela counted down the days the way an inmate would anticipating his release from prison. It was now the last week in June and she still hadn't heard from Levi. Each time her cell or house phone rang her heart skipped a beat. But when she saw the caller ID display it sank like a stone.

She'd become an actress, pretending nothing in her life had changed. When Traci invited her and Levi over for dinner with her and Reggie, Angela gave her an excuse that Levi was working double shifts and preparing to return to New York. What made the lie believable was that he actually was going to leave at the end of the month.

She refused to cry and in the end the pain really did make her heart ache. She loved Levi, loved him more than she could've imagined loving a man, and for that she was grateful. If she hadn't met him, then she never would've experienced what it feels like to be in love.

Try as she might, Angela broke her promise and when June thirtieth dawned she dissolved into a crying jag. Angela called Traci to tell her she wasn't feeling well and spent the entire day in bed, refusing to answer her phones and deleting voicemail messages without listening to them. Her pity party lasted twenty-four hours and when she finally forced herself out of bed she was ready to face the world.

Angela shared the Fourth of July with her parents, laughing, eating and when she returned home she gave Miss Divine an extended massage, then sat down to complete her manuscript. She cried again, this time it was tears of relief. Angelina Court-land would deliver her latest project two months before the dead-line.

Miriam Jabin, as promised, had overnighted her travel itiner-ary. A driver would pick her up from her house, drive her to the Louisville airport where she would fly first class to New York. A driver would meet her flight in New York and take her to a hotel where Miriam, Angela's agent and publicist would meet her for dinner. She would spend three days in New York before returning to Louisville. That would give her enough time to do some shopping and sightseeing.

Angela adjusted her shoulder bag and walked into the hotel restaurant. "I'm here to meet my party. The name on the reser-vation is Jabin."

The maître d' nodded. "Come right this way, madam."

Her eyes met those of the women seated at a table in a se-cluded corner of the restaurant. She shook hands with Miriam, then hugged her agent and publicist.

Miriam peered at her over a pair of half glasses. She had a gray boyish cut, a misshapen cotton blazer and character lines that surrounded a pair of sharp blue-gray eyes when she squinted. Her style confirmed that the brilliant editor was no-frills and no-nonsense.

"Sit down, Angela," Miriam ordered with a dismissive wave of her hand. "You're a lot prettier than I thought. It's a damn shame you're hiding behind a silly-ass pseudonym."

Angela sat up straight. "My private life will remain exactly what it is—private. Even my parents don't know I write, so the subject is closed."

"Damn," Miriam said, smiling. "So there's some fire under

that sweet, Southern, sugar-wouldn't-melt-in-your-mouth charm," she said in a perfect Southern drawl. Everyone laughed, including Angela. It put everyone at ease.

Over dinner, two bottles of wine and a very dirty martini for Miriam, Angela realized why she'd been summoned to New York. Her agent and editor had shown the proposal to a television network executive who wanted to option the novel for a made-for-television miniseries.

Angela slumped back in her chair, pressing a hand to her chest. "I don't believe it."

"Believe it, Angela," said her agent, who was only a few years older than Angela. "Miriam is going to work closely with the scriptwriter to make certain he hits all the plot points in the novel."

Brad Linden, a highly regarded publicist, spoke for the first time. Brad and her agent were partners in and out of the office. "I plan to put together a spectacular marketing package that will guarantee that this novel makes all the major lists."

Miriam tapped her glass, signaling to the waiter she wanted another martini. "And because the network really wants this project, they're willing to offer you an obscene amount to option it." Picking up a pen, she wrote an amount on a cocktail napkin, then pushed it across the table to Angela. "Do you think you can live with that?"

For the second time in minutes Angela was at a loss for words. The cable network was offering to pay her seven figures for a miniseries based on her yet-to-be-published novel.

"It looks good."

"You bet your ass it's good," Miriam said. "It's insane."

"Are you saying my book isn't worth what they want to give me?"

Miriam shook her head. "I deal with books, not movies. I've never signed off on a million dollar advance, but I've seen million dollar royalty checks. You're one of those rare writers that will get both. You have an enormous talent, Angela, and I respect you for wanting to keep a low profile. But you're going to have to ask yourself how long can you hide. It may come back to haunt you."

Angela wanted to tell her that it already had haunted her. Whenever she thought of Levi she remembered the look on his face, the pain in his eyes when he believed she didn't trust him enough with her secret.

Brad leaned close to the waiter when he brought Miriam's martini. "Can you please bring us four glasses of your best champagne?"

Angela groaned inwardly. She'd drunk two glasses of wine, and a glass of champagne was certain to put her out for the count. Then she realized she wasn't driving. All she had to do was walk out of the restaurant to the elevator that would take her to her hotel suite.

Angela woke up with a headache the next morning, but after swallowing two aspirins she was ready to take on the Big Apple. She took the open-air, double-decker sightseeing tour bus, viewing the city from the top deck. She returned to the hotel, showered, changed into a shift dress and ballet-type flats, then walked across town to Macy's to select gifts for her mother and Traci. Angela had decided to get a large bottle of her mother's perfume and a maternity outfit for Traci that she could wear after she delivered her baby.

The first thing Angela noticed about New Yorkers was that they always seemed to be in a hurry. Even women in five-inch stilettoes walked fast. Macy's was crowded with shoppers and she had to literally push her way to the escalator to ride up to the maternity department floor.

Angela had just stepped off the escalator when she saw him. Levi was standing with a woman with an obvious baby bump. She must have made a sound because he looked directly at her.

"Move lady!" she heard someone shout behind her, and Angela moved aside as she watched Levi close the distance between them.

It was no wonder he couldn't stay in Kentucky because it was obvious he'd gotten someone in New York pregnant. That's why he'd said so explicitly that he would take responsibility for *not* getting her pregnant. The woman held up a top and Angela noticed her left hand was bare. So Levi hadn't married his baby mama.

Levi felt a flood of emotion sweep over him when he came face-to-face with the woman who'd continued to haunt him—night and day. He reached out to touch her, but she pulled back.

"What are you doing in New York?"

"I came to meet with my editor, agent and publicist."

"I called you, Angie, but you didn't call me back." Why, he thought, did she have to look so delicious?

"I probably deleted the voice mails."

"Probably."

"Okay, I did."

"Why?"

"I don't know, Levi. Your girlfriend is looking at us."

Levi glanced over his shoulder. "Crystal's not my girlfriend. She's my cousin."

"Your cousin?"

"Yes." His eyes narrowed. "Did you think I'd sleep with you if I'd gotten another woman pregnant?"

"I don't know what to think, Levi. Right now my life has been a little crazy."

"It appears as if we have a similar problem. Come, let me introduce you to my cousin." He extended his hand and wasn't disappointed when Angela placed her hand in his. "Crystal, I would like you to meet Angela Chase. She's the woman I've told you about. Angie, my favorite cousin, Crystal Eaton."

Tall, slender, with black cropped hair and velvety dark skin, Crystal stared at the woman who had no idea of the power she held over her cousin. She inclined her head. "It's nice to finally put a name with a face."

Angela smiled. "Congratulations."

Crystal rested a hand on her rounded belly. "Thank you. I know Levi hates shopping, but he offered to come with me to pick up some clothes to hide my rapidly expanding waistline."

"I came to pick up some for my cousin who also can't fit into her regular clothes."

Crystal's eyes lit up. "There's a designer who has a line of separates that can be worn as maternity clothes and after the baby is born. Some of the tops can be worn as dresses or tunics. There are also leggings and cropped pants."

"That's what I'm looking for."

Crystal took Angela's arm. "They're over here on this rack."

Crossing his arms over his chest, Levi watched the two women go through racks of clothes as the piles over their arms became bigger and bigger. He'd promised to bring Crystal into Manhattan so she could meet with her attorney to draw up papers naming him legal guardian of her unborn child in the event something happened to her. As much as he'd pressed, she refused to divulge the name of her baby's father.

They'd stopped to eat lunch and were ready to take a taxi back to Grand Central Station when Crystal suggested stopping at Macy's so she could do some shopping.

"We're finished," Crystal announced proudly.

Levi took the pile of clothes from her and made his way to a register. He pushed his credit card across the counter when the clerk totaled the purchases. He signed the receipt then stepped aside when Angela placed her pile on the counter. He knew he shocked her when he handed the clerk his card. "I'm paying for this, too." The woman's eyes shifted from Crystal to Angela. "One is my cousin and the other is my fiancée."

The clerk flushed in embarrassment. "I... I..."

Levi winked at her. "It's okay. I know what you were thinking."

"Shame on you, Levi," Crystal chastised when they headed for the elevator. "How did you know what she was thinking?"

"She probably thought I was a pimp and you were my girls."

"You don't look like a pimp," Angela said.

Levi stepped aside to let the two women precede him into the elevator. "How many pimps have you seen?"

"I've seen movies."

Moving closer, Levi dipped his head, inhaling Angela's perfume. "That's just Hollywood's version. I know pimps who look like Wall Street executives."

Angela turned to look up at him. "You hang out with pimps?" she whispered.

He resisted the urge to kiss her until she lost her breath. "We'll talk about this later. Where are you staying?" Angela gave him the name of her hotel. "What room?" She gave him that, too. "As soon as I take Crystal home I'll come back into the city to see you. We need to talk."

"Why, Levi?" she whispered. "You said all that needed to be said last month."

"No, I didn't. And if you hadn't erased my voice mail messages you would've known that. I'll see you later."

They exited the elevator on the first floor. Levi led Crystal out the revolving door to the street to hail a taxi, while Angela went over to the perfume counter to buy perfume for her mother.

Levi wanted to talk and she was willing to listen.

Chapter 21

"Angie, please sit down."

She stared at Levi as he sat in a deep armchair. He looped one leg over the opposite knee. "Why?"

"You're making me nervous."

"You're a doctor, Levi. You don't get nervous."

"It's different with you."

"Why?"

"Because I'm not personally involved with my patients."

"Are we involved?" Angela asked, continuing to pace back and forth over the deep pile carpet.

"Of course we're involved. We're involved and in love."

She stopped, resting her hands at her waist. "What is love without trust?"

"What is trust without love?" He stood up and held her shoulders in a firm grip. "When I called you it was to apologize. I only thought of myself when I accused you of not trusting me. But, that was before I spoke to Traci."

Angela blinked as if coming out of a trance. "What does Traci have to do with us?"

"When you didn't return my calls, I called Traci and asked her about your writing. And, because she'd assumed you'd told me she told me how you wanted to remain anonymous because you didn't want your personal life to become public like some celebrity authors. I had no right to judge you. And I'm sorry."

Biting her lip, Angela cast her eyes downward. "And I'm sorry it didn't work out, Levi. We could've had the time of our lives if things had turned out differently."

His hands tightened on her shoulders. "It still can."

She looked up at him. "No, it can't, Levi. Not with me in Louisville and you here in New York."

"I'm only going to be in New York until tomorrow."

"Where are you going?" There was a hint of panic in her voice.

"Home. I'm moving to Louisville. I've accepted the position to become head of pediatrics at Clarke County General. Close your mouth, baby. I only came back to New York to sell my interest in the medical group partnership. I know I won't make the kind of money in Kentucky that I made in New York, but that doesn't matter. I'll still earn enough to support my wife and the children we'll have in the lifestyle to which she is accustomed."

"Who is this wife?"

"I believe I'm looking at her. That is if she'll have me."

Tears filled Angela's eyes and she tried blinking them back. "I thought you were old-fashioned, Levi."

"I am."

"Then, if you want me to give you an answer, then you better ask me properly. After all, I am a Southern belle."

Taking her hand in his, Levi bent down on one knee. The smile on his lips had reached his eyes. "Miss Angela Chase aka Angelina Courtland, will you do me the honor of becoming my wife? I promise to love, support and protect you with my life."

Angela sank to the floor on trembling knees. "Yes, Levi Eaton. I will marry you and become the mother of our children."

Gathering her in his arms and pressing her to his chest, Levi brushed his lips over hers as if he feared she would break. "When are you leaving?"

"Tomorrow. I have an eight o'clock flight."

"I'm driving, so can you cancel the ticket?"

"I didn't pay for the ticket. My publisher paid for me to come to New York."

"Is that the norm?"

"No." Angela had shocked Levi yet again when she told him about her book and movie deal. "You don't have to worry about taking care of me, because financially I'm in a very good place."

"Your money is yours and mine is ours. Whatever you make you can put aside for our children's education."

"Even if we have two children I don't believe their education would add up to seven figures."

Levi chuckled. "It would if they decide to become doctors."

She poked out her lips. "I didn't think about that."

"Now that you're going to ride back with me, I think we should get up early and see about buying you a ring."

"You want to do the whole ring and engagement thing?"

"Why not, Angie? You deserve a ring, an engagement and then have your father walk you down the aisle to give you away to a man who'll love you for life. The only other thing we have to agree on is when you want to get married."

Angela's smile was radiant. "How about Christmas? I've always fantasized about having a Christmas wedding."

"That gives us about five months to pull everything together." He kissed the tears on her lashes. "This time it's for real, baby."

Looping her arms around Levi's neck, Angela buried her face against his shoulder. She couldn't have written a better ending.

Angela Chase and Angelina Courtland would have to share a hero. But there was more than enough for the both of them.

"Is this the part when the hero sweeps the heroine up in his arms and takes her to bed where they make mad, crazy love to each other?" she asked, smiling.

"Damn, baby. You must have read my mind."

Levi rose to his feet, pulling Angela up with him. He carried her into the bedroom, closed the door with his foot and lowered her onto the bed. He took his time undressing her, gazing adoringly at her naked body. His hands were shaking when she rose to her knees, brushing his hands away and removed his clothes with an agonizing slowness that tested his willpower. This time there was no foreplay as they came together in an explosive joining that would be repeated over and over until they ultimately became one.

* * * * *

REQUEST YOUR FREE BOOKS!

2 FREE NOVELS
PLUS 2 FREE GIFTS!

KIMANI
ROMANCE
™

Love's ultimate destination!

YES! Please send me 2 FREE Kimani™ Romance novels and my 2 FREE gifts (gifts are worth about $10). After receiving them, if I don't wish to receive any more books, I can return the shipping statement marked "cancel." If I don't cancel, I will receive 4 brand-new novels every month and be billed just $4.94 per book in the U.S. or $5.49 per book in Canada. That's a saving of at least 21% off the cover price. It's quite a bargain! Shipping and handling is just 50¢ per book in the U.S. and 75¢ per book in Canada.* I understand that accepting the 2 free books and gifts places me under no obligation to buy anything. I can always return a shipment and cancel at any time. Even if I never buy another book, the two free books and gifts are mine to keep forever.

168/368 XDN FEJR

Name	(PLEASE PRINT)	
Address		Apt. #
City	State/Prov.	Zip/Postal Code

Signature (if under 18, a parent or guardian must sign)

Mail to the Reader Service:
IN U.S.A.: P.O. Box 1867, Buffalo, NY 14240-1867
IN CANADA: P.O. Box 609, Fort Erie, Ontario L2A 5X3

Not valid for current subscribers to Kimani Romance books.

Want to try two free books from another line?
Call 1-800-873-8635 or visit www.ReaderService.com.

* Terms and prices subject to change without notice. Prices do not include applicable taxes. Sales tax applicable in N.Y. Canadian residents will be charged applicable taxes. Offer not valid in Quebec. This offer is limited to one order per household. All orders subject to credit approval. Credit or debit balances in a customer's account(s) may be offset by any other outstanding balance owed by or to the customer. Please allow 4 to 6 weeks for delivery. Offer available while quantities last.

Your Privacy—The Reader Service is committed to protecting your privacy. Our Privacy Policy is available online at www.ReaderService.com or upon request from the Reader Service.

We make a portion of our mailing list available to reputable third parties that offer products we believe may interest you. If you prefer that we not exchange your name with third parties, or if you wish to clarify or modify your communication preferences, please visit us at www.ReaderService.com/consumerschoice or write to us at Reader Service Preference Service, P.O. Box 9062, Buffalo, NY 14269. Include your complete name and address.

KROM11B

"Gwynne Forster writes with a fresh, sophisticated sensuality that raises romance from the ordinary to the extraordinary heights of breathtaking fantasy."
—*RT Book Reviews* on *SEALED WITH A KISS*

ESSENCE BESTSELLING AUTHOR

GWYNNE FORSTER

For artist and free spirit Naomi Logan, sexy radio call-in host Rufus Meade is the wrong man at the wrong time. His conservative views drive her crazy! But despite their differences, Naomi awakens feelings in Rufus that he's never felt before. It seems that opposites not only attract, they ignite!

SEALED WITH A KISS

Available March 2012 wherever books are sold.

KIMANI PRESS™

www.kimanipress.com

KPGF4720312